THE BEST OF XER☉

THE BEST OF XERO

EDITED BY PAT AND DICK LUPOFF

TACHYON PUBLICATIONS
SAN FRANCISCO, CALIFORNIA

THE BEST OF XERO

TACHYON PUBLICATIONS
1459 18TH STREET #139
SAN FRANCISCO, CALIFORNIA 94107
(415) 285-5615
www.tachyonpublications.com

SERIES EDITOR: JACOB WEISMAN

ISBN: 1-892391-11-2

FIRST EDITION: JULY 2004

⟨⟩

PRINTED IN THE UNITED STATES OF AMERICA
BY PHOENIX COLOR CORPORATION

1   2   3   4   5   6   7   8   9   0

To Thomas Alva Edison, inventor of the mimeograph

The Best of Xero
Table of Contents

Introductions:

The Best of Xero:

INTRODUCTION

HOW PROPELLOR-HEADS, BNFS, SERCON GEEKS, NEWBIES, RECOVERING GAFIATORS AND KIDS IN BASEMENTS INVENTED THE WORLD WIDE WEB, ALL EXCEPT FOR THE DELIVERY SYSTEM.

ROGER EBERT
NOVEMBER 2003

In grade school I had a paper route, and one of the homes where I threw the Champaign-Urbana *Courier* was a tarpaper wartime housing unit occupied by two University of Illinois students from Poland, and their mother. When I came around to collect (20 cents a week), they'd invite me in and quiz me, perhaps because I was an odd and talkative kid who amused them. They read science fiction, and when they moved out at the end of the school year they gave me a big cardboard carton filled with old issues of *Astounding* — old even then, from the 1940s, with names like A. E. van Vogt, Robert Heinlein and L. Ron Hubbard on the covers. For a time they sat in the basement, to be taken up, looked at, and put back down. I was still into *Tom Corbett, Space Cadet*. But when I was 11 or 12, I started to read them, and then I bought my own first prozines. *Amazing* was the one most to my liking, and when a new issue hit the stands I regarded it with a certain curious quickening of attention that a year or so later I would come to identify with sexual feelings. It offered the same kind of half-understood forbidden world. I read every word of every issue, flat on my stomach, sprawled on top of the bedspread. In one of those issues there was a column reviewing new fanzines, and I sent off a dime to Buck and Juanita Coulson for a copy of *Yandro*. This was one of the most important and formative acts of my life.

By then I was reading all the prozines — *Analog, F&SF, Galaxy, If, Infinity, Imagination, Imaginative Tales, Fantastic Universe* ... see how I can still name them. I waited impatiently for the installments of Hal Clement's *Mission of Gravity* in *ASF*. Emsh and Freas, tiny signatures at the bottom of the covers, began to mean

ROGER EBERT (1942-) was a teen-aged science fiction fan when he wrote poetry for Xero. He went on to write the screenplay for Beyond the Valley of the Dolls, a film regarded by some viewers as a parodistic masterpiece. As film critic for the Chicago Sun-Times he has also written numerous books about cinema, including Roger Ebert's Book of Film (1997) and The Great Movies (2002). He is best known, however, as the pioneer (along with the late Gene Siskel) and by far the most highly regarded and influential practitioner of the art of film-criticism-on-television, illustrating his critiques with clips from the films under discussion.

a lot to me — and Chesley Bonestell on *F&SF*, of course. I have hundreds of mags in a closet even now, all with a little sticker on the inside cover that says *Roger Ebert's Science Fiction Collection*. Every five years or so, in the middle of another task, I'll look at them and a particular cover will bring memory flooding back like a madeleine. The cover of *If*, for example, illustrating the story about a toy that zapped paper clips into the fourth dimension — and what happened when they started leaking back into this one. I bought the Ballantine paperbacks by Arthur C. Clarke and Robert Sheckley, and the Ace Doubles by Murray Leinster and Eric Frank Russell. I bought the anthologies by Groff Conklin and H. L. Gold and the legendary John W. Campbell, Jr. I founded the Urbana High School Science Fiction Club; we rented *Destination Moon* and showed it in the auditorium, we went to a speech on the campus by Clarke and got his autograph, and we made a tape recording of H. G. Wells' *War of the Worlds*, complete with sound effects and a performance by my classmate Dave Stiers, who later became David Ogden Stiers of *M*A*S*H*.

But all of that is beside the point. Prozines and fanzines were two different worlds, and it was in the virtual world of science fiction fandom that I started to learn to be a writer and a critic. Virtual, because for a long time I never met any other fans; they lived only in the pages of mimeographed fanzines that arrived at 410 E. Washington St. and were quickly hidden among the hundreds of sf mags in the basement, on metal shelves that cost four books of Green Stamps. "Hidden," because at first I concealed my interest in fandom from my parents. Fanzines were not offensive in any way — certainly not in a sexual way, which would have been the worst way of all in a family living in the American Catholicism of the 1950s, but I sensed somehow that they were . . dangerous. Dangerous, because untamed, unofficial, unlicensed. It was the time of beatniks and *On the Road*, which I also read, and no one who did not grow up in the '50s will be quite able to understand how subversive fandom seemed.

Most fanzines had a small circulation of a few hundred, but they created a reality so intriguing and self-referential that, for fans, they were the newspapers of a world. Looking through old issues of *Xero*, which during its brief glory was one of the best

BEATNIKS, *Steve Stiles*

STEVE STILES was a prolific fan cartoonist and illustrator with a background in advertising art and layout. He collaborated with Dick Lupoff on a short-lived comic-strip, "The Adventures of Isidore," and on a proto-steampunk graphic novel that was serialized in Heavy Metal magazine before book publication as Aether Flyer.

fanzines ever published, I was stunned by how immediate and vivid my reaction was to names not thought about for years: Harry Warner, Jr., Mike Deckinger, Guy Terwilliger, Gene DeWeese, Bob Lichtman, bhob Stewart (how evocative that "h" was!), Walt Willis, Bob Tucker, "Ajay" Budrys, Ted White. I met Donald Westlake as an adult (we have been on a couple of cruises together) and he was surprised to find that I was already reading him in *Xero*. I found established professionals (Harlan Ellison, Donald A. Wollheim, Anthony Boucher, Fredrik Pohl, Avram Davidson, James Blish) happy to contribute to a fanzine, indeed plunging passionately into the fray. I confess happily that as I scanned pages and pages of letters of comment ("locs"), my eye instinctively scanned for my own name, as it did 40 years ago, and when I found it (Blish dismissing one of my locs), I felt the same flash of recognition, embarrassment and egoboo that I felt then; much muted, to be sure, diluted, but still there. Locs were the currency of payment for fanzine contributors; you wrote, and in the next issue got to read about what you had written. Today I can see my name on a full-page ad for a movie with disinterest, but what Harry Warner, Jr. or Buck Coulson had to say about me — well, that was important.

Wilson (Bob) Tucker was the first fan I met. He lived in Leland, a hamlet south of Bloomington, not far from Urbana. In the summer of 1958, still in high school, I was working as a reporter for the Champaign-Urbana *News-Gazette*, and was assigned to drive to Springfield to cover something at the state fair. I made a detour past his house. Bob and Fern made me feel right at home, and to meet them again I concocted a sort of fraud on my newspaper. We had a Sunday article on interior decorating, and I convinced an editor that I should write a piece about the household arrangements of one of Downstate Illinois' major writers. Well, Tucker *was* major! In the endless fanzine debates about whether sf was really literature, *The Long Loud Silence* was always cited as real literature. Bob was a movie projectionist in Bloomington who wrote in his spare time (a writer with the same talent would be a best-seller today). The Tucker home was a modest two-bedroom suburban house with attached garage — "turn left off the highway when you get to the motel." I photographed the high points of the interior decoration, which to my eye consisted of Bob's typewriter, his desk, his shelves of books, his piles of sf magazines, his framed movie posters, and the Tuckers, standing in front of various compositions of the above. This article actually ran in the paper.

A year or so after that I joined Tucker and Ed Gorman, a fan from Cedar Rapids, on a trip to the MidWestCon in Cincinnati. We drove in my family's Dodge, nearly skidding off a road in Indiana, talking all the way about fandom in a giddy rapid-fire exchange of inside jargon. At a motel in Cincinnati I made people laugh with my reproductions of Bob and Ray routines, and drank a little beer, which felt like a lot of beer to an inexperienced drinker, and — here is the earth-shaking part — *I actually met Buck and Juanita Coulson, Dick and Pat Lupoff, and Harlan Ellison!* The Coulsons struck me as two of the nicest people I had ever met, the kind of people where you would like to move into their spare room, and the astonishingly long run of their *Yandro* was one of the monuments of fandom. The Lupoffs were enormously funny and smart New Yorkers — that city that the novels of Thomas Wolfe had forever colored in my daydreams. Harlan was — how old? Twenty? Young and cocky, with the color proofs for the cover of his new paperback that Berkley Books was about to publish, and as he showed me the glossy reproduction, I knew envy of a desperately sincere kind.

The summer of 1961, now a student at the University of Illinois, I made my first trip to Europe on a $325 charter flight, and in Belfast visited Walt and Madeleine Willis. They invited me to tea—tomato sandwiches and Earl Grey — and took me around to meet James White, another of Belfast's BNFs (Big Name Fans), whose prozine collection was carefully wrapped in brown parcel paper, year by year, and labeled ("F&SF 1957"). Fandom was a secret society and I had admission to friends everywhere who spoke the same arcane language.

In the summer of 1962 I found myself going to South Africa as the press agent for a tour of wheelchair athletes from the University of Illinois. After the long bus trip from Urbana, we stopped overnight at a motel near LaGuardia, and I called Dick and Pat Lupoff. Because this visit was immortalized in *Xero 9*, I drop briefly from my own narrative to allow Dick to see me through his eyes.

ROGER EBERT BREEZES BY

DICK LUPOFF

There was a Fanoclast meeting June 15, and when Pat and I got home the baby sitter told us that Rog Ebert had called. Rog Ebert! We hadn't seen him since the 1961 MidWestCon, and had hardly heard from him since. He'd contributed several of his curious hybrid prosepoems to *Xero*, but the last of those had appeared in number 6, last September. The return number for Rog was the hotel at LaGuardia Airport, and by furious calling and calling back we managed to get in touch with him Saturday, June 16. That night Rog came over for a visit, as did, coincidentally, Coast Guard Al Lewis and Larry Ivie, the latter carrying a Tarzan painting and John Carter painting that he was using as samples. Rog seemed to have matured considerably since that MidWestCon. Actually, meeting him at the North Plaza Hotel had been my first contact with him. Prior to that, just from reading his fanzine material, I had conjured a slim and sensitive, tall, sallow hypochondriac, slow of speech and manner. What a surprise! Rog is built like a football player, is full of energy, talks incessantly, and is forever telling bad jokes. At that MidWestCon he had turned a contour chair in the Seascape Room into a space-jockey's bucket, turned his glasses upside down, and had half a roomful of people in hysterics.

But on this trip he had calmed down. After all, he's twenty now.

Rog is terribly, terribly Aware Politically, full of the usual liberal line. He is also an immensely talented young man, and a hustler on top of it. What was he doing in New York in June, for instance. Well, right after the end of the spring semester at the University of Illinois Rog had engineered himself a job as publicity man for a team of paraplegic athletes en route to New York for the annual Wheelchair Games, made a tour at the behest of a South African philanthropist out to start a rehabilitation program for injured persons in his country.

While there, Rog told us, he was going to do the research for an article on student unrest, already all but sold to *The Nation*. When he got home, Rog will have to go to work to write an article on a long-lost-but-now-rediscovered folk singer which is slated for *Show*.

After a full evening of talk, we arranged to meet the following night at a Chinese restaurant in Times Square, following which Rog could get a tour of the two areas of New York he is eager to see: Times Square/42nd Street, and Greenwich Village. By the time the crowd was assembled in the Chinese Republic (Nationalist, of course) it consisted of Walter Breen (who drew a small crowd on the sidewalk before dinner; people kept waiting for him to start a hellfire sermon), Lin Carter and his poopsie, Gary Deindorfer, Lee Hoffman, Ted and Sylvia White, Rog, Pat and myself. It was a pretty good meal, full of plusdoublegood fannish talk, following which the group became unfortunately separated in the surging mob of 42nd Street. All right, so it was Sunday night. There's always a surging mob on 42nd Street.

Lin and his poopsie Claire, Pat and I, and Rog, made our way back and forth on the Street for a while, but all that happened was that gay types kept trying to pick Rog up because he looked so wholesome and innocent. Then we gave up and went to the Village. Rog's item, "Snippets," is a faithful record of the evening's events from that point on onward, and if you don't know the rest of the feghootling that keeps popping up every few lines, it's to your benefit not to find out. Monday, Rog flew on.

FIDEL-MAN, Steve Stiles

And here, as advertised, is my item "Snippets:"

... and —
* they're showing charlie chaplin movies*
*   by god,*
in the front part, let's go
* and see them!*
--yes, but —
*   haahaaha ... but you're*
the only one
* laughing, dear*
*   --yes, haa —*
* but*
--which one was ours? —
*   (in red, that one; there)*
* --our check? —*
... and this fellow collected roots, kept them in
*   bottles,*
*   labeled and all — collected them from*
all over the
* world ...*
* one dollar and eighty-three cents —*
(one doesn't want to bore one's poopsie, does one?)
*   --but you like Sylvia ... —*
* (that's not true of marie)*
*   pure middle-class; i do not like that kind of person —*
(i don't consider you a fan; you're sort of nationalized
*   by right*
* --rite? —*
*   of marriage)*
*   i like conventions ...*
after the fanoclast meetings the cigarette
*   butts stay*
*   until the next fanoclast meeting ...*
* look, they're showing charlie chaplin movies, by*
*   god*
--... (and so when he died his son thought it would
* be a good idea to have a casket made of all*
* these roots, and so he hired a carpenter to*
* build the casket, but when ...) ... —*

twenty-three cents apiece,
thank you, ma'am.
... we went to bed, and then the doorbell rang. It
it was george nims raybin and 27 little teenage fans ...
(i know i'm early but i have noplace else to go)
... oooooh ...

These meetings, these connections and conversations, were important because they existed in an alternative world to the one I inhabited. Fandom grew out of and fed a world-view that was dubious of received opinion, sarcastic, anarchic, geeky before that was fashionable. In those years it was heretical to take comic books or *Captain Video* seriously. Pop culture was not yet an academic subject. From Lenny Bruce, Stan Freberg, Harvey Kurtzman, Mort Sahl and Bob and Ray we found an angle on America that cut through the orthodoxy of the fifties and was an early form of what would come to be known as the sixties.

I published my own fanzine (*Stymie*), cutting the ditto masters on an old L. C. Smith and paying an office supply company a few bucks to run it off for me. My freshman year in college I published *The Spectator*, a weekly "newspaper of politics and the arts" at the University, and this was a descendent of my fanzine. If I had only known it, I had stumbled on the format of the alternative weekly, but I didn't know enough to give it away, and the ads and circulation income weren't enough to keep it afloat; at the end of a year I sold it for $200 and joined the staff of *The Daily Illini*, then as now a great independent campus paper, and it took so much of my time that, little by little, fandom drifted out of sight.

From time to time I've heard from friends from those days. I spent time with Ed Gorman during a visit to Coe College; he became a mystery writer and wrote a novel about two movie critics who had a TV show. Harlan Ellison and I have had dinner in Los Angeles — once in the home of the eccentric film collector David Bradley, who had a concrete bunker filled with prints behind his house, and showed us the rare early cut of *The Big Sleep*. I ran into Dick Lupoff in San Francisco during a book tour — he has a show on Pacifica Radio — and we remembered that New York visit, when he and Pat seemed so incomprehensibly metropolitan to me. I actually sold two stories to Ted White when he was editing *Amazing* and *Fantastic*, circa 1970.

But fan friendships, for me, were mostly long distance and conducted by mail, and the influence of fandom was on my writing voice. I became critical. I wrote smart-ass locs about other people's writing, and read them about my own. I was in a world that stood outside the mainstream. Science fiction was the occasion for fandom, and often the topic, but the subterranean subject was a kind of kibitzing outsider world view. Because of fandom, we got to 1967 ten years before most of the non-fan world.

For that matter, we were online before there was online. It is perfectly obvious to me that fanzines were Web pages before there was a Web, and locs were message threads and bulletin boards before there was cyberspace. Someday an academic will write a study proving that the style, tone and much of the language of the online world developed in a direct linear fashion from science fiction fandom — not to mention the unorthodox incorporation of ersatz letters and numbers in spelling, later to influence the naming of computer companies and programs. Fanzines acted uncannily like mimeographed versions of Usenet groups, forums, message boards and Web pages — even to such universal design strategies as IYGTFUI (If You've Got the Font, Use It). Some of the same people segued directly from fandom to online, especially to places like the Well — not surprisingly, since many computer pioneers were also sf fans.

Today fandom survives on the Web, where it is no doubt World

1. LOOK, ITS HARLAN ELLISON PLAYING SKITTLES!

2.

3.

4. YAY HARLAN ELLISON

5.

6. GREAT GAME HARLAN!

7.

8. THANKS!

a nostalgic moment in the summer of 1960 when harlan played skittles in greenwich village all alone one afternoon after he discovered that his audience had only been waiting for a bus and just rode off...captured here by andy reiss

Wide, and some very slick fanzines have segued into prozines. Are there still analog (paper) publications called fanzines? I haven't heard that there are. That world has moved on. How long did *Yandro* last? How much is my first edition of the *Fancyclopedia* worth? Today a 12-year-old kid in Urbana has other ways to connect with alternative ideas, other worlds to explore. No doubt they are as exciting as fandom was for me. God knows what we would have given in 1958 for the Web.

But for the years of their existence, what a brave new world fanzines created! There was a rough democracy at work; no one knew how old you were unless you told them, and locs made it clear that you either had it or you didn't. First, of course, was the hurdle of getting your stuff accepted. When Lupoff or Coulson or Deckinger printed something by me, that was recognition of a kind that my world otherwise completely lacked. To look through these old pages of *Xero* even today, and find Harlan Ellison right about *Psycho* when the world was wrong, and Blish taking on Amis, is to realize that in the mimeographed pages of a fanzine created in the Lupoff living room there existed a rare and wonderful discourse, and it was a privilege to be part of it.

SKITTLES, Andy Reiss

ANDY REISS, whose wry and observant cartoons quickly established him as a sometimes biting commentator, went on to a distinguished career as an art critic, curator, and historian.

INTRODUCTION

WE DIDN'T KNOW WHAT WE WERE DOING

RICHARD A. LUPOFF

RICHARD LUPOFF (1935-) worked as a journalist in both print and broadcast media, a technical writer, and a filmmaker before becoming a full-time author. He has written more than fifty books and 100 short stories including science fiction, mystery, fantasy, horror, and mainstream fiction, as well as criticism and literary history.

What you're holding in your hands, *The Best of Xero*, is the pure distillate of one of the best fanzines ever published. I say this in all modesty, as my wife, Patricia, and I were the editors and publishers of *Xero*.

That's a pretty extravagant claim, to be sure, and in fact there have been many fine examples of the form in the seventy or so years since the first identifiable fanzines appeared. Still, just look at the list of authors on the contents page of this book and you'll see a remarkable list of bylines.

We created this periodical in the summer of 1960. I was recently out of the army and striving mightily to climb the pyramid of the industrial world. Pat had even more recently received her college degree and was working at the then-semi-mandatory role of full-time homemaker and prospective mother.

In later years we would both change our career goals.

We were living in New York at the time, and moving on the edges of the city's literary community. I was a science fiction fan of some years standing and had even published some very small, very crude fanzines as early as 1952. Pat had read science fiction but had no idea of the existence of the fan community.

Soon we made the acquaintance of the local fan groups, were intrigued by the fanzines that we saw, and decided to publish one of our own.

Thus, *Xero*.

And we truly didn't know what we were doing. We thought we were publishing a science fiction fan magazine. But just look at the first issue of *Xero*. The cover illustration was a drawing of Kublai Khan's stately pleasure dome, furnished by our friend Joe Sanders. Pat and I composed most of the issue ourselves, a common practice among new fan publishers who lack the contacts to get outside contributions. Pat wrote two pieces, a review of a book by Sax Rohmer, the king of sensational yellow peril novels, and an essay on Mervyn Peake, the British fantasist then almost unknown in the US. I wrote an essay called "The Big Red Cheese," musing fondly on the comic books of my childhood. And Harlan Ellison, our only outside contributor, gave us a review of *Psycho* – not the novel by Robert Bloch but the movie based on that book, directed by Alfred Hitchcock.

So if *Xero* was a science fiction fanzine, where was the part about science fiction?

It wasn't there!

With later issues we did add material about science fiction, most notably in the form of many, many book reviews, but *Xero* was never really a true science fiction fanzine. Looking back at the experience Pat and I had publishing *Xero*, and leafing through a bound set of copies, I realize now that *Xero* was a review of popular culture and contemporary events.

UNION MAN, *Steve Stiles*

In the early 1960s, the era when *Xero* was published, the stylish trend, or trendy style, in fan publishing was something called *fannishness*. Or, if you were very, very *fannish*, to the point where you were considered a *faan* rather than merely a fan, you and your publication were *faanish* or even *f-a-a-a-n-i-s-h.*

The earmarks of fannish writing were a lightness of tone and sharpness of wit, a cynical disregard for the mundane or non-fannish world, and a correspondingly high degree of self-concern. The Platonic ideal of a fannish essay would be one so brilliantly hilarious as to leave the reader rolling on the floor in hysterics while simultaneously gasping in admiration, yet that would have *absolutely no substantive content.*

From the first issue, *Xero* took a course counter to this model. In seeking material for the magazine we placed no limits on the topics contributors could address, providing only that they write about *something,* and that they write about it interestingly. We were not out to bore our readers.

This is not to say that *Xero* was the only fanzine that published substantial material. It wasn't "us against the world." There had been a long-standing tension in the fan community between those who regarded fanac (fan-activity) as something to be taken with at least a degree of seriousness, and those who regarded it as nothing more than an excuse for a perpetual party.

There's something to be said for seriousness, of course, and there's a good deal to be said for partying. Seems to me that people who take either attitude as an inflexible rule for living shut themselves off from much of what makes existence worthwhile.

I think I'd better interrupt this narrative for a moment in case you're wondering what the heck you've got yourself into. Maybe I'd better explain what a fanzine is. Or was. And if you already know, please bear with me, because not everybody does.

Fanzines came into being in the 1930s when a group of young aficionados borrowed the technology of amateur journalism. Inspired by the periodicals recently created by Hugo Gernsback — *Amazing Stories, Scientific Detective Monthly, Science Wonder Quarterly* and the like — they began publishing magazines of their own. Some were miniature scientific journals and some were actually scaled-down science fiction magazines. As the

fan community became increasingly self-aware the focus of its publications shifted in large part to fandom itself.

"*DAMON KNIGHT*", *Lin Carter*

Even so, printing equipment was bulky and expensive. Then fans discovered the mimeograph (and to a lesser extent its cousin, the hectograph). Here was a machine that could be bought for a few dollars and mounted on a desk or table-top. It didn't require any type. Instead of assembling thousands of little letter-shaped lead pellets for each page of a magazine, the publisher would roll a mimeograph stencil into his typewriter and punch the keys as if he were creating a manuscript. Once the stencil was completed, it was mounted on the outside of a revolving drum, ink was forced through the holes punched by the typewriter, paper was passed beneath the drum, and — *voila!* — you could make as many copies as you wanted.

Thus was born The Mimeograph Revolution, and shortly was born the classic fanzine. Mimeo'd on standard 8.5" X 11" paper, "bound" with an ordinary office stapler, the result was a magazine, modest in appearance but functional in nature. The classic fanzine was published between the late 1930s and some time around 1980. Don't quarrel with me about the years, please. We're not talking about discrete events here but an ongoing process.

Fanzines are still published, or so I am told, but they don't much resemble the fanzines of the classic era. The computer has completely superseded the mimeograph and now the internet and the e-zine are rendering the printed fanzine itself an endangered species.

But in its heyday, oh, in its heyday the fanzine was really something.

That first issue of *Xero* ran to thirty pages. We had planned on a circulation of 100 copies but — remember, we didn't know what we were doing! — we forgot to allow for spoilage, file copies, or the proverbial "office use." Consequently, the circulation of that first issue was closer to 90 copies.

The World Science Fiction Convention took place that year in Pittsburgh. Pat and I loaded our ninety *Xero*s in a carton and lugged them off to the convention. We planned to give them away and establish an instant presence for ourselves in the fanzine publishing world. The trouble was, nobody wanted to take one.

I remember earnestly chasing fans down the corridors of the convention hotel, pleading with them to take a copy of *Xero*. We somehow managed to get rid of all the copies, so at least we didn't have to bring any home with us. I don't know how many of those ninety copies survive, but they do turn up occasionally on auction sites. Last I heard, the going price was around $200 per, which may someday seem cheap.

This all strikes me as weird. It was just a fanzine, for heaven's sake.

Well, the first issue was out, the die was cast, and to our delight letters of comment ("locs" in fannish argot) poured in. Pat and I had worked out a division of labor whereby she would edit the ongoing letter column, a standard feature in the fanzines of the era. We'd heard complaints from other faneds (you can work that one out for yourself, I'll bet) that they couldn't get enough locs, but we got plenty of them, and they were unanimously supportive of our editorial policy.

We had expected opposition, and soon we got it, but for the most part *Xero* was welcomed by a loyal, growing audience.

With the second issue, *Xero* expanded to 50 pages. The magazine was spruced up somewhat with drawings by Dave English and Sylvia White, two prominent fans of the day. As *de facto* chief designer and production manager of the magazine, I was learning how to handle arcane devices like styli, lettering guides, and shading plates, and developing a least a rudimentary sense of design, as well.

We also discovered that writers were eager to have an outlet which welcomed essays, memoirs, and reviews, writing that was *about something*, in the still-prevailing climate of fannish narcissism and insubstantiality. Science fiction and mystery writer Larry Harris became our regular book reviewer. Ted White, then at the outset of a fine career as novelist and editor, followed up on the theme of old comics with a splendidly researched essay on M. C. Gaines, a pioneering comic book publisher. And a young New Jersey fan named Mike Deckinger contributed an essay — included in *The Best of Xero* — on his childhood fascination with the *Captain Video* television show.

Deckinger's essay set off a chain reaction or topic thread, one of many that developed in *Xero*. The third issue featured "The Secret Files of *Captain Video*," bylined *Arthur Merlyn*. It did not take long for the truth to emerge: Arthur Merlyn was a pseudonym of James Blish, one of the leading science fiction writers of his generation. Blish, or Merlyn, had been a lead writer on the *Captain Video* series, and had brought in many of his pals as fellow writers.

We also had more fan artists contributing to the magazine, most notably bhob Stewart, an immensely talented cartoonist and designer. After another issue bhob would assume the title of art editor, but he really assumed full control of the magazine's appearance and proceeded to raise it to remarkable heights. In time bhob and Pat and I became so thoroughly integrated a team that we simply designated bhob as a third editor.

The name "bhob," by the way, has a story behind it. So much in fandom does. There were several fans named Robert Stuart or Stewart, and to avoid confusion they worked out a system of nomenclature. There was Bob, Bobby, Robert, and – *our* Robert Stewart – bhob. With a silent *h*.

Within three issues *Xero* had established itself as a leading fanzine. We were getting essays from professional writers like Blish, Harris, and Otto Binder and publishable letters were pouring in. The physical appearance of the magazine had once been an embarrassment; it now became a point of pride.

The page count kept growing — eventually it would reach 100. The circulation kept growing, too, despite our efforts to keep it down. *Xero* was a hobby, you understand. I had a day job – tech writer for a computer manufacturer — and eventually added a second job, editing for Canaveral Press. The first of these put bread on our table and kept the rent paid on our apartment. The second was a total joy, surely the happiest employment situation of my life.

By the beginning of 1961 Pat was pregnant. She was pretty sick for several months but she hung in there and our first baby was born in September of that year.

The first few issues of *Xero* had been mimeographed for us by a company called Metropolitan Mimeo Service, run by — Ted White. Yes, the same fellow. The fan community was small and you kept running into the same people in different contexts. After a while we bought a machine of our own which ultimately saved us money and added to the fun of fan-publishing. All those hours of standing next to the machine, adding ink, changing stencils.

Once we had all the pages run off we would lay them out in stacks around the perimeter of our dining room table and start marching around the table assembling copies of the magazine. At first we did this ourselves, but as the page-count and circulation both grew, we began drafting volunteers including fan-friend and small-time pro writer Hal Lynch and our sometime cover artist Larry Ivie.

We also managed to hoodwink Donald and Elsie Wollheim into joining our collating parties. Don and Elsie had been fans in the late 1930s. Don went on to edit a series of pulp magazines, then run the Ace Doubles program, then create DAW Books. Don and Elsie are both gone now, and their daughter Betsie runs the company.

Every copy of *Xero* meant extra work and extra expense. At first we offered copies only to contributors, including letter writers, or as trade for other people's fanzines. We came under severe pressure to offer copies for sale, and finally felt that we could yield to the pressure and still discourage buyers by charging an unreasonable price. Many fans were young and poor, and we felt that we could simply price ourselves out of their reach. More affluent fans would be outraged by our greed and refuse on principle to buy the magazine.

That was our plan.

Standard price for fanzines in that era was 25 cents per copy. Subscriptions were four for a dollar, sometimes — a bargain! — five for a dollar. So, crafty devils that we were, Pat and I offered *Xero* for 35 cents per copy, subscriptions at three issues for a dollar.

The plan backfired. Suddenly our mailbox was clogged with envelopes containing quarters and dimes and dollar bills. One of our subscribers at the time was Art Spiegelman, who would someday win a Pulitzer Prize for his graphic novel *Maus*. Another youngster who would have subscribed if only he'd known about *Xero* was Michael Chabon, who won *his* Pulitzer for *The Amazing Adventures of Kavalier and Clay*. Chabon missed out on the magazine but when the comic book essays were collected in a book called *All in Color for a Dime*, the young Chabon slept with a copy under his pillow.

One well-to-do subscriber sent us a sizable check along with several pages of names and addresses, and instructions to mail copies of *Xero* to each person listed, with his compliments. We returned the check with a note explaining that *Xero* was a labor of love and was intended to give pleasure to its creators and its readers, *not* to bolster his ego by servicing his personal mailing list. We never heard from him again.

A pair of twins tried to enter dual subscriptions and we accepted their money and entered a joint subscription for them to share.

We received an odd document from the New York Public Library. It was a conditional purchase order. We were to fill out a set of forms that would have done the IRS proud and return them to the library along with a sample copy of *Xero*. If the grand poobahs at the library decided that *Xero* was worthy of inclusion in their collection they would then send us a *real* purchase order and, presumably a check.

For thirty-five cents?

After looking over the mandatory paperwork we decided to forgo the honor of being catalogued by the New York Public Library, and simply tossed their correspondence.

Despite our best efforts, circulation of *Xero* grew to 300, and would have grown a lot more than that if we'd let it. Three hundred copies doesn't sound like much, but in the then-tiny pond of fandom, it made for a very big frog.

We kept our subscribers list on a set of index cards carefully filed in a little tin box. And when it came time to mail out each issue we faced a problem. We didn't know anything about bulk mailing permits or other postal arcana, and we really didn't want to get involved with another bureaucracy. Instead we ordered a rubber stamp that said *Fourth Class Mail*. When a new issue of *Xero* was ready to go out we would stuff copies into manila envelopes, write out subscribers' names and addresses, affix stamps, and hit each envelope with our *Fourth Class Mail* indicia.

Then what?

We didn't want to deal with the authorities so each night we would fill a suitcase with copies of the magazine. Later, in the wee small hours, we would take the elevator downstairs in our building and stroll through the neighborhood. At each mailbox we would slip a few copies of the magazine through the receptacle. Three or four or five copies in a small mailbox, ten or twenty in a large one. Constantly looking over our shoulders like amateur spies.

We would repeat the process night after night until all the copies were mailed, shaking in our boots at the thought of Postal Inspectors turning up at our apartment and demanding to talk with us, or worse yet stopping us at a mailbox and demanding to know what we thought we were doing.

Fortunately, it never happened.

You can see that our lives were busy. I would come home from the office, doff my business suit and don sweatshirt and jeans. Pat would put some dinner on the table and I would scarf down my meal. During her pregnancies Pat was often too sick to eat much. After dinner, or what passed for it, we would turn to *Xero*, sorting through locs on the last issue and submissions for the next. Then we would rev up our little Smith-Corona electric portable typewriter — it's still in the family, by the way, after all these years — and one of us would start typing stencils while the other worked feverishly with lettering guides, shading plates, and mimeoscope. This last was a device consisting of a sheet of frosted glass angled over a light bulb. You would place a mimeo stencil on the glass and go to work with an array of styli, creating display lettering or tracing illustrations.

The improved production quality of the magazine attracted more talented artists, three of particular note. One was Steve Stiles, a near neighbor of ours in Manhattan. Steve developed into a superb cartoonist and would later make a place for himself in the comics world. We also created a feature together which would eventually run serially in *Heavy Metal* magazine, by then edited by Ted White, and was then published as a graphic novel. Another was Larry Ivie, whose cover for *Xero 5* was adapted as the dust jacket of *The Best of Xero*. Ivie also worked in comics, as well as painting covers for scores of magazines. The third was Andy Reiss, who would go on to a distinguished career as an art curator, critic, and historian.

On Saturdays Pat and I would trek out to the Pace Paper Company in Brooklyn. This was a one-man business run by a strange, elderly man who furnished our paper stock at bargain prices. Or we would ride the Staten Island ferry to the home of Larry and Noreen Shaw. There wasn't room for a mimeograph in our little Manhattan apartment and Larry and Noreen let us keep the machine in their basement, rent free, and come out and use it any time we wanted. In exchange, they got to use the mimeo when we weren't using it.

I said a while ago that we had expected opposition to our policy of seeking substance in *Xero*, and that we would get it before very long. Now it started, but it came from an unexpected source. We had anticipated criticism from the ultra-fannish camp, and there were a few snide remarks and self-congratulatory snickers, but these soon disappeared. Clearly, the "about something" concept brought about a resonance on the part of the fan community.

But what to do when we received a postcard like this one, written by a prominent fan named Art Castillo —

Dear schizophrenics:

An excerpt from a card sent to Donaho: "There seems to be a mass-surge among the cattle recently to bandy about comic-book statistics like baseball averages. I hope this regressive idiocy dies out with the conditions that prompted it. I'm afraid these people confuse regaining childhood spontaneity with the morbid imbecility foisted on children by adults. So far (aside from Nelson) the only one who's had anything to say on the subject is Boggs (Xero 3) ' ... All around you is a society seething, begging not only for a critical evaluation of its fundamentals but for a re-construction of those very fundamentals, and you people sit on your ass and discuss comic books.' What's wrong with you, anyway?"

Donaho, in case you're puzzled, was a leading fan publisher. Nelson was, and still is, Ray Nelson, a fan cartoonist then and an accomplished novelist and short-story writer in later years. Boggs was another brilliant fan writer who disappeared into some murky literary depths long before his death.

Pat and I didn't trashcan Castillo's postcard or relegate it to the letter column. We ran it as a full-page guest editorial. That might have rubbed salt in Castillo's wounds. When we didn't hear from him we wondered if his contributor's copy of *Xero 4* failed to reach him, and even invited him to write an essay for the magazine. He responded with another terrific postcard that became a guest editorial in *Xero 5*:

No, haven't gotten Xero but can well anticipate the attitude. I have no intention of telling you how to run your magazine. I merely comment in passing that there is a good deal of difference between a quality magazine that publishes material which is both interesting and has something to say and a Sunday supplement which publishes items simply because they are "interesting." The latter phenomenon is simply part of that relativistic dadaism (of which Life is the outstanding example) into which Western culture is rapidly disintegrating. Dwight McDonald or G. Legman, for instance, can write interestingly about comic books but they have something to say about comic books ... in context ... against a background with a specific hierarchy of social values. Would you ask me to contribute to True Confessions or Men's Sweat because a certain level of mentality found them "interesting?" Oh, come now. Mature your definition a little bit and maybe I'll reconsider ... Cheers,

We were enchanted with Art Castillo's phraseology, and thereafter adopted a subtitle for *Xero*. It was thereafter *Xero: the*

Fanzine of Relativistic Dadaism. Alas, we never heard from Castillo again. I guess he gave us up as a hopeless cause.

But a lesson was learned. We had been attacked (gently) from one side for being "serious and constructive" instead of lightly and wittily fannish, and from the other side for, I suppose, not being "serious and constructive" enough. We decided that *Xero* would find its own audience and its audience would find it, which in fact was already happening. Both the ultrafannish and the hyperserious could go their own ways.

We weren't above or apart from the fan community, of course. Probably the most popular fan in the world was an Irishman named Walter A. Willis. A group of American fans had raised a fund in 1952 and brought him across the ocean to attend the World Science Fiction Convention in Chicago. Ten years later the US fan community duplicated that effort and brought both Willis and his wife Madeleine to the Worldcon. A variety of fund-raisers were staged to finance the Willises' trip.

Pat and I published a special "Willish" — Willis-issue — of *Xero*. It was *Xero 6*, featured a portrait of Willis on the cover, and sold for the breathtaking price of $1 per copy. All receipts went to the Willis Fund. Even contributors were asked to buy their copies instead of receiving the usual complimentary contributors' copies. Pat and I went so far as to buy our own file copies of the magazine. Marion Zimmer Bradley accused us of blackmail, but the issue sold out.

Xero published essays for the most part, in one form or another, along with cartoons and other graphics. We published very little fiction — one story, as I remember — and an occasional poem. Our most prolific poet was a teen-aged fan from the Midwest named Roger Ebert. When Roger had a stopover in New York Pat and I as sophisticated adults in our twenties had the pleasure of entertaining Roger and showing him the bright lights of the big city.

Forty years later when Roger agreed to write his introduction to *The Best of Xero* he asked me for a copy of the report I published, on his visit. I'd completely forgot about writing that report, but there it was, in the fading ink of my own salad days. Roger has interpolated it into his introduction. I must say that my political and social attitudes have changed drastically in the past four decades, and I was tempted to revise the copy for republication, but that, obviously, would be to falsify history, so my youthful words will have to stand.

Around this time we also received a brief essay by a young professional named Donald E. Westlake who was making a name for himself as both a science fiction and mystery writer. In fact, Westlake had approached me at a cocktail party and offered to send me his manuscript. I kindly offered to look at it. Hah!

The screed was called "Don't Call Me, I'll Call You." In it, Westlake effectively resigned from the science fiction world. To make sure that his bridges were thoroughly burned he told some damning stories about John W. Campbell, Jr., at that time the most influential editor in the field. He also told off the other leading editors just to make sure they would never buy a manuscript from him again.

Westlake's agent wailed that "Don has killed himself (professionally)." And in fact the essay was explosive. When it was reprinted in *Mystery Scene* magazine in 2003 I had occasion to reread it for the first time in forty years, and it is *still* explosive. But Westlake somehow managed to survive, as the row of best-selling mystery novels and the screenwriting Oscar on his mantelpiece attest.

As *Xero* grew in both size and circulation, it also became increasingly elaborate in design and production. Our friend Chris Steinbrunner, film manager for New York's TV Channel 9, got us access to a wonderful machine that converted drawings to mimeograph stencils electronically, bypassing the whole stylus-shading plate-mimeoscope process. George Scithers, a fan who would later become founding editor of *Isaac Asimov's Science Fiction Magazine* and serve at both *Amazing Stories* and *Weird Tales* as well, furnished us with several packets of brilliant incandescent paper stock that we used for *Xero* covers.

ANGEL-DEVIL, *Steve Stiles*

And we began sending out artwork to printers, collating the results into our magazine either as covers or as interior illustrations. We used this process for a brilliant satirical comic strip by Landon Chesney and to reproduce a huge, ancient magazine photograph of a circa-1900 stage production called *A Yankee Circus on Mars*. This latter went along with an essay titled "The Greatest Shows Un-Earthly" by Norman Clarke. Clarke later expanded the essay into a book, *The Mighty Hippodrome* (1968), one of a surprising number that grew from *Xero*'s pages.

Lin Carter was at the outset of his own career, during which he would become one of the most prolific and most popular novelists in the field, churning out pastiches of the works of Edgar Rice Burroughs, Robert E. Howard, and other authors of fantastic adventures. For *Xero*, Lin wrote poetry, book reviews (when Larry Harris retired from the task), and a series of essays titled *Notes on Tolkien*. The series was collected and expanded to become a Ballantine book, *Understanding Tolkien and the Lord of the Rings*.

The essays about old comics became two books, *All in Color for a Dime* and *The Comic-Book Book*, co-edited by Don Thompson and myself. Some of James Blish's trenchant essays were incorporated into later volumes of his criticism.

Most of the essays that we ran were relatively gentle, first-person reminiscences, or else, like Norman Clarke's pieces on theater history or Chris Steinbrunner's articles about radio drama and movie serials, were effectively research papers, written in a populist style for the lay reader rather than in academic jargon. Just about everything was well-received, although a paean to fantasist Clark Ashton Smith, written by Haywood P. Norton, brought some complaints.

But two items in *Xero* set off major firestorms. The first was Don Westlake's "Don't Call Me, I'll Call You." This brought letters of protest from L. Sprague de Camp, Frederik Pohl, Avram Davidson, and Donald Wollheim, as well our usual population of fan readers and correspondents, the most prolific and emphatic of whom was Richard Kyle.

The second was a review of Kingsley Amis' book *New Maps of Hell*. Amis' survey of the science fiction field was controversial in its own right. Then James Blish reviewed the book for *Xero* and the missives flew hot and heavy, variously in support or condemnation of Amis and of Blish.

Wow, was it ever fun!

But by the time we produced *Xero 8* — May, 1962 — we realized that something drastic would have to be done. We had produced eight issues of the magazine in eighteen months. *Xero* never had a formal publication schedule. Each issue would appear when we had enough good material to fill it and enough time to go through the elaborate process of production.

There was no problem, by now, in obtaining fine essays by well-known writers plus ever-better graphics. All of this in a truly amateur atmosphere — we never paid a contributor a dime. But as the magazine grew in girth, in elaboration, and in circulation, the production of each issue became increasingly burdensome. Having reached the level we had reached, we didn't want to back off to a more modest plane, so we announced that there would be two more issues, numbers 9 and 10, and that would be the end of *Xero*.

Some readers complained about this. Some asserted that we should have kept going full-bore and then simply stopped without making the announcement that we did. But it seemed, at least to Pat and me, that it would be more seemly to bring this wonderful adventure to an orderly landing in our home port than to end it *in medias res.*

Those last two issues were thoroughly up to par. They included Norman Clarke's superb essay, "The Greatest Shows Unearthly," complete with a gatefold illustration, as well as Ebert poetry, a brilliant Sax Rohmer parody by Lin Carter, a splendid piece on the workings of the publishing industry by Charles M. Collins, an astonishing blast at editorial stupidity disguised as a book review by Wilson Tucker, and a fine, comprehensive survey of the life and works of Sax Rohmer by Bob Briney.

Xero had come full circle. Pat Lupoff raised the topic of Sax Rohmer in the first issue; Bob Briney brought the subject to a close in the tenth and final issue.

Well, "final" is a slippery term. Sometime novelist Dave Van Arnam had promised a major piece on Edgar Rice Burroughs for the tenth *Xero,* but the issue grew so large, and Van Arnam's essay so bulky that we left it out of *Xero* proper and issued it as a separate volume, *The Reader's Guide to Barsoom and Amtor.* The circulation of this went up to 500 copies and the price to five dollars. The book — for that is what it really was — sold out overnight and a second printing was planned but somehow never quite happened.

We also published a special index edition of *Xero,* giving readers one last chance to get in their locs.

Shirley Camper, a feature writer for *Cosmopolitan* magazine, came to our apartment to conduct a lengthy interview, ostensibly to gather material for a feature article in *Cosmo.* The article never appeared, but Ms. Camper urged us to make *Xero* a fully commercial magazine.

It was an intriguing notion, but the longer we considered it the less we were inclined to proceed. It would, in fact, have meant a complete revamping of *Xero*. Instead of trying to hold circulation down we would have had to boost it as high as we could, increasing our print run at least tenfold to start out and another tenfold as soon as we could.

That in turn would have meant the end of our whole procedure involving stencils, lettering guides, shading plates, mimeoscopes, correction fluid and stencil cement, duping sessions (you can figure that one out!), and treks to the Pace Paper Company in Brooklyn and to Larry and Noreen Shaw's house on Staten Island. It would have meant the end of those collating parties with their endless circlings of the dinner table, and of the thrilling late-night missions to the corner mailbox.

These chores may sound like an office slavey's version of Hell, and if we'd been performing them for pay they might indeed have been boring at best and agonizing at worst. But we were doing them because we loved publishing *Xero* and each task, however menial and repetitious, was part of that love affair.

Instead we would have to send manuscripts to a typographic service. Remember, this was long before the era of home computers and desktop publishing software. We'd have to engage a graphic designer. Our first choice would of course have been bhob Stewart, if we could get him to stay on.

Xero had never included many advertisements, and the few we did run were featured *gratis* for worthy fannish causes. We would, of course, have to reverse that policy and work aggressively to get as many ads as we could, and to charge market rates for them. Our first targets would have been book publishers, of course, followed by record companies, movie producers, and assorted entertainment venues. The automobile and vodka ads would have come later.

We would have had to arrange distribution to get the magazine into bookstores and onto newsstands. And of course the little tin box with the index cards would have to go. Subscriptions would require a businesslike procedure, probably farmed out to a so-called "fulfillment house" in the business of handling subscription lists for periodical publishers.

We would certainly have paid our contributors. This would have placed us in direct competition with every other publication in the field, from *The Saturday Review of Literature* to *The New Yorker*. It's unlikely that we could have matched their pay rates. Paradoxically, it might have been more difficult for us to get material of the quality we wanted by paying for it than it had been when we "paid" only in contributor's copies.

In fact, we would have been publishing a new magazine. It might have been very good but it wouldn't have been *Xero* any more. Thinking back to those days, I believe that, had we moved into professional publishing, we would have wiped the slate clean and started afresh with Volume One, Number One of — something different.

Our Manhattan apartment was not far from Lexington Avenue, and I think that we might have published *The Lexington Review*. Yes, I rather like the sound of that. It smacks of upscale, Revolutionary War America, Paul Revere, Nathan Hale, the Minute Men and all that. Yet it would have had a direct geographical connection to our base of operations.

But our second child would arrive in 1964. Pat was already busy with Ken; Kathy would make her life far busier. And I was struggling with my own demons. I was making good money in the computer business and my career was on the upswing. *The Lexington Review* would have been a full-time occupation and I was clinging for dear life to my regular paycheck: I couldn't just walk away from my job.

It was 1970 and our third child, Tommy, had arrived, before I was finally able to make my break from the computer industry. By then I was writing books on a pretty regular basis, and the idea of going into the magazine business (or going *back* into it) was simply beyond the pale.

Xero had won the Hugo award at the World Science Fiction Convention in 1963, but by the time of that convention the magazine was already defunct. In later years Pat and I were approached repeatedly by editors and publishers aware of the treasure trove of material in the back files of *Xero*. Some of them proposed reissuing the full run of the magazine in facsimile. Others felt that a "Best of" volume was a more practical and appealing approach. But none of them ever came to us with a firm and attractive offer.

Of course there were many other fine fanzines in the same era, and an enterprising publisher might do well to look at them as a source of terrific and even important writing that is in danger of being lost forever. Titles come trippingly to the brain: *Habakkuk, Lighthouse, Void, Hyphen, Slant, Cosmag, Oopsla!, Quandry, Inside, Grue.* Were they as good as my memory tells me they were? Someone else will have to make that determination. Were there still others that I never knew about, or that I simply fail to remember? Without a doubt there were.

But you have to start somewhere, and I'll confess that Pat and I had pretty well decided that a *Xero* facsimile or a *Xero* anthology would remain an unfilled dream.

That is, until Jacob Weisman of Tachyon Publications proposed to publish *The Best of Xero*. He not only offered to take on the project, but to do so in a hands-on manner. Jacob has been the chief laborer in selecting material from the files of the magazine. The letters, for instance, were selected and edited once by Pat, forty years ago. Jacob filtered them again to reach the selection in this book.

The general contents of the magazine were originally procured through both Pat's efforts and my own. If we'd had to select the material for *The Best of Xero* I'm convinced the project would have grown to unwieldy size and collapsed of its own sheer weight. As in the letter selections, Jacob provided a "re-filtering" of the general contents of the magazine, to arrive at the contents of *The Best of Xero*. I could, frankly, wail at the top of my lungs, "How can we publish this book without including _____?" (Fill in the blank.)

But these are the realities of the publishing world, and I offer *The Best of Xero* with pride and without regrets.

Still, I'll let you in on a little secret. If you visit our home and find your way into the cellar, there on an old kitchen table lurking beneath an oilcloth cover you will find a half-century-old Gestetner mimeograph. In the drawer beneath the mimeo are a small but tasteful selection of lettering guides and shading plates.

And once in a while I wake up the middle of the night, slip out of bed so as not to waken Pat, and creep silently down to the cellar and stand there, just stand there, looking at the old Gestetner and thinking, *Well, maybe, maybe one of these days, just maybe …*

INTRODUCTION

THOSE WERE THE GOOD OLD DAYS
PAT LUPOFF

Fandom in the early sixties was a lot of fun. There were the serious fans like the Lunarians who had formal meetings with a gavel to start them and a written agenda of topics to be discussed. Then there were fans like us; we were in a group called the Fanoclasts who got together because we enjoyed each other's company. We talked and gossiped about the latest fan scandals. We drank beer and sometimes a group of us would get on the New York subway in the middle of the night and go and eat Chinese food at a little restaurant in Chinatown called Sam Wo's. Then we would pile back on the Lexington Avenue line of the subway and get home at about two o'clock in the morning.

In the early sixties this was a perfectly safe thing to do. So our decision to start a fanzine seemed to be a perfectly normal thing to do.

Our first thought was to call our fanzine *Xanadu* but — alas — we learned that name was already taken so we settled on *Xero*. As Dick said, we pretty much wrote the first issue ourselves. I had recently been turned on to the Gormenghast trilogy written by Mervyn Peake, by fellow fan Joe Sanders, and also while book scouting with Dick had discovered the sinister world of Sax Rohmer. This provided me with lots to write about in the early issues of *Xero*. When tons of mail started coming in all about the first issue of *Xero*, Dick asked me to become the letter editor. I had lots of fun reading and sometimes commenting on all of *Xero*'s correspondence.

The volume of correspondence was huge and most of the letters were remarkably apt. I tried to keep the published correspondence on topic, comments on articles in the previous issue, without becoming too repetitious. Some letters came from otherwise anonymous fans in various parts of the country and the world. Others came from very prominent figures in the science

PATRICIA LUPOFF (1937-) pursued scholarly interests ranging from archaeology to contemporary fantasy literature to Western Americana, publishing a number of important papers on the latter subject. She worked as a journalist in San Francisco in the 1970s, returning to the world of books as a buyer and manager first for an antiquarian book dealer, then as manager of the children's department of Cody's Books, one of the leading independent bookstores in northern California. As co-founding editor of Xero she was the first woman ever to win the Science Fiction Achievement Award (Hugo).

fiction field. I tried to make my choices based on the quality of the letters rather than the fame of their authors.

I learned from Dick how to cut stencils on our electric typewriter, a skill that I was asked to perform at a temporary job at an insurance company in the seventies. I learned how to apply corflu with a heavy hand in both instances.

I also learned how to feed a group of people and not poison them. (Cooking had not been a skill that I had been taught while growing up.) Spaghetti and salad was a meal that I could cook safely and not set our apartment on fire, something that I almost did while broiling a steak earlier in our marriage.

Sneaking out of our apartment late at night with our suitcases full of *Xero*s stamped and ready to be mailed, and depositing them in different neighborhood mailboxes, sometimes with our small and noisy Cocker Spaniel in tow, only added to the fun. I do wonder what our elevator man thought of all of this, but he never asked. We tipped him generously at Christmas and sometimes brought him cups of hot coffee or chicken broth when he stopped on our floor and we were up late at night.

When I became pregnant with our first child, Ken, my share of the work on *Xero* was done at very odd hours. I was "morning sick" off and on throughout the day, although the later in the day that it was the better and hungrier I became. One time I was editing letters late at night when I desperately craved egg rolls. Fortunately, since we lived in Manhattan, there was a Chinese restaurant right around the corner from us that stayed open till about two in the morning. Dick was very kind and ran downstairs to buy me egg rolls so that I could continue my work on *Xero*.

When our fanzine publishing became too serious and some of the thrill and the fun had gone out of publishing it, we decided to quit while we were still ahead. Sometimes I, like Dick, will sneak downstairs to the basement and peer wistfully at our mimeograph machine and then return upstairs and stare at my computer, but I really think that publishing *Xero* was a product of the sixties.

It's a different decade now, in fact it's a different century. Whole generations of fans have come and gone in the past forty-odd years. I'll leave it to today's fans to run fandom the way they see fit.

PSYCHO

REVIEWED BY HARLAN ELLISON

HARLAN ELLISON (1934-) was one of the noisiest and most conspicuous members of the fan community in the late 1950s and early 1960s. Some fans (and pros) admired his brashness and obvious talent, others regarded him as a pest. Nobody, but nobody, ignored him. He moved from fandom into the ranks of professional writing with – well, maybe it was a short story called "The Glow-Worm" in Infinity Science Fiction *for February, 1956. He has been a prolific and steady producer for half a century, using at least seven pseudonyms, writing hundreds of short stories and not a few novels, screenplays, comic book scripts, and critical pieces. He has also edited anthologies, his* Dangerous Visions *books becoming one of the most important and influential series in the history of the field. He insists that he is not "a science fiction writer" but rather, and simply, a writer, some of whose works happen to fall under the science fiction*

Now, to begin, let's set the ground rules: you're a guy who makes his living writing, you know all the cliches, all the phony starts, and you can usually second-guess the movie-scripters every time out. You are over twenty-one, find the mockings and mewlings of Lugosi and Chaney more pitiable than frightening, and the last time you were really scared was when the platoon leader wakened you for guard at four in the morning out on bivouac. Further, you've read the book, know the author is a greater wit than weirdie, and you're all set to be bored. Ground rules set. Witness in point: this reviewer. I went to see the Bloch-Hitchcock *Psycho*.

Frankly, I had the shit scared out of me.

No two ways about it, Charlie, this time they've pulled off the Indian rope trick. It starts out like a below-par chapter of *Stella Dallas* and pretty chop-chop leaves all reality behind as the fit of terror wraps around your windpipe. If you've read the book, be assured the moon pitcher follows pretty faithfully (they've extended the opening to give you some drool-invoking scenes of Janet Leigh in her bra and half-slip, and they've taken literary license with the character of Norman, the son who runs the motel). (As to the license taken with Norman's character, I feel it is all to the good as warmed-over by Tony Perkins: brooding pensive, darkly intense, engaging, altogether terrifying in its simplicity and naturalism.)

If you haven't read the book, the gravest disservice will be done you by the trap-mouth who spills the plot. Far be it from me to kill the goose. However (he said, remembering how annoyed he used to get in high school when oral book reports were concluded, "And if you want to know what happens, you'll have to read the book."), the scene is the Southwest, the opening gun gets fired as Miss Leigh, full in the midst of an affair with a young divorced cat from a small town somewhere, heads out with a bagful of her employer's loot. She stops, in her mad flight, at a run-down motel operated by likable but lopsided Tony Perkins, who has nasty fights with his Mother, seen as a shadow through the window of their brooding, Addams-like mansion on the hill ... under the scud-filled cadaverous-grey sky.

rubric. Xero *was lucky to catch him in 1960 in a relaxed moment, early in his career.*

That's it. That's all you get. From there on out, you had better bring the Miltown out of your weskit pocket. Because at that point Hitchcock uncorks some of the most brutally gagging detail work ever to grace the screen. Consider: on TV and suchlike, murder is a fairly uncomplicated matter. You want someone dead, you stab or shoot him ... once ... and down he goes. Life just ain't like that, Charlie. In the real world (the one where you have to carry out the garbage or it begins to smell fairly bad) murder can be mucho difficult. Just consider again: the guy doesn't want to die. He fights you as you try to stab him. He grabs your arm. You struggle. He throws you off balance. You get in slight slashes to the arms in an attempt to land a fatal blow. Blood begins to spatter. The struggle goes on. Reality.

That's right, Charlie. That's what Hitchcock has given us in *Psycho*. And this, this grotesque pathological attention to the sensational aspects of reality combined with obscure camera angles and stream-of-consciousness music leaves the viewer in a state of debilitation and shakenness.

It was so painful ... the suspense, the horror of it all ... that twice I felt compelled to get up and leave the theatre. I *literally* could not stand it. And to top it off, the ending is in the finest tradition of the macabre. If *Diabolique* with its eyeball-thumbing scene scared you, this picture will stop your pump permanently, I can say with all sureness that *no one* will escape terror at this show.

It was filmed the smartest way possible (for this sort of flick) in black and white, and the cast is brilliant. They all have dimension and purpose, and what befalls each of them (even the unseen Mother) matters — to you.

Go then, Charlie, with my best wishes and my condolences. Because after you've seen this film, you'll be scared to ever take a shower in a motel again. And that, Charlie baby, is a promise.

EPISTOLARY INTERCOURSE #1

CONDUCTED BY PAT LUPOFF

HARRY WARNER, JR.

I missed *Psycho* for unavoidable reasons, but this is the best review I've read of it. I wonder how many individuals failed to attend it because of the preview. I saw that, and it was the most dismal five minutes I've ever spent in a theater.

DAVE ENGLISH

Harlan's review of *Psycho* has the distinction of being the best review I've read of the film I've seen. The other was Bosley Crowther's, which somebody showed me the other day. Both reviews, each in its own way, say the same thing: that Mr. Hitchcock set about to make a horror movie and succeeded very well. So damned if I can see what all the crabbing is about, especially when I compare *Psycho* to something like *Circus of Horrors* which I inadvertently showed up at last week — a wretched collection of violent deaths and sundry ugliness piled one on top of the other without taste or logic whatever.

As soon as everybody who's going to gets to see this film, I hope somebody will really take and review the thing. I think it deserves a bit more detailed discussion: in fact, one of the most frustrating experiences in recent days has been wanting to talk it over with a number of people, none of whom have seen the blamed thing.

The article on Captain Marvel was lovely and I agree completely as to the superiority of Marvel over Superman. Such was my feeling, too, back in the days when I was reading for the first time, and was responsible for many heated, often bloody debates in my neighborhood.

As matter of fact, it was on the comic book that I first learned to read. I don't mean to say that reading was something that I picked up on my own, before the school system had a go at

BATMAN, Ajay Budrys

AJAY BUDRYS was, yes, the same person as Algis Budrys, who had a long and distinguished career as novelist, short story writer, editor and critic.

teaching me, but I remember vividly an occasion when I picked up a Marvel comic which no one would read to me at the time, and poring over it suddenly discovered that instead of laboriously spelling out individual words, I was actually and literally *reading*.

DONALD ANDERSON

Harlan Ellison's review of *Psycho* stuck a nerve, as my reaction to this movie was much the same as his. As the plot advanced to each murder, I found myself attempting, unsuccessfully, to avert my face from the screen. Movies *just don't scare me* — but this one did.

TOM CONDIT

"The Big Red Cheese" was the real highlight of the issue, and gives me a beautiful opportunity to make a public announcement. A group of us in New York (me and Martha Adkins, to be precise) have formed the idea of reviving Captain Marvel. The motive for this is simple: with the possible exception of the Heap and the Spirit, Captain Marvel was the greatest of all comic book characters. We therefore have resolved to form the *Marvel Family Revival Association* (and the religious sound of the name is deliberate) for the purpose of urging and aiding the revival of Captain Marvel, with Eando Binder hired at whatever fabulous salary he demands to write the continuity. The headquarters of the above association is provisionally in care of me. There is only one membership requirement: that you write a letter to Fawcett Publications urging them to revive Captain Marvel. We're considering making up a letterhead, etc. Why must we do it? Because it is *not* there.

OTTO BINDER

Might mention in passing that Anthony Boucher bowled me over by revealing he was a Captain Marvel fan of long standing, as it's being first-rate "fantasy."

THOSE HIGH-FLYING SPACESHIPS

MIKE DECKINGER

Seven o'clock in the evening used to be a sacred hour for me.

No matter what else I was doing I stopped then. I divorced myself from all outside pleasure, broke away from games I might have been engaged in, folded up comics, and even left the dinner table.

That was when *Captain Video* went on and at the time I could think of no fate more unbearable than missing an installment.

Just as the housewives of today keep themselves glued to the daily fare of mediocrity and banality dished out by the soap opera, I was a devotee of space opera, reveling daily in what it had to offer.

Captain Video was the first.

He had to be, I can't recall anyone I watched before him, though there were many I know of who succeeded him.

"Captain Video," as played by Al Hodge, was a dashing, skilled, intelligent adventurer who, with the assistance of his Video Ranger (a Robin type, aiding but not overshadowing the principle hero), sought adventure in outer space and helped combat evil. The early shows were a combination of live and filmed action. All the interplanetary scenes were filmed, most of them being repeated endlessly day after day, and having the same shot of a spaceship taking off and landing. Captain Video's portion of the show was live and rather than being treated as a typical half-hour adventure, it was a serial, progressing from one improbable event to another, until a climax was reached, which never made much sense, but which was a pretext for starting some new adventure.

Prior to watching the show, my only science fiction indoctrination had been through the medium of comics, and you

MIKE DECKINGER (1943-) was a native New Yorker who moved to placid, bucolic New Jersey at the age of seven. "I became enthralled with science fiction in my pre-teens," he states, "and from there drifted into the fan world. In the early '60s I published several unmemorable fanzines, Hocus and Bedlam, and feverishly wrote tons of even more profoundly unmemorable material for other publications." Deckinger is excessively modest: his essay on Captain Video provoked James Blish to write his own Captain Video memoir (as Arthur Merlyn), which led to what a later generation would refer to as a rich discussion thread. The too-modest Deckinger and his wife have lived in San Francisco since 1971, having been "lured by the seductive spell of the receding hippie era."

can easily realize how this could have an adverse effect.

Most of the sf comics I had read tossed caution, facts, and logic to the winds in bringing across their stories, and my head became so filled with these inaccuracies (walking across the moon without a spacesuit, normal gravity on a spaceship in free fall, etc.) that I was prepared for anything the good captain had to offer in the way of scientific details. And there were many inconsistencies that filled the screen, though it's doubtful whether I even noticed any of them then.

The serial format of *Captain Video* gave the good captain the opportunity to indulge in as many interplanetary adventures as he desired, without destroying the continuity of the show, such as it was. I can remember one set of episodes devoted to the search for a Philosopher's Stone by a young spaceman who heard voices from the stars talking to him. By the time this particular series was done, there was so much doubletalk and unresolved ending that I *never* found out whether the young man found his Stone.

Doctor Pauli was a diabolical mad scientist whose chief claim to infamy was his evil little laugh. He didn't like Captain Video at all. Well, this naturally meant that the captain had to do everything in his power to bring the criminal to justice, and I can't remember to this day whether Doctor Pauli was disposed of once and for all or not. I tend to think he wasn't; it would have been too much of a letdown to see an invincible archfiend like him nabbed by Captain Video.

Another recurring character was Video's boss, first Commissioner Bell and later Commissioner Carey. The commissioner was to Captain Video very much what Perry White was (and is) to Superman. The commissioner was a symbol (and an amusing one at that, considering that this was a juvenile show) of all exasperated-but doggedly-pompous brass in high places. He was simply unable to comprehend why the good captain hadn't located the crooks yet and made it seem as if he was preparing to bust the lawman to something lower than private. He ranted and raved and was instrumental in switching all juvenile emotions not otherwise committed to the favor of Captain Video. Naturally we kids were aware that the commissioner was really a nice guy and that anyone would act like that if he had the kind of twenty-four-hour-a-day job the commissioner had, sitting constantly by the viewer screen to receive calls from Captain Video. Secretly, we still admired the commissioner, but we never let it show.

There were several gimmicks filling the show that deserve mention. Since *Captain Video* was being shown at the height of the western rage — and since tired western footage is vastly cheaper than live action — a portion of every show was given over to "contact" with the special "western Video Ranger." What was done here actually was simply to show an old western, a few minutes of it each day, the hero of the western automatically becoming a special agent of the captain. When a film was completed, we would "contact" another "western Video Ranger" and a new western would begin. I wonder how Gene Autry felt, knowing that he was a special western agent of Captain Video.

Premiums are always big business, whether they are offered in Cracker Jack boxes or on TV, and *Captain Video* managed to drag more premiums and giveaway toys onto the show than anyone else in his time. Who can forget the beaming face of announcer Fred Scott as he described in delightful, liquid, yet still masculine tones, the address to which you send your quarter and the required number of Powerhouse candy bar wrappers for the free premium they were offering.

Most of the premiums had actually been used by the captain himself in one or another of his adventures, which proved how valuable they were. I may have been a gullible youngster at the time, but I point with pride to the fact that I succumbed only once to this hard-sell advertising, to order a special card which has the negative image of a man, and makes use of some principle of optics to give you a positive image against a blank background if you first stare intently enough at the card. No matter how many times it was mentioned on TV, I could not figure the gimmick out, so I finally sent away for it. It was not entirely useless, because the day after I received it I watched Captain Video apprehend a notorious criminal through its use.

Most of the props on the show were pretty bad, and easily

recognizable as poorly simulated gadgets. Captain Video had a paralyzer consisting of a futuristically styled gun with an underslung trigger. When the trigger was pressed a beam of light shot out, accompanied by a low buzz, all generated by two flashlight batteries located in the muzzle of the gun. The reason I know this is that I had purchased the exact same thing several weeks before for $1.29 at a local store. Whenever Captain Video shot anyone with the gun, the victim would freeze in his tracks, sometimes toppling over to make things worse. It was a last-resort weapon; it would even penetrate walls, and no one could escape the lethal blast of Captain Video's paralyzer. All mine ever did was light up dark places and produce a very annoying buzz faintly akin to the sound of a horde of angry bees about to zero in for an attack. I could never understand the reason; when the captain was operating the same I was, why did he get that nice paralyzing effect while all I got was a light and a buzz? It just didn't seem right, and one evening after unsuccessfully trying to paralyze several cats, I carefully dissected the gun in such a thorough manner that I was never able to reassemble it.

Since *Captain Video* was intended for us action-loving juveniles who generally deplored mushy romance, he was depicted as a man's man who shunned womanhood. He was trustworthy, loyal, helpful, kind, etc, but he simply refused to be shackled with any woman. We saw no mushy clinches between the captain and *any* female, while the captain's fanatical regard for the Video Ranger was so great as to suggest homosexual tendencies. But being youngsters, we didn't know of such things, and if we did, we forgave him.

After all, the captain was my hero.

Until recently. Recently when I saw Al Hodge working as a phony dentist in a TV commercial. My whole world crumbled about me as the good captain explained about toothpaste. "Where are your spaceships," wanted to cry out as he held up the tube of toothpaste and with a keen smile explained its better qualities.

But there were no spaceships, no more commissioners, no more robots, no more ray guns, no more Video Rangers.

And no more *Captain Video.*

EPISTOLARY INTERCOURSE #2
CONDUCTED BY PAT LUPOFF

BOB LEMAN

Somehow I managed to miss the comic books entirely, except for a few *Famous Funnies*. When I was in the army, the sex-and-sadism comics were in vogue, and I recollect that during basic training there was a brisk trade in these things going on. I tried to read them a time or two, but of course they were intended for semi-literates. Still, in later years, when I read Wertham's book damning the comics as the source of all juvenile delinquency, it seemed to me to be a pack of damned nonsense. I only wish I'd been a comics fan, so I could wander down nostalgia's perfumed path as I read this series.

RUTH BERMAN

I loved Mike Deckinger's article "Those High Flying Spaceships." I happen to have as many pleasant and nostalgic feelings toward *Video* as he does. I never left the dinner table when *Captain Video* came on. I sat down in front of the TV with my dinner tray five minutes before the Captain came on to make sure I wouldn't miss him. For years the carpet before the TV had a mashed-potatoes hue.

Perhaps there are some snide folks in the readership (it seems unlikely, but there just might be) who would say that Mike ... and Ted White ... and me, too, are just being nostalgic at great length about our childhoods. Right! Can you think of anything pleasanter? Outside of dreaming of the future? The high-flying spaceships are gone, but they've left ghosts behind.

WHERE DO YOU GET THOSE CRAZY IDEAS?

LARRY M. HARRIS

LARRY HARRIS (1933-2002) may have been a pseudonym of LAURENCE M. JANIFER. Or maybe it was the other way around. Ask any three of his friends and the first two will disagree while the third will tell you that he was really Alfred Blake, Andrew Blake, Mark Phillips, or maybe Barbara Wilson -- since he used all of those names. His first novel, Pagan Passions *(1959), was the first of four collaborations with the late Randall Garrett. Like many commercial novelists, he divided much of his output between science fiction and mysteries. But he also wrote sexy paperbacks and ghost-wrote several joke books and autobiographies.*

The fact is that nobody ever asks me that question. They all assume they know. Maybe they do. I wish they'd tell me, though, because I don't.

Somebody comes up to me and says: "Gee, that was a funny idea of yours, about those poodles and the TV guy. I guess you figured a lot of people are interested in TV, and a lot of people own dogs, so it would be popular, huh?

So I say yes. Because what else is there to say? I wrote a book called *The Pickled Poodles* (Random House, $2.95, advt.) and it deals with a TV guy and some dogs and some other things, and do I know why I wrote it? No. I picked the TV guy because I needed someone with money and a large business orientation, and TV is something I know a little about. I needed such a character because somebody once said to me, by a slip of the tongue as lovely as it was unexpected, "I saw this great play on TV last night. There's this guy, see, and he's being blackmailed but he doesn't know it … "

Even if that hadn't been what the play was about (and it wasn't), I had to figure out some way to make the idea work. A man being blackmailed, who doesn't know he's being blackmailed … the idea has a certain charm. In order to work it out, I found I needed a character with certain business appurtenances. Hence, the moneyed man. Hence (because the money and the business organization have to come from somewhere, and my knowledge of Wall Street is not very extensive) the TV guy.

And the dogs? I said to myself: "I would like some dogs in this book. Large, drunken. I think they would be very pleasant to have around." So I put in some dogs. Then I had to plot the rest of the book, but it was easier going, since I had so many known factors — the dogs, the TV guy and the blackmail bit, and so on.

I write books because I like writing books, and I write the

RAY GUNS, Dan Adkins

DAN ADKINS was a film scholar and archivist as well a scholar and critic working in the graphic arts when he came to Xero. His works were often surprising realistic, not at all as "cartoony" as one might have expected.

books I write because those are the ideas that occur to me. I carried around the notion of super-talented juvenile delinquents for two years, trying it in story after story, because I liked it. When Garrett and I did *Out Like a Light*, I realized what I liked about my delinquents: they were funny. Indeed they were. I had a lot of fun with them, and apparently the readers of *Astounding* did.

That Sweet Little Old Lady is part Campbell's idea, part mine, part Garrett's; at this distance, I can't reconstruct it any better than that. The entire book was written in about sixty hours, counting sleeping and eating time, with Garrett doing draft one and me doing draft two. *Out Like a Light* took a lot longer: eight days. (But for two of those days we didn't do any work at all; we worked four, goofed two and worked two.) *Occasion for Disaster* seems, in retrospect, to have gone on forever; for the first time we had complicated rewrite problems, and the book staggered toward final completion like James Barton, in his old drunk act, reaching for a lamppost. Once again, the basic notion was Campbell's, but the decorations (seventy-nine thousand, nine hundred and ninety words) were ours, and I don't know who did what any more. I do remember that Garrett originally created Queen Elizabeth I (Rose Thompson) and that I created Dr. Thomas O'Connor of Westinghouse Labs. Malone and Burris are joint creations, and who, if anyone, is responsible for Brubitsch, Borbitsch and Garbitsch I cannot possibly say.

As for *Pagan Passions* ... well, this was our notion, originally, but you'd never know it. Horace Gold provided the main plot-line, Garrett provided much of the mythology — and several unsung heroes provided that list of musical instruments, which took twenty-four hours of intensive and slightly drunken research. I listed every instrument I could come up with; Garrett added a few of the kazoo variety; and then I began calling friendly musicians and music students.

Ah research ... now here is something I do very little of. In *The Pickled Poodles*, the entire action is laid in Chicago and Topeka. I'd had Chicago described to me (never been there) but knew nothing about Topeka. I called some friends, but they had never been to Topeka either. One of them (I think Garrett) sad "It's a typical middle-western town." On that sentence, my total research for the book, I based two chapters.

Lee Wright at Random did correct some of my more egregious errors regarding poodles. I have never owned a dog, and don't even like them very much. I dreamed up a poodle and set it going; Lee made it plausible, much later.

But sometimes I do a little research. Just a little, not enough to be dangerous (because research, like garlic, is best in small quantities; a lot of it simply overpowers everything else in the mixture). I still remember how to say: "American s.o.b." in Russian, which Garrett and I needed for an early draft of *Occasion for Disaster*. (The scene no longer occurs in the book.) I know a number of deadly poisons, and some which ought to be and aren't. I know the names of all the major Greek gods. I even know how to name a race-horse, and the best was for a female impersonator to pretend to mammary development (any name containing fourteen letters or under, and use a brassiere filled with birdseed to give natural heft and motion). Most of this has come in handy for various stories.

But this does not answer the major question.

Where do I get those things, those crazy ideas?

They come to me. Sometimes Garrett or Campbell arrives bringing them. Sometimes they come under their own power. I was thinking of vampires the other night (it's a peaceful subject, like the family tree of the Hohenzollerns or the poison techniques of the more pushy Borgia offspring) and new ideas up and bite me. So maybe I'll write it.

Also, the other night, as I was dropping off to sleep, the world's single most horrible notion struck me. I sat up in bed, going: "Wheep, wheep," in a terrified fashion and flapping aimlessly. Then I spent some time rationalizing the notion. Then, next day, I called a publisher.

Maybe there's a book in this notion. I'm beginning to think

there is. The publisher also seems to think so.

So when you read it, don't ask me where I got the idea. It came and bit me. They do that sometimes. I write in several fields — mysteries, sf, unpublished plays, westerns, confessions, humor, horror, men's adventures, crossword puzzles ... because You Never Know. The next idea is likely to be anything at all.

Like the idea for this article, for instance. Dick Lupoff asked me to write it, so I did. I took me twenty minutes. It runs one thousand words. When I finish it I am going to send it to *Xero* and go inside and get a drink and drink it.

Then, later, or maybe tomorrow or so, I'm going to get to work on another idea.

There are lots of ideas floating around.

All I have to do is weed out the ones that demand research. Then I get to work on the other ones. This saves time and labor, and makes being a writer easier and more fun.

But, of course, not everybody can be a writer. Here is a test:

When you look at a beautiful girl (girls, make that a handsome man) — when you look at a beautiful girl (and for you people of both sexes — oh, the hell with it) — when you look at a beautiful girl, do you get ideas?

Of course you do.

Do those ideas invariably lead you to a typewriter, or to a pen and paper?

They don't? So don't be a writer. Mine, damn it, do.

THE SECRET FILES OF CAPTAIN VIDEO

BY JAMES BLISH WRITING AS ARTHUR MERLYN*

Nostalgia is busting out all over, and especially in the sercon journals, of which suddenly there are once more a good many. Redd Boggs' *Discord* has followed up a Jim Harmon article about "I Love a Mystery" with a complete script of one of those shows, demonstrating — to me at least — that those of us who missed it were lucky; and now we have these acres of copy about comic books in *Xero*. No doubt about it, this is National Back-to-the-Womb Year, with a vengeance. Kind of hard on us types who are rowing, more or less desperately, in the other direction.

But I have to confess that Mike Deckinger's piece about *Captain Video* caught me in the treacly toils. As I bit into the madeleine, all unknowing, my mind went reeling back to the days when I was writing the show. I may recover, but I don't think I can count on it.

Mike's essay stops short of the real golden days of the show's history: the period when the little gobbets of old westerns were thrown out, and the program was revised to consist of new stories each 15 days (three weeks) long, each by a different author. This change took place when the advertising agency for General Foods, the main sponsor, assigned to the show a new producer-cum-account-exec, a dark intense woman named Olga Druce.

Olga had heard of s-f somewhere and began to bring in s-f writers to do the scripts under the new format. For a long time she depended upon Bryce Walton, who did — as she gradually began to recognize — a very sloppy job. I remember one sequence in which Walton gave new names, and new and impossible orbits, to all the moons of Jupiter, thus greatly confusing my (then) eight-year-old, who had had them straight for almost a year. Olga doubtless didn't know the Jovian satellites any better that Bryce did, but she objected powerfully to the amount of violence in the Walton scripts; whenever he ran out of ideas he stage a fist-fight, which meant about every other day. She began scrounging around for other s-f writers.

JAMES BLISH, aka ARTHUR MERLYN (1921-1975) was a science fiction fan in the 1930s and had become a professional writer while still in his teens. His many novels and short stories include the classic A Case of Conscience *and the "Cities in Flight" cycle. Despite his high standing he never lost his interest in the fan community and participated generously in its rough and tumble with thoughtful essays and critiques. He was one of the first critics to treat science fiction with rigor and intelligence, and several collections of his criticism have become recognized classics in their own right.*

During the succeeding year she used three-week scripts by R.S. Richardson, Walter M. Miller Jr. and me (and this is by no means a complete list). Some of these stories were good, and the Miller, if I can trust my memory, was downright distinguished. Furthermore, they were fun to do — which was lucky, for the pay was not precisely princely: $100 for each half-hour script, or $1500 for a three-week story. In those days, and maybe even now, the Dumont network was called "Channel 5-and-dime," and deserved it. Of course as a lump $1500 looks like a fair sum of money; but 15 half-hour television scripts come to about 120,000 words, or twice as long as the average novel.

(The job did enable me to charge off my first television set on my income tax as a business expense; maybe that ought to be counted in.)

Stories usually evolved over dinner with Olga and the director — the latter a quiet, beefy man who turned into a shouting fury on the monitoring bridge. Olga drank numberless Scotch Mists and carefully explained the pitfalls. Of these the main one was the character of Captain Video, which could not be allowed to change in the course of a story. This made him so wooden that the first temptation for a writer was to drop him down a deep, dark hole in Episode 1, and not let him out until Episode 15. This, Olga said firmly, would not do; the good Captain had to be in the midst of the action all the time. We qualled (a useful word invented by Bob Lowndes circa 1946, covering the same ground as "croggled" but with more overtones) and said Okay, Olga. And then, there were those fist fights; the word on them was Nix.

There were some open areas, however. Olga had no objection to the writer's giving the Captain a sense of humor, providing that it was quiet situational humor and not wise-cracks or sight-gags. A good deal could also be done with Commissioner Carey, the Commissioner of Public Safety who was ostensibly Video's boss: a bumbling type who could nevertheless be made rather wistfully funny if you took care with him. (Walton had made him a repulsive office tyrant who never did anything but pound his desk and fume, which Olga wanted to get away from.) The Video Ranger, the Captain's young sidekick, could be allowed a certain amount of irreverent humor so long as it wasn't directed against the Captain.

There were also some more technical outs. One of the standard characters was the communications officer, Rogers, who was announcer Fred Scott; he opened the show on camera, thus: "Good evening, Rangers. This is Rogers, speaking for Captain Video," (Anyone for Boskone?). In the course of doing my own stint on the show I discovered that he could be used as a character in the main body of the script, at no extra expense; an innovation, to the best of my knowledge. Fred was, it turned out, a very resourceful actor and every script thereafter used him extensively. Then there was also the television institution of the "five-liner," but I'll delay describing that until a little later.

The actors were almost uniformly excellent, especially considering the handicaps under which they labored as a matter of course. Viewers often complained of the frequency with which they stammered or blew lines; but without considering that Hodges, Scott, *et al.* were required to memorize a half-hour script each and every day — a frightful chore which they performed well and cheerfully, on the whole. I was unaware of the pressure under which they operated until after my three weeks of scripts were all written, and so threw many roadblocks in their way — in particular the name of the spaceship involved, the *Telemachus*, over which they all fell repeatedly. Commissioner Carey never got it right even when it was syllabified for him on the teleprompter. By the time the show was running I was frantically rewriting the last week of it to remove as many of these barriers as I could, as soon as I became aware of them in rehearsal. (There was only one rehearsal for each day's show.)

In addition to the regulars (Video, the Commissioner, the Ranger, Rogers, and a character name Craig invented by Walton who was a sort of opposite number for the Ranger and whom I retained because — unlike the others — I could make him grow and change), my show involved several "outsiders" who were hired for this three-week sequence only. One of these was a girl, Lois somebody, a charming tyke who handled her role very well and greatly enlivened the rehearsals with all sorts of fantastic horseplay with the Ranger. The other was a British emigre, Malcolm somebody, who played my villain with great gusto, and whom I encountered later in more expensive TV shows; for instance, he played the friend of the deceased Great Author in a Hallmark dramatization of Maugham's *Cakes and Ale.* As Jason, my space pirate, he sneered and fleered with every evidence of enjoying himself. His end, alas, was horrible; some years later his hotel room was broken into and he was beaten to death with bottles. As far as I know the murderers have yet to be caught, and I doubt that anybody is looking for them anymore. At the time he could hardly have had more than ten bucks in his wallet, for he had been out of work for more than a year.

Hodges himself was delightful, and I doubt that I will ever forget him. The woodenness of the character he played was an injustice to him, for he was very fast on his feet, and responded with gratitude and virtuosity to any little subtlety the writer could manage to give his role. He was also magnificent with the kids who visited the show; if they worshipped him on TV, they went away from a personal encounter convinced that they themselves had been ennobled. He was as pure a case of what type-casting does to an actor as I have ever encountered; I am perfectly convinced that no role exists that he couldn't have done well, but his identification with Capt. Video was so complete that he has never since been given a decent chance.

Meanwhile, however, back at Capt. Video's secret base, there were rumblings, followed finally by an explosion. General Foods' agency withdrew its sponsorship, leaving behind only a gaggle of spot commercials plugging candy bars and other small change. With the cornflakes went Olga Druce, never to be seen again.

Dumont, convinced that nothing could kill *Captain Video*, went on as before, engaging a former movie director name Frank Telford as both producer and director. He was rather impressive. He introduced a number of technical tricks to the show, including a technique of rear projection which vastly expanded the kinds of backdrops a writer could call for; and on the bridge he was as quiet as a mouse, in sharp contrast to all the yelling which had gone on up there before. He also worked out a number of ingenious ways to keep the main characters in the story while they were actually away on vacation; I vividly remember the two weeks during which Commissioner Carey was tied up on the floor of a runaway spaceship (a still photograph given action by rolling the camera viewing it on gimbals).

Telford also developed the Saturday show, *The Secret Files of Captain Video*, which ran at 11:00 A.M. This completely broke with many of the former canons of the series by using the good Captain only as a minor character; Telford's notion was that in this way he could dramatize famous s-f short stories in such a way as to keep the kids, but perhaps attract some adult s-f fans as well. I did the first script for this, and adaptation of my story "The Box," with a great deal of assistance from Telford; and it was here that I was introduced to the five-liner. There are, it seems, three kinds of actors that can be used on TV according to union rules, each one of which costs the producer a fixed sum. Between major characters (who may say anything at any length) and extras (who are not allowed to open their mouths) there is the five-liner, who may deliver five lines and no more. The length of the line doesn't matter, as long as it is a single sentence; it's a good thing Henry James or William Faulkner weren't TV scriptwriters. It's surprising how much can be done with this device, though. Eight characters in "The Box" were five-liners, including my hero's wife; and nobody I have ever talked to who saw the show would believe that Meister's wife didn't talk as much as Meister himself, or any other of the major characters. It was a good show, and besides I got $300 for it, though it was only a half hour script. *Variety* liked it too. Hot dog!

But the decline in *Cap't Video*'s fortunes went remorselessly on. The other sponsors followed General Foods out the door like so many sheep, and soon nothing was left but public service departments. At last Dumont forced Telford to cut the daily strophes to fifteen minutes, but even this didn't help. Not even the candy bars were with it anymore. The last story was Damon Knight's, a good one — his second for the project and as far as I know the only one to be written for the fifteen minute format.

(The dropped fifteen minutes of that half hour, by the way, were filled in by an exceedingly funny domestic comedy called

Ethel and Albert, slightly sick, largely adlibbed and many years ahead of its time. It strongly resembled Mike Nichols and Elaine May. It died, too.)

Dumont kept Al on as the MC for a cartoon show, in which he used a robot prop left over from Knight's first script. As far as I know this still continues, though I wouldn't swear to it; and I believe Fred Scott is also still an announcer for Channel 5. But I miss the old days — the show much more than the money, which was never very inspiring. It was fun. If Mike Deckinger never saw any of the stories that ran after Cap't. Video's Western Agent was dropped, he missed some good yarns, some of them a hell of a lot better than anything that ran on *Tales of Tomorrow*. And I will further bet that nothing Rod Serling has done yet on *Twilight Zone* has been half as good as Walter Miller's stint for *Capt. Video*, which was not only purequill adult s-f, but remarkably poetic and moving throughout.

I still choke on cornflakes, now and then.

*Of course Arthur Merlyn isn't his real name. The customary Xero prize, a free copy of Flying Saucers, *to the first person who successfully identifies Merlyn. Another article by the same author — under his real name — will appear in Xero 4.*
-R.L.

EPISTOLARY INTERCOURSE #3
CONDUCTED BY PAT LUPOFF

JAMES BLISH

My *Video* piece administered a few unintentional slights (and a few intentional, I freely admit). I had meant to give as complete a list of the people who wrote the show that year or so, but I must have been typing too fast. I don't think I can reconstruct a complete list after this many years, but I do recall that among the people who wrote sequences — in addition to Richardson, Walton, Miller, Knight, and myself — were Jack Vance, Bob Sheckley, and Arthur C. Clarke. Several of these did two sequences before the debacle — Walton of course did a whole string of them — and there was one instance of one of the boys rewriting another, at Olga's request. (Not me, Doc, not me!)

One last note: one of the glories of the show for the writer was the model shop. Hollywood models are usually very elaborate — a spaceship model, for example, may run six feet long, just in case somebody might want to count the rivets — but on TV that's not necessary because of the degradation of the image. *Captain Video* spaceships rarely ran longer than a foot and cost very little; and the man who made them also did the shooting, and was good at it. This meant that the writer could call for all kinds of tabletop and other process film without so much as a blench from the producer. It was regarded as part of the normal cost of the show. My script called for a planet-wide earthquake, and the model shop turned out quite a terrifying one.

STEVE STILES

Glad to hear more about the good *Captain Video*. The sheer beauty of the series came to me yesterday when I was contemplating "Flash Gordon" in my quiet intellectual way. It was the continuity, the cliffhanging element which held my interest; like eating peanuts, bigosh, how could you stand missing a show, when in the last adventure the Ranger was being assimilated alive?

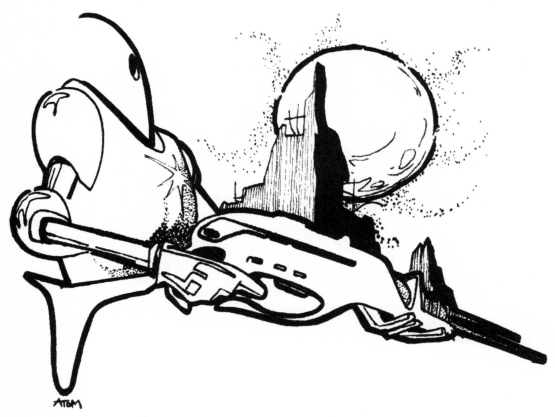

BOB BRINEY

ATOM was the signature name of Arthur Thomson, a popular British fan artist. Without question he was talented enough to establish himself professionally, and in fact he did have a few professional appearances, but for the most part he directed his works to the fan press.

I enjoyed the inside view of *Captain Video*. Since I never saw any of the programs and have not read any of the books or comics, there are no personal memories and no nostalgia to tie in with the discussion, but I found it very interesting anyway. I'll refrain from attempting to guess the identity of "Arthur Merlyn" — but if it's the same author who has used this name before (for example: in *Super Science* in the early '40s), then it is no wonder I enjoyed his article. I can't recall anything by Bl---, er Merlyn, that I haven't enjoyed reading.

DON THOMPSON

Larry Harris is a far better fan and reviewer than he is an sf writer. Possibly it's merely his collaborating with Garrett that gives me this feeling; Garrett is just playing around, prostituting his talent and infecting science fiction with social diseases in the process. Harris, in this article, shows evidence that he cares about science fiction and I think that Mark Phillips and Kenneth Malone ought to die natural deaths and Harris should strike out on his own.

Blish's article is quite interesting, though I doubt that *Captain Video* was as good as he makes it out to be. I saw only a few installments, since my family succumbed to TV only recently, and I thought it stank. Personally, I think westerns are the best-done things on tv (with rare exceptions such as *Twilight Zone* and news-features by Huntley-Brinkley or Murrow-Friendly), probably because producers, writers, and cameramen have more experience with horseshit and gunsmoke epics than any others. People are used to westerns, so you can start making them adult. People are not used to science fiction, so it's for kids. Serling is trying to start feeding TV viewers a dose of adult sf, even though they've had none to eat in years, since they were on the *Captain Video* pablum. I don't think TV viewers are ready for science fiction, except for occasional appearances. They'd rather watch hoods mowing down cops for fifty-five minutes before Eliot Ness devotes the last five minutes to mowing them down.

On to another topic: Magazine sf is not quite dead, but it's dying. I will not be content with books alone because I like short stories and won't get short stories without magazines. Regret, not remorse, describes my feelings here.

My favorite prozine is *F&SF*. *Amazing* is better than it used to be, but every sf magazine is better than *Amazing* used to be. The magazine looks great compared to the Fairman, Browne, and Palmer versions, but it still prints a great quantity of crap. The recent novel by Dr. Sam McClatchie (I'm still not sure that's not a pseudonym of Moskowitz') is an archaic, clumsy, stiff and self-consciously "cute" hunk of crud. Maybe it had a good middle and end, I don't know. I started feeling queasy in my stomach halfway through the first installment. How many great stories has *Amazing* published lately? How many have they published that are unreadable or barely readable? I read every word in *F&SF* and even *Galaxy* and *If*, but I skip over at least one story in every issue of *Amazing* and *Fantastic* because I find it dull, stupid, or corny — or not even remotely science fiction. And the covers, for Christ's sake — and the way Lobsenz snickers about the mundane reaction as an intelligent, mature person, pick up a copy of a magazine with that stupid cover of a planet-head swallowing a spaceship?

And those "artsy" little monstrosities by Bunch ... Jesus, Mary, and Joseph. Yet they look arty, so everybody praises them, despite the fact that they are all alike.

Amazing Stories a good magazine? Come on now. You've got to convince me of that. I think it's in about fourth place, below *F&SF*, *If*, and *Galaxy* and it's superior to *Analog* only because Campbell is determined to make it a vehicle for his own crackbrained beliefs.

SOME COMMENTS WITH REGARDS TO
NEW MAPS OF HELL
BY JAMES BLISH

NEW MAPS OF HELL, KINGSLEY AMIS. HARCOURT, BRACE & CO., NEW YORK, 1960. 161 PP., $3.95

This volume is now very well known, as it deserves to be, since it is the only existing serious study of science fiction of any weight to be undertaken by an outsider. The books by de Camp and Knight, and Avent's *The Science Fiction Novel*, are all three of great value, but they are each the kind of book that can be read with greatest profit by a practitioner, that is, another science fiction writer. Amis is rewarding in this respect as well, but he addresses himself primarily to the reader — particularly the prospective reader.

Amis is not, of course, the complete outsider that some of his reviewers have implied. He has been reading s-f since about 1934, and his text refers to magazine stories which appeared well before that year (plus, if course, works of Wells and others which appeared before he was born.) He is a member of the three-man board of selection of the British Science Fiction Book Club, an organization with a considerably better record than its American counterpart; and it is perhaps indicative that *New Maps of Hell* is dedicated to Bruce Montgomery, widely unrecognized in the U.S. under this, his real name, as Britain's leading s-f anthologist.

NEW MAPS OF HELL,
Andy Reiss

Many of the comments I have seen on the book, however, praise or damn it for quite irrelevant reasons, as well as some that are simply untrue. There has, for instance, been a tendency to laud the book for having wrung from *Time Magazine* the first faintly friendly notice ever accorded s-f by that ill-written and dishonest journal. Why the friendship of *Time* should be considered valuable is beyond me, but in any case it has nothing to do with the merits of Amis' book. Writers who are praised by Amis praise him back, in one instance to the point of endorsing a guess of his which is patently untrue; those he damns (or worse, simply ignores) respond with steam-whistle screams. (Hell hath no fury like a woman who can't even find her name in the index.) This is understandable, but again, irrelevant.

The book has many strengths, not the least of which is its wit — as was to have been expected from the author of *Lucky Jim*. It is anything but "considerably" arrogant, as its most arrogant critic unluckily alleges; indeed, Amis has no use either for intellectual slummers or for people who see s-f as the greatest of art forms, and is at pains to dissociate himself from both types. Furthermore, he is aware of the existence of gaps in his knowledge, if not always of their extent, and admits them readily. No more can I see why opinions which have been in formation over a period of twenty-six years should be labelled "ill-considered;" the book is in fact extremely reflective in cast, no matter how many of its conclusions one may disagree with.

The same critic alleges "unconsidering slovenliness of research," which is nonsense (and leads me to the suspicion that the three accusations involved are not so much the product of critical judgment as of the game being played with the verb "to consider"). There are, to be sure, some errors, and some omissions, but they are quite minor. On page 46, for instance, Amis is unable to remember the title or author of Hal K. Wells' "The Cavern of the Shining Ones," hardly a crucial lapse; and he spoils the anecdote at the top of page sixty by making its protagonist a s-f writer instead of a *Weird Tales* writer, thereby missing an interesting but altogether minor psychiatric point. In general, it is quite plain that Amis has read far more s-f than most of his critics. He is also immensely better read in the mainstream, which gives him a great advantage over people with only one string to their bows, but not, it must be added, an unfair one. For documentation see the index, which by the way is excellent.

The book has also been criticised — for once, relevantly — for its marked bias toward the *Galaxy* type of story. This is in part a product of the author's personal taste, about which nothing can be done; but in part, too, many of those doing the complaining have only themselves to blame. In the course of preparing the lectures at Princeton which resulted in the book, Amis sent extended questionnaires to many writers and editors in the field; and report has it that the returns came largely from the Pohl-Ballantine-Gold Axis, thereby heavily skewing the data Amis had to work with.

This is nevertheless a real weakness. What seems to appeal most to Amis in s-f is social satire, so much so that he readily swallows a great deal of work ranging from the pathetically inept to the downright awful. It is this bias that leads him to his now notorious deification of Frederik Pohl, which I suspect is already an embarrassment to both men and is likely to become more so as time goes on. Of greater consequence than overestimating an individual writer, however — for on such a matter there is often no possibility of honest agreement between one critic and another — is the encouragement this bias lends to further proliferation of the social satire in s-f, a sub-class which had reduced itself to a cliché and a bore some time before Amis came on the scene to lend it his endorsement. I at least would maintain that rather than calling for better examples of the type, as Amis does, what is needed is a moratorium on the damn thing; it has already been done very well, middling well, not well at all, and absolutely miserably, *ad nauseum*.

Personal taste, skewed data or both also bias the book toward the one-punch type of story, of which the work of Robert Sheckley is properly singled out as the best example. This bias, unlike the previous one, is surprising in a sophisticated s-f reader, simply because such a reader is usually almost impossible to surprise. It is characteristic of a Sheckley story, as it is of the work of less polished writers of the same kind, that the punch can be seen coming some pages ahead of the moment when the author delivers it (the reader knows, for instance, that when a character mutters, "There's something wrong here, but I can't quite put my finger on it," there is a large hole in the story's logic immediately adjacent to the remark, out of which hole the author will pull his surprise at the end); and if the punch is all the story has — as is almost invariably the case — nothing remains but Sheckley's incidental wit (or in the lesser writers of the same kind, nothing at all).

I would further disagree with Amis' contention, on page 101, that satire on individual persons and corporations is universally absent in s-f. I'll not resist the temptation to point out that my own *They Shall Have Stars* — which furthermore was first published in England — devotes about a third of its wordage to a personal attack on McCarthy, a point U.S. McCarthyites were quick to recognize. Corporations? Well, the higher echelons of General Electric were in no doubt whose ox was being gored in Kurt Vonnegut's *Player Piano*, as I know from having worked for one of their public relations agencies that year, and this book we can be sure Amis has read (see page 149).*   These examples could be multiplied; McCarthy was indeed quite a favorite target of American s-f, as was only to have been expected; for instance see Kornbluth's "Takeoff," or the more recent *The Manchurian Candidate.* I would not go so far as to maintain that it is a common feature in s-f, but it's there. Whether or not we need more of it is another question.

One of the problems in this kind of thing is inbreeding, or to put it more bluntly, incest, a conspicuous failing of quite a sizable body of s-f. Writers in this field quite frequently put each other in their stories, sometimes to express friendship, but more often to criticize or even to pay off old scores. Thus — to cite an example of each — we find Anthony Boucher making Judith Merrill the heroine of a story, Fritz Leiber satirizing both L. Ron Hubbard and A.E. van Vogt as a peculiarly revolting villain (in, luckily, and utterly revolting story). These examples, too, could be multiplied. The outcome may be interesting to those in the know, but for most readers it is more likely to be simple bafflement. This type of *roman a clef*, in which the necessary key is virtually inaccessible, is far more common than it ought to be in s-f, and any general move toward personal satire is likely to multiply it.

Despite these dissents, however, *New Maps of Hell* strikes me as a job that badly needed to be done, and for the most part has been done wondrous well.

*Nor was Chas. Pfizer & Co., Inc., in any doubt about who was being satirized in my own *The Frozen Year*, which appeared in England as *Fallen Star* with an Amis jacket endorsement. In fact, they damn near fired me.

EPISTOLARY INTERCOURSE #4
CONDUCTED BY PAT LUPOFF

AJAY BUDRYS

Blish on Amis was a nice, clear note of sanity on the subject. I noted some other lapses in Amis; for example, whenever he summarizes a story, then apologizes for not remembering the title and author, he's usually slighting Phil Dick. But these are, as Jim points out, minor quibbles. *New Maps* is a demanding job rather well done.

In fact, I'm much less troubled by Amis' bias for Sheckley than Jim is. Sheckley never talks about his work or his motives, and rarely mixes into the large kaffee-klatsches that go on all the time among other professionals. The result is that much progress and hard work has managed to get by unnoticed, especially since most of the brilliant critical insights in this field — with one or two significant exceptions — are gained by bending the ear at these gossip-mongerings. Sheckley badly needs critical re-evaluation; if he was not as good as his original notices, he was never as insipid as he was later made out to be, and he is a good deal closer to John Collier now than he once was to O. Henry. He may not be a science fiction novelist — frankly it's hard to tell, the way portions of his career have been managed — but he can handle any other length in sf, and I have read one Sheckley adventure novel that I'm sure Jim would find even more interesting than I did. It may be that Amis, standing well away from the staple critical notions that exist here, has a better chance to notice who is playing well and who is merely dragging the same old bow across some badly slackened strings. Amis has some decidedly peculiar notions about where the important talents in sf lie, true — or rather, about how much attention should be paid to people like Kuttner, Kornbluth, and Heinlein, or Sturgeon — but I don't think he can be fooled into seeing talent where there is none. I naturally — and selfishly — believe that Jim can't either, but Sheckley is so quiet — and he has no self-appointed press agent working for him — it's easy to forget how many years it's been since the AAA Ace Stories.

El FACE,
Cathy Bell in collaboration
with bhob Stewart

CATHY BELL was a friend of bhob Stewart's; her collaboration with him on the El "Face" may have been her only work in the fan press.

ROG EBERT

Blish is very irritating in his review of *New Maps of Hell*; he manages to climb over and around and — very nearly — through the only cogent issue: was Amis right in his pronouncements on the relative worth of various stf writers? I think Blish's opinion on this would be more important than a three-page grab-bag of loose ends busily being uncluttered.

ANTHONY BOUCHER

I very much enjoyed *Xero 4* — partly for the startling experience of finding myself in complete agreement with Blish on a matter of criticism (and in a minority position at that).

HARRY WARNER, JR.

You're serving a most valuable function in preserving facts that might get lost to the world in the next few decades, and just think how collectors will bless you a half-century from now, when the dime comics of the 1930s and 1940s are as rare and expensive as the dime novels today, and *Xero* is the only major source of information about the genesis of the characters and the names of the writers and so on.

I didn't read *New Maps of Hell* from beginning to end. But it occurred to me that most of the criticisms directed at it were prompted by disappointment that it wasn't a history of the prozines, a task which Amis obviously didn't attempt. Aside from that, there has been only the inevitable carping about favorite authors being snubbed. Too few fan reviewers have emphasized the most important thing of all, how lucky we were that this first major study of the field was written by somebody who likes sf.

LEWIS FORBES

Your editorial pleased me no end. Boiled down to "this is my zine and I'll damn well publish anything I damn well like." This is an attitude I would enjoy even more in some of the professional, slick, high circulation, scared-stiff stuff which wanders into my

home on occasion. And I'd flip if it showed up on television.

Don Thompson's comments on Garrett's writing are a beautiful piece of wordsmanship, and appropriate. And as far as television — occasionally one of the local stations will goof and stage a concert, or schedule a worthwhile play from one of the networks. They do this with abject apologies. I don't have a set. Every once in a while I watch a show or two on my folks' or Judy's set; this reminds me why I shouldn't get one.

As for *Xero Comics*: The artwork in this section is the best in the book. The attitude toward the subject (nostalgic, informative, and more than slightly tongue-in-cheek) makes what could have been a very boring article interesting. As for how long this kick will last: someday you're going to run out of characters to write articles about.

I was a trifle young and innocent when Wonder Woman passed under my eyes. Anyway, I never recognized it as lesbian pornography. Seems a shame, too. Now that I look back she was a trifle off-color.

Contention, Sylvia White

SYLVIA WHITE was a talented artist who entered the science fiction community, was married for a time to fan-turned-pro writer and editor Ted White. She graced a number of fanzines with her carefully crafted drawings, and then drifted away from the science fiction world.

contention

what would
the
martians think
of a
dog

lifting his leg

on mars? not
much, i
should
t h i n k
...un-
less he
(happened)
to be a
girl.

        - rog ebert

FOURPENCE EACH AND ALL IN WRITING

ERIC BENTCLIFFE

ERIC BENTCLIFFE (1927-1992) was an English science fiction fan who apparently regarded American fandom and its growing interest in comics in the 1960s with a spirit of detached bemusement. He was a talented writer and fan publisher in his own right. Copies of his fanzine Bastion *are treasured by collectors. His popularity in the fan community was such that he won the Trans-Atlantic Fan Fund (TAFF), an institution which brought British fans to American conventions and vice versa each year. Having missed out on the primarily American phenomenon of comic books, Bentcliffe dredged up childhood recollections of the "boys' papers" and other mass literature of his own childhood, adding a rich perspective for readers on both sides of the Atlantic.*

There weren't any comic books available over here back in my misspent youth, and, indeed, apart from a few which came over from the States as "Ballas" (as occasional s-f magazines did) during wartime, I never got to see any until it was too late for them to cast their seemingly magic spell on me. I'll leave it to the audience to decide whether this is a good thing or not!

However, the discussions in *Xero* on the topic have led me to do a little research of my own — into just what *I* was reading when most American fans were reading comic books.

There were the t'uppeny bloods, of course, the story-magazines which catered for children of varying ages. *Hotspur*, and the like, which had a fair literary standard and featured many stories with a fantasy or s-f slant. I well recall reading in this paper an extremely long serial (I think it lasted almost eighteen months) entitled "Last Rocket to Venus", which still sticks in my mind as one of the most enjoyable s-f stories I've ever read — at the time, naturally; I don't expect I'd classify it as such if I were to read it again today. And lest someone suspects me of having had a retarded childhood maybe I'd better date this yarn as near as I can, and the period I'm dealing with. I haven't any copies of *Hotspur* now, or any of the other boys' papers I used to read with such gusto, so any attempt at dating must be a guess. The period 1936 to 1939 is as near as I can get ... way back when I was 11 or 12 or something.

Catering for a slightly older boy were several semi-slick story magazines which I gradually graduated to. *Modern Wonder, Buzzer, Modern Boy*, et cetera. *Modern Wonder* frequently featured articles on space flight, and one of its regular story writers was John Beynon — better known today as John Wyndham. I'm fairly sure that at least one of his s-f stories from that magazine was subsequently featured elsewhere as adult fare, but titles escape me for the moment. *Buzzer* also had several rather good s-f stories featured, and I recall a back cover cartoon strip of the Captain

Future type. *Modern Boy*, well, *Modern Boy* featured one of the favorite characters of my youthful reading — Captain Justice.

Captain Justice wasn't exactly a Superman, he was more of a gentleman-adventurer type who liked to set wrongs right ... in a scientific way. He had the usual cohort of what seems now rather stereotyped henchmen (but which didn't seem so at the time of reading), O'Malley the jovial Irishman, Midge the youngster who was always getting into "scrapes," Len Connor the Radio Operator-Inventor, and ... dear old Professor Flaznagel, who was always blowing up his laboratory and inventing super weapons which would be made off with by Foreign Spies and Evil People. Old Flazzy, as he was frequently called (behind his back) by the irrepressible Midge, was responsible for at least half of the wrongs Captain Justice had to right, not ever intentionally of course.

I don't have any copies of *Modern Boy* these days either, but I do have one or two of the s-f stories of my youth in pocket book form — as they were published in the *Boys Friend Library* and the *Schoolboys Own Library* circa 1938/1939. At four pence each.

Two of these relics feature Captain Justice, which is why I've been able to go into some detail up above, and leafing through them I'm almost tempted to reread the darn things. Certainly their standard of writing and logic was far greater than that of the current so-called "original" s-f pocket books published over here, and these latter are intended for adults. The author of the Captain Justice yarns was Murray Roberts; I don't know whether this was a house name or just one person — the output was pretty high so it could have been a house name.

Number 629 of the *Boys Friend Library* was "The Ocean Robot," published July 7th '38. Old Flazzy had invented a super robot of rather gargantuan dimensions. "A giant robot!" declared Justice. "A metal monster carrying guns, searchlights, and probably a crew of several men."

"A blinkin' walking battleship!" exclaimed the red-haired youngster. (Midge of course.) Professor Flaznagel was rather apt to spring his latest inventions on them suddenly!

However, all is not well: an evil scientist has purloined the plans and made an identical model which ravages the shipping lanes, and is only caught up with after a South American Revolution, A Kidnapping (of Midge), and much amusing adventure. Like all good stories its ending left room for a sequel, and this was forthcoming in number 633 of the Library, "The Rival Robots."

Garth Leopold, Evil Scientist, has licked his wounds and built himself several dozen more giant robots and once more he challenges Justice — in more ways than one. He's still after that South American Republic, he has a hidden underground base up the Amazon, and manages to cause some considerable consternation before he's brought to book. "Leopold's agents have been putting in some hot work. They've smothered the town with placards and bills announcing that Justice has gone over to Leopold, and Leopold is about to advance on San Romas with an army of ten thousand men, umpteen tanks and planes, and a whole flock of robots."

Perhaps not quite the sort of stuff which would get a Hugo today, but you must admit that it was good clean fun for the kiddey-winkies. And I recall, but don't possess, several Captain Justice yarns which were verging on space opera with Pirate Asteroids and all the thud and blunder of *Planet Stories*.

Murray Roberts' Captain Justice wasn't the only stfish character abroad in those boys books, although he was one of the best. I've unearthed another couple of the *Boys Friend Library* titles which I've kept for their s-f connection — and because they were favorite reading of mine long, long ago. "The Lion At Bay" is one, by Roger Fewey. Published July 7th '39 by that Library.

This is a super-invasion yarn in which Asiatic Hordes by the Chinese invade the United Kingdom and Europe. They do so by means of giant submersibles equipped with caterpillars for land use, wireless heat-rays, and "pipe-planes") — these latter being a pretty fine depiction of today's jets. The land submarines also carry large numbers of "beetle-cars," a type of fighting machine very similar to Sam Merwin's 'pippits' in the "House of Many Worlds." The plot isn't terribly novel; the two heroes, two schoolboys at home for the hols, meet up with an inventor who has a "triple-gun" capable of piercing the immense armour of the submersible. They help him get it to the right authorities, and see considerable action as it is tested out.

After several thousand words of WOTW type writing the Federals (Asiatics) are defeated and the boys are awarded the V.C. Put baldly like that, it doesn't sound much of a story, but leafing through it reveals that quite a few passages still evoke the old sense of wonder — and it's a plot I wouldn't be at all surprised to see revised in the near future.

This one had a sequel, too. "The Lion's Revenge," in which our heroes, accompanied by the British Army, invade China and eventually destroy the Federals completely. The two boys undertake a Secret Service mission to penetrate the enemy headquarters, and after some quite Harrisonesque adventures succeed in their objectives. Quite frankly, I'm surprised how well these two yarns seem to have held up over the years; much of the boys fiction of those days was written in a very goshwowoboy style, but these two stories in particular have a terse, quite documentary tone. I'm tempted to re-read them even now.

Perhaps more typical of that era of schoolboy stories are four other boys pb's I have here. Those are products of the *Schoolboys Own Library*, the series which was responsible for the famous (over here) *Greyfriars School* stories of author Frank Richards, which featured such characters as Billy Bunter (later awarded a TV series of his own), Harry Wharton, Bob Cherry, and their chums of the Remove.

The four titles I have here are not by Frank Richards, but by one Edwy Searles Brooks. They could, however, have been equally well written by the Greyfriars author. They tell of the adventures of a group of public (Private!) schoolboys who go off in their hols for a tour of the Solomon Islands in a yacht belonging to Lord Dorrimore, a wealthy patron and ex-boy of the school. In, unfortunately, the typical schoolboy style of the day ...

"Been talking to the pater over the phone!" he grinned. "It's all serene!"

"What's all serene?" asked Handforth.

"Haven't you heard?" said Pitt, in wonder.

"Of course he's heard!" put in McClure. "But the ass won't believe it. And anyhow, he says he wouldn't go to the Solomon Islands for a pension!"

The stories *moved* though... First of all the boys are ship-wrecked, and play Robinson Crusoe on a desert isle, which is invaded by cannibals. They fight off the cannibals only to have to face a volcanic eruption, from which they are rescued in the proverbial nick of time by Lord Dorrimore who had been hauled aboard a passing tramp-steamer at the time of the shipwreck, and who has had his yacht repaired. Dorrimore has a friend who has a dirigible named *The Flying Fish* which also helps in the rescue; this friend is en route to the Antarctic on a voyage of exploration — nothing loath, the boys embark with him for the frozen South.

There they find a "hot river," which leads them to not-one-but-two long-isolated kingdoms by way of an underground cavern, in which dwell monsters. And they help to fight a war between the two kingdoms before they return to school for the next term!

They don't write stories like that anymore, you might well say!!

And you'd be right. And I'm sorry they don't, for the boys, anyway. Today, the main fare offered to the kids over here seems to be similar to that offered to the kids in the states. Comic books. And while I'm not saying that comic books are not an art form, I'd rather see the older children, at least, reading *words* than just looking at pictures.

But maybe I'm old-fashioned, and anyway this article hasn't been written in an attempt to sermonize but rather to provide some comparison of what the older UK fans were (probably) reading when you-all were immersed in the wonders of Marvelman, and Superman.

THE INCREDULOUS EYE

ED GORMAN

As an onlooker I've been watching and reading *Xero* with quite a lot of interest. I'm not a comic book collector, nor what you might call a true aficionado. I read the Marvel stories, and the DC's, but I was never one to hunt through dingy stories to find #31 of *Billy Batson Bops* or *Marvel Meets Konky*.

I did derive quite a lot of pleasure from comic books, though. For instance, one issue of *Superman* clings solidly in my memory, because on the day I received it, my grandmother was being buried, and my parents presented me with an issue to offer me a reprieve from a situation which my young mind couldn't grasp. Superman proved a superlative host, and my feelings changed from drably depressed to excited as I read through it.

But today I can no longer read *Superman*. And I don't think it's just because the writing staff (of DC) has changed and alleged quality met with a decline. This goes for all the "hero" comics. I find myself eyeing them all with incredulity. Why? Well, mainly, I can't identify with them, and as I go through them, I'm as passionless as a Doc Smith creation. I'm no Superman, or Green Lantern, or whoever — I am myself, a mere human being, who, when faced with a problem must solve it any (human) way I can. I can't fly, nor can I look to a magic ring for guidance; I must bumble through a serious development with my rather low mentality working at full speed. Therefore, when I relax and look for escape in reading matter, I *do* want something that can uplift me from my daily problems, but also I want heroes with whom I can sympathize.

When I read about Superman [and I use him as an example because (1) he is the most popular of all super-humans and (2) he personifies the whole "Mighty Man" cliché] I think along these lines: I don't like Superman because he's arrogant. He is not human to begin with. He is an individual who was placed on Earth by fate and who, after realizing and improvising his various talents, has found that he can derive quite a lot of pleasure by

ED GORMAN (1941-) was a teen-aged fan when he wrote for Xero and for the next quarter century maintained his amateur standing while working in the advertising business in his home town of Cedar Rapids, Iowa. Then he burst on the publishing scene with a mystery novel Rough Cut *(1985). Once started, he became amazingly productive; to date his output includes well over fifty novels and a half dozen or more collections of short stories. A versatile writer, Gorman writes mysteries, westerns, and horror novels, and even makes an occasional foray into science fiction. He was the founding editor and publisher of* Mystery Scene, *a highly influential literary newsmagazine.*

keeping the native population in shackles. He's become a minor god, and fighting his foes has taken on the tones of a chess master checkmating tyro opponents.

It's true that not all these comic book idols can fly, or crash through walls, or read minds. But the ones I'm centering into view are those who solve their disastrous problems with gadgets; whether they be mental or physical gimmicks makes no difference. Because I am a human being, I like to identify with those who have problems, but must solve them as I would. I like extraordinary problems for my heroes to face, and I really don't mind if they solve their woes with some scientific or mystical power which they've either improvised or discovered in the course of the story. But I detest those who can readily challenge and defeat any foe by culling a super-weapon which awaits their call at any time, at any circumstance. It's for this reason, I believe, that Superman's editor introduced "kryptonite" — this is an enemy, one thing which can block the otherwise all-powerful creature. But even this menacing alloy is not enough. Not for me, anyway. A human being can die a thousand ways. At any step of the way, fate can cash him in, pick up his option and he's through. Superman and the other superhumans have no worry. Few things can stop them, and everyone knows they'll win in the finish anyway, so the suspense angle is cut down even more drastically.

Perhaps I have been tainted by what Jim Harmon calls "vainglorious pride." Perhaps I have never been a true appreciator of melodrama, no matter what form it appears in. But I don't think so. I read pulps, for example, and like them. But I enjoy contemporary stf more than I do that of, say, *Planet*. Why? Well, the humans presented are much more credible. I still know they are going to win, most of the time, but they're being understandable and real, a feature of these stories which makes me want to read the yarns and enjoy them to their finish.

Stf has evolved, but I don't think comic books have. I've never read any of the old, *old* comic books such as those that Jim Harmon, Ted White, and Don Thompson discuss, and maybe if I did I would realize what they're talking about. But with the knowledge I have, and through the way *I* interpret the comics, I think that a successful comic today would be comprised of mortal-facing-superhuman problems, and not vice versa.

The picture is worth the proverbial thousand words. I think that's why comics are both a successful and potent medium. It's the same with television. A printed story is most often marred by failure of characterization, but on television characters are far more easily rendered believable, short of their being provided with invalid dialog and assuming that the casting director is not a nincompoop.

But basically, it is relatively easy to accept the credibility of characters on television because they move and breath before you, walking, talking, acting as *Homo sapiens*. In comics it is the same, although in a more limited sense. The possibilities of a narrative in illustrated form are tremendous. Great things, with capable writing and illustrating, could be produced. But why waste these potential gains on fly-happy finks who have wondrous powers? I'd rather see this talent directed at human beings and their problems, rather than something I cannot understand.

Stf has always had trouble with backgrounds. The description wasn't accurate and detailed enough for everyone to picture. But in the comics the artist interprets the writer's thoughts so clearly than an illustration evolves. Half the sense of wonder has been captured right here; the other half depends on the characters. See what I mean?

This is not a complaint against Jim Harmon, Ted White, or Don Thompson. Their "All in Color for a Dime" articles have been greeted with pleasure from this quarter. Rather, this piece is a conclusion, which I have reached because of comic book reading and the aforementioned articles.

Finding specific cases of what I mean is unfortunately difficult, but I think that a more subdued EC would be a fitting example of what I have in mind. Balance the accent between characterization and mood-effect and you've got a winner. Be lopsided on either one, and the end result is sterility. And by that I mean exactly what the word implies.

There are, of course, sharp limitations in comics. The dialogue must be precise and must follow the story line. But EC did it for their Bradbury adaptations, and many others have done it at various times, in various publications.

And speaking in dollars-and-cents, I think that a comic book such as I would design would be successful, even though it would be published for the, umm, the "gourmets" of the comic book followers. I *know* that Superman is popular, and probably will be for a long time to come. But Superman and all the other superhero types appeal primarily to children and to those adults-in-term-of-years whose taste has never grown up.

Attempts at adult-directed comic books have always failed in the past, but I believe that this has been due to poor execution, distribution, etc., rather than to any invalidity of the basic idea.

What I am intimating is a fairly credible comic, with good writing and choice illustrating. Something not necessarily pitched at the immature mentality.

See you in the letter column.

HE SWOOPED ON HIS VICTIMS AND BIT THEM ON THE NOSE:

AN ODD LETTER FROM MR. DAVIDSON

Lupophoi:

You will probably get this days later because I've got no stamps and better things to do with my money — the few coins between me, starvation, and that messianically distant era when Randy Garrett starts paying his debts — than to buy stamps with it for letters of comments (I've just learned to call them locs, hee hee, but am too shy for such ingroup terminology) on fanzines.

Thanks for asking me to write something for *Xero*, but (a) I can't think of anything (b) I have no right to take the time from what I should be doing professionally (letters aren't writing!) and (c) there are a few publications which are ahead of you in case I decide I have both time and subject matter.

Commend you on layout and general appearance, sometimes much too good for the subject matter (*Captain Crudd Comics* — reeeaallly). Too bad that such a good cartoonist as Andy Reiss has to suffer from reproduction difficulties (give him my regards and my address and ask him to communicate if he likes). (I mean, I'd like him to.) [Andrew Joel Reiss, Avram Davidson's address is 410 West 110th Street, NYC 25.]

Now, leave us see. J. Blish, gentleman, savant, scholar (writer, too) attributes the Amis "marked bias for the *Galaxy* type of story" to the fact that "Amis sent extended questionnaires to many writers ... returns came largely from the Pohl-Ballantine-Gold Axis, thereby heavily skewing the data Amis had to work with." Which may be — is, for all I know o contrare. Let me note for the record that, while I've sold no stories to Messrs Pohl and/or Ballantine, I did sell five to *Galaxy*, of which either all five or four were in print at the time Amis sent out his queries. I know he sent them to, among others, Wm. Tenn and Robt. Sheckley, (much more frequent *Galaxy*

AVRAM DAVIDSON (1923-1993) was a character as fabulous as any of his fictitious creations. He served in the United States Navy in World War II, fought in the Israeli War of Independence, and wrote science fiction, fantasy, detective stories, and history books with equal facility, brilliance, and an inimitable style and world view. Regarded as a "writer's writer" he was held in esteem approaching worship by his colleagues, but never achieved the wider acceptance and rewards that he deserved. A decade after Davidson's death, his onetime wife and literary executor, Grania Davis, sparked a revival of his works, introducing this astonishing talent to a new generation of readers.

writers, of course; bigger by far names, of c.) but none to me. So he was exercising selectivity even before his replies could come in. His privilege. I hope nobody thinks my pride was hurt, because it was.

I think JB is not quite correct in utterly condemning SF writers who include SF writers as characters. This seems quite legitimate, providing the characterization is done so well that no "key" is needed. Surely no one missed much essential in not knowing (as I did not, at first) that Somerset Maugham's *Cakes and Ale* includes Thomas Hardy and Hugh Walpole.

The cartoon by "bhob" captioned "Even kings must live by nature" reminds me of my grandmother's expression for the water closet. A former subject of His Apostolic Majesty, Francis Joseph, she called it "Where the kaiser goes on foot."

In re Margolin on Deckinger on *Psycho* and *Caligar* — anybody remember a moom pitcher from mid-30's or a bit earlier, which it was entitled *Mad Love*? It was made abroad, I think in France, though I was at that time incapable of recognizing French when I heard it. The only English lines were delivered by Edmund Brophy, a bald, hubbin-nosed little American who — in this country — played comic hoods — only in *Mad Love* he was a strangler. Guillotined. Peter Lorre played a physician who, if I recall, was going nuts (a) for dearth of some popsie and (b) on general principles. This was one of the first films to use such tricks as Unseen Voices (if you know whattamean), Rippling Vision, etc. Not physician, dopy: surgeon. Yes. The popsie loved a pianist who had his hands crushed in a train wreck just as the axe plopped on Brophy's nape. Lorre promptly took off Brophy's hands and grafted them onto the wizard of the keys. Who soon began to strangle people... I forget how it ended. Why do I bother? Well, I, uh, like, didn't ever see either *Caligari* or *Psycho*, and I got to talk about *something*, don't I?

Margolin speaks of the British film *Dead of Night*. I quite well remember the ventriloquist/dummy part — there were three or four stories, unconnected, in the picture — but not the bits BM mentions as accompanying it — spook mirror, ghost boy, "gold incident." [Err, Margolin's "reference" to a "gold incident" was just a typo. What he originally wrote was "golf incident."] But I *am* sure one of the sequences contained Thomas Mitchell as "Septimius Podger, Professional Chiromancer," who was reading palms at a party, guessing the unguessable, predicting the unpredictable-but-just-then-proven-true, until he came to the palm of Edgar G. Robinson — & refused to say what he'd seen. EGR bugged him until he got the one word, "Murder." wandered the dark streets of London wondering whom he was going to kill — and for crisesakes WHY? — this EGR being a gentle type, in this film. Till one night he met whom but S. Podger on London Bridge, had words with him, and knocked him fatally into the mucky old Thames. Will someone correct or corroborate my belief that this bit was based on a story by Oscar Fingall O'Flaherty Wilde?

["I will," says Larry M. Harris. "The Septimus Podger story was not in Dead of Night, but The Night Has a Thousand Eyes. It was based on a story by "George Hopley." (Cornell Woolrich) of which I have a copy which you may borrow if you wish."]

BM also uses "unbeknownst." The use of this odd form seems increasing. Is it legitimate? Why won't "unknown" do? I've also seen "unbeknown." Hmm.

Before the Comic Books as a genre unto themselves appeared, lo, there was *Famous Funnies*. Remember? This simply reprinted the Sunday sheets of various all-known funnies in each issue. Among them was one called "Nipper" and one called "Desperate Ambrose." I seem to recollect dimly that Ambrose had appeared in some newspaper in the NY area — maybe in my local Yonkers one — but long years before I saw it in FF. "Nipper." I'd never seen nor have I seen it since. I regarded it as a superior strip, without compeers, unique in its flavor, zippier, devoid of funny paper or comic strip cliches. It dealt with the doings of a small boy, who wore shorts — it always seemed summer — and lived in a very small town. Can anyone tell me anything at all about "Nipper"? Ambrose was also a small boy, but highly stylized. He was always threatening to do something desperate. The father of the family was preternaturally tall and thin … About two, three years back Jean Shepperd asked, Did anyone remember the comic strip in which everyone was always sitting down to eat tripe? At once I got the picture. I could

HE SWOOPED ON HIS VICTIMS AND BIT THEM ON THE NOSE, bhob Stewart

BHOB STEWART did double or triple — maybe quadruple — duty at Xero as chief designer, art editor, illustrator and cartoonist. He also worked in advertising art, and subsequently pursued a career in the comic industry.

see it clearly. The tripe looked like black spaghetti, was in bowls, and there were loud complaints... But I couldn't recall the name, dammit, it was haunting, frustrating ... and if Shephard ever said it, I missed it. He is Very Good, but I can only take small doses of him, somehow. Well sir, it now stands in my mind that Desperate Ambrose may have been the funny wherein the family seemed always about to sit down to tripe. Anybody confirm or deny? Anybody able to tell anything about Desp. Ambrose?

There were LOTS of good funnies in the days before *Dick Tracy* blight spread far and wide; and so many which I never see mentioned in the histories and articles. Who remembers when Blondie and Dagwood were just characters in *Dumb Dora*? The dowager Mrs. Bumstead being Violently Opposed to their marriage. I'm quite certain that I remember the first appearance of Popeye the Sailor in *Thimble Theatre* (it would have been not earlier than c. 1929, or I couldn't have been able to read the dialogue) he came and took Olive Oyl away from her brother Castor's friend, Ham Gravy. Castor was as short as Olive was tall, but more than this I can't remember. And nothing about Ham Gravy remains in my mind.

Tailspin Tommy? Poo. Who remembers *Mescal Ike*, the cowboy who hung around in a general store which had funny signs hung about it? And who had an elderly pal with jutting chin whiskers who was always whittling? Who remembers fat *Clarence*, and his pretty, slim wife? Who remembers *Brutus*? And the female — wife? Friend — Cleo? Who, *Pa's Son-in-Law*? The s-i-l was an Englishman, Cedric (of course), an awful simpering boob with a monocle and a long cigarette-holder. Pa was always beating him up. Pa's name was Lemuel Splutterfuss (oh Lupoffs what are you doing to me? Things I haven't thought of in YEARS). The horses and cows in *Brutus* had, instead of hooves, long flat feet. And the favorite expression was "Gleeps."

Happy Hooligan (Opper? Gropper?) is well-remembered, but who remembers a companion strip that ran along the top or bottom of the full HH sheet (a common practice in those days) — *Hee Haw and Her Name Was Maude*? Maude was a mule. I was (if you'll excuse the expression) cutting up some old touches a while back with Randy Garrett, and we were trying to think of the name of the kid or What-Was-It in *Parlor, Bedroom, & Sink* (I may have that *all* wrong). Kid always wore a long baby robe but spoke adultly, had a hug nose, and was always being kidnapped by a hulking villain named Fagin, a tattered-tramp figure, who had whiskers not unlike *Moon Mullins*'s Uncle Willy (Lady Plushbottom was in those days Miss Erma ... no, dammit Emmy — yes — Miss Emmy Schmaltz, kept a boardinghouse, and her favorite expression was "I'll smack your sassy face!" Does she still say it?). The kid in the nightie bore these abductions with patience and fortitude, remarking only, from time to time, sadly, "Fagin, yous is a viper." Don't know why the beak. His natural parents (on the rare occasions we were permitted to see them, or they to see the kid) were normal-looking, and very very young. Poor, too. I think they had to cook on a gas-ring which led via rubber-buster gas-*jet*. Well, *I* couldn't remember the kid's name. But Randy could. Bunky. Hey, all you good people out there in Funny Paper land — anybody remember Bunky?

... Lupoff, yous is a viper ...

Later, much later, there was *Peter Piltdown*. This was over 20 years ago, mind, before Piltdown man was kicked out of the Evolution Club for cheating at cards), a sort of forerunner of *B.C.* Only it was peopled just with kids, one of whom was a bit speech-impedimented and a bit of a feeb, too, but kept saying that he loved "alimals." ("aminals," etc.) And as for your low-down, no-count, trashy *Bat Man* — any of you remember the ORIGINAL Bat Man? He appeared in *Hair-breadth Harry* and stalked Harry's girl, Belinda — and just about anybody else stalkable, I guess. He wore a stovepipe hat and a long black cloak, and he *lurked*, Jesus*, did he ever lurk! In tree, like for instance. And then he swooped on his victims, bit them on the nose, and the nose then swelled up to horrid red proportions (I am *not* making this *up*). I freely admit that this scared the piss out of me — the only thing of its kind which ever did. It may be that I was still too young to read when I was looking at it, seem to recall its being read to me.

You can see that we had *whole*some comics in them days.

How is the rerun of *Barnaby* doing these days? I was crazy for it when it first appeared, before WWII, but don't even glance at it now. Time and past to secure, and get back to *The Price of Blood*, which maybe Ellery Queen will buy, and so enable me to put off dissolution for yet another fortnight. So goodbye, thanks for *Xero*, and you understand why I can't comply with your request that I write something for you.

Peace and Blessing,
Avram Davidson

*I refer, of course, to Jesus ben Sira, author of the book of Ecclesticus. Ecclessiasticus? You could do better?

Dear Mr. Davidson, Sir:

Sad we are that you found it needful to turn down our request for material for Xero. However, any time in the future that you still cannot write for the magazine, feel free to not write for us in the manner of the preceding pages.

Yours regrettingly,
Pat & Dick

ABSOLUTE XERO

IN WHICH I GIVE (OR MAYBE GET) A COURSE IN HOME DECORATING ...

BY PAT LUPOFF

Once upon a time, back in the days before *Xero* (which was only a year ago, has anyone noticed?), Dick and I and of course Snoopy (there never was a time before Snoopy) lived in a huge three room penthouse-mansion. Surrounded by conventional pieces of furniture: beds, bookcases, chairs, tables ... yet we were lonely. There seemed to be something missing. The empty nooks and crannies of our spacious mansion seemed spooky and gloomy.

For almost a year we had lived in the penthouse, for all that time this dreadful state of affairs had continued. We were beside ourselves. We tried everything to dispel the gloom: charcoal cookouts and moonbathing on the terrace in the summer, crackling fires in the fireplace accompanied by fine stereo music in the winter ... nothing seemed to work.

Until one day a voice was heard echoing loudly through the mists of gloom: "O, YE MOST SILLY ONES, WHY DON'T YOU PULL YOURSELFS TOGETHER AND PUBLISH A FANZINE?" Just like that. Not even "yourselves." "Why don't you pull yourselves together and publish a fanzine?"

Why not indeed? We told the voice why not. It was dirty, messy, expensive to publish a fanzine. It consumed every spare cent, and moment of money, energy, and time available. It would fill every cubic inch of space allotted to it and to a dozen other activities. It would cut us off from our numerous mundane friends, drain our enthusiasm for a hundred varied interests. Wreck our lives. Yes, wreck them.

We made a foraging party, briefly, through our palace to collect all the equipment needed in fanzine publishing. After a thorough search we finally emerged with one item of equipment: a typer (formerly known as typewriter). Of course we had all the mundane equipment, such as pens, pencils, and erasers, but obviously this would not do. First we needed a symbol of inspiration. This we acquired at the Pittcon after a heated battle with the formidable Fritz Lang Frau in Mond, Chris Moskowitz. A lovely work by Frank R. Paul, a peaceful pastoral scene of a spaceman surrounded by some graceful grey bems rather resembling sorely overstuffed bats, dancing around inside an iron-mongery on Mercury or Iapetus or maybe on Vulcan.

ABSOLUTE XERO, Steve Stiles

Dick wanted this masterpiece in our bedroom; I was not so sure, so we deferred decision until after returning home, via TWAirliner. However, we had no way of wrapping the Paul, and with its bare glass face hanging out, we feared to check it through with our package. The stewardess and the other passengers on the place kept glancing out of the corners of their eyes at us and our burden as we rose into the atmosphere and headed east. After a few furtive glances they began to look more frequently, more directly, more incredulously. Fortunately it was a short flight, or we might have had to skyjack the plane in order to get home. The painting now does hang over the bar. It has frightened one or two imbibers out of overdoing the drinks.

Next, we realized that more practical things were in order. I decided to surprise Dick on our anniversary, even if it meant a gift of romance and beauty, with a mimeoscope. It cost as much as a fine pair of cufflinks, several good shirts, or three Bronzini ties, but the gift seemed to fill Dick with a heavenly inspiration. Each night for a month or more thereafter, Dick would arrive home a little late, with a mysterious, albeit somewhat dazed, smile on his face, and a stylus, shading plate, or lettering guide in his hand. No money for dinner, but happy nonetheless. "Look," he would say, "it's an A.B. Dick 468 and it writes like this."

Or, "Darling, it's a 1629 medium splatter."

Or, "It's a Gestetner 144 half-inch Egyptian."

Eventually we became practical again and procured stencils and lots of correction fluid. After we became proficient in the use of all these foreign objects we dragged a bridge table from a closet and set it up as a temporary desk. It is still standing in the same spot, a full year later.

At last the great moment had arrived. We set out to produce to first issue of *Xero*. Dick sat down to write an article about Captain Marvel. To bolster his recollections (and also because it might provide a few hours of nostalgic fun) he bought a few old *Captain Marvel* comics in a back-issue shop downtown. I sat gloomily in the corner. "What's the matter?" Dick asked me. "Captain Marvel is just a big red cheese," I replied, "Now Captain Marvel *JR* and Mickey Mouse, *they* had brains." While not fully agreeing with me, Dick set out and brought home some *Captain Marvel Jr., Mary Marvel,* and *Walt Disney* comics. Comic books multiply like hopped-up rabbits.

BIRTH CONTROL MAN,
Steve Stiles

From a neat pile completely concealed behind a chair in a corner of our bedroom, we now have what resembles three side-by-side Leaning Towers of Pisa.

Finally the ultimate moment in published arrived. After paying for four issues of *Xero* produced on the Q'Press, and one on an ancient ABDick 90, we decided that *we* needed a mimeo all our own. So Dick put a few dollars on a stock he knew of, and lo! — a mimeo. No kidding, actually and literally, all you have to do to make money in the market is buy cheap and sell dear; I don't see why people think it's complicated.

Now we looked around our somewhat fuller mansion ... where would we put our proudest possession? But alas, all the once empty nooks and crannies in our home were bare and gloomy no more. They were filled, even bursting with cheerful objects. A stack of comics here, of pulps there. A huge mound of fanzines. Several boxes of prozines. Books. Shading plates. Lettering guides, stencils, styli, bottles of corflu and stencil cement. The mimeo went to the basement of Larry and Noreen Shaw.

So we now spend each Sunday carefully reading the classified ads for larger apartments. Our few remaining mundane friends simply assume that we need an extra room for the baby whom we expect in a matter of days. But fans know better. Any well-adjusted mimeo needs a room of its own in order to perform to perfection. Wish us luck.

EPISTOLARY INTERCOURSE #5
CONDUCTED BY PAT LUPOFF

RICHARD KYLE

The mimeography was rather erratic in my copy — which is probably to be expected on a new machine — but I should imagine you'll probably have everything straightened out next issue.

I haven't read *Rogue Moon* yet, although I have it on order (I skipped it when it first came out because Gold Medal's science fiction is usually inferior, but Blish's review in *F&SF* sold it to me), but some of Blish's observations strike me as faulty.

I don't think the overwhelming majority of science fiction readers have made it clear that they actively distrust and dislike emotional content in stories, "even in the rare instances where the author has it under perfect control." I do think they actively distrust and dislike science fiction stories where the particular emotional content does not bear any coherent relationship with the physical situation of the story. This is a major flaw in the work of every one of the writers Blish cites, except Stuart — and the Stuart stories *were* popular and well received. A romantic love story is irrelevant to science fiction, just as much as a Mickey Spillane style murder is irrelevant to the romantic love story. Which isn't to say that people in science fiction can't be in love or death should be secondary to the primary theme of the stories and emotionally consistent with it. I've read too many stories by the authors Blish mentioned in which the characters and settings have had all the consistency of a Jane Austen love story with George S. Patton, Jr. as the hero. It isn't that the characters are poorly drawn, it's that they belong in wholly different stories.

And I frankly question just how much craftsmanship had to do with the success of "Heinlein, Kuttner, and del Rey." Laurence Manning was as good a craftsman — and for that matter, an imaginative craftsman — but his style and viewpoint and emotional insights belonged to a previous generation. Heinlein and Kuttner and del Rey were just with it, that's all. They were steam engines and it was steam engine time; Manning was driving a damned fine horse and buggy. I suspect they would have been successful if they had written with all the finesse of Norvell Page.

Going back to *Xero 4*, Blish's comments on *New Maps of Hell* provided the only blood pressure rise for me in the issue. I have great admiration for Blish as a writer, and — usually — considerable respect for him as a critic; but I cannot understand his support of Amis' book.

If someone were to write a "survey" of the modern mystery story deifying George Harmon Coxe, exalting Henry Kane, brushing aside Raymond Chandler, ignoring Dashiell Hammett, upbraiding Arthur Conan Doyle for the paucity of sex and sadism in the Sherlock Holmes stories, and completely dismissing the contributions of Ellery Queen as an editor and anthologist, we can be sure — no matter who the author might be — that the book would provoke no more than a snort of amusement and a sigh of regret and soon find itself remaindered away to the 10¢ each, 3 for 25¢ tables of ill-managed second-hand book stores.

Yet *New Maps of Hell* thrust greatness on a shoulders of a competent Frederik Pohl, enthuses over Robert Sheckley's superficialities, scarcely mentions Robert A. Heinlein (the excellent index James Blish speaks of lists four entries under Heinlein's name — Robert Sheckley has nine — and two of these merely notebook titles), speaks not at all of Olaf Stapledon, one of the founding fathers of modern science fiction, condemns some of H.G. Wells' most powerful stories because they were not satirical, and describes the founder of modern magazine science fiction, John W. Campbell, Jr, as a "crank;" and expresses the hope that he be kicked out of science fiction (Amis had previously written of the emergence around 1940 of increased quality in magazine science fiction: "Why this happened when it did, or at all, I am not sure") — yet *New Maps of Hell* does all this in its survey of modern science fiction, and rather than merriment, it produces shouts of praise and screams of outrage, and instead of dying on the remainder tables, it sells *en masse* in the drugstores and newsstands across the country.

Why? Mainly, it would seem, because the author's name is Kingsley Amis, and science fiction — after all these years still dressing on public occasions in its out-of-date and threadbare inferiority complexes — defers to "important people" the way poor relations do to the rich, either fawning servilely or by leaping for their throats.

It is beyond me, though, why James Blish, who is certainly no poor relation and who knows the history of science fiction as few current fans and writer do, chooses to praise this ineptly organized and shabbily researched book (and it *is* shabbily researched, regardless of the number of questionnaires Amis sent out: it was his responsibility to get the facts, not the writers' to send them to him). Certainly, it is written with charm and style; but charm cannot make up for a lack of factuality, and style of itself, no matter how pleasing, makes no book good. Blish speaks, too, of the many years Amis has read science fiction, but familiarity with a body of literature does not insure understanding of it (witness the legions of western story readers who know nothing about the western as an art form). Aside from that, the bins of "Yank Magazines: *Interesting Reading"* in the English Woolworth stores of the middle '30s are not likely to have provided a rounded view of American science fiction, or a chronological one, if the English magazine displays on American newsracks of the time offer a parallel; at any rate, there is no evidence in *New Maps of Hell* that they did.

The truth is that Kingsley Amis no more understands science fiction than the man who describes *Moby-Dick* as "that fishing book" understands Melville. And because he does not understand, and because his literary reputation is what it is, his ill thought-out utterances are bound — by their very lack of accuracy — to do science fiction more harm than good in the long run.

The literary reputation science fiction deserves — in the measure it deserves — will be determined by time and truth, not by any man, no matter what his name.

I think it is time science fiction took a good, direct look at itself and its history. I think it is time the field showed proper respect for the men who made it. H.G. Wells was a far better writer than he is given credit by the literary critics and by Amis. Stapledon still influences the field. And John W. Campbell, Jr. (whatever one's opinion of his current editorial work may be) created the modern magazine science fiction story.

Anyhow, some of us who were reading science fiction in the late '30s and early '40s remember what Campbell did. We remember what came before him. I wish James Blish did.

JAMES BLISH

XERO 5 WELCOMED HERE WITH GASPS OF AWE.

Ebert's question — "was Amis right in his pronouncements on the relative worth of various stf writers?" — is not in my view "the only cogent issue," obviously, or I'd have paid some attention to it in the review. It would have been absolutely impossible for Amis to please everybody, or even a majority on this subject. Budrys' list of people Amis has slighted (Kuttner, Heinlein, Kornbluth, Sturgeon) almost completely overlaps mine; and it would be at least a tenable argument to note that in a literature of ideas, a critic might evaluate the contributors at least in part by what they have contributed that was new and/or influential in the field. In addition a critic who is also an expert fiction writer (like Amis) might have been influenced by who-made-purely-technical-contributions. I'm speaking about writing techniques, not technological background: van Vogt, for example, doesn't know enough science to put in a thimble, but as a technical innovator he was enormously inventive and influential. All four of the men mentioned by Budrys qualify on both counts, where some of the people Amis praises have visibly been followers all their lives.

From these twin grounds I continue to think that Amis over-emphasizes Sheckley. Talent, sure, that's been visible from the beginning; and the man handles the language very much better than most of us; in addition, he's inarguably witty. But in terms of contributions? The field is no different now than it would have been had Sheckley never existed. (A completely untestable and hence empty judgement, I know.) It might of course be argued that he started the trend toward what I now think of with horror as the *Galaxy* type of short story, but that bias pre-existed in the editor; since he was certain to publish that kind of story anyhow, I suppose we should be grateful that he got much of it from as skillful a writer as Bob.

For the rest, it seems to me that taste enters in to so great an extent that this question can never be the central one. For example, I personally believe Amis gives Fred Pohl somewhat more than his due, but since Pohl plainly has contributed both ideas and techniques to the field in overflowing measure, perhaps more of both than nearly everybody else still practicing, I have no objective grounds for complaint, and have to retreat to Pearlman's admirable formulation, "De gustibus ain't what they used to be."

I do think that Amis sent out his questionnaires on some sort of frequency principals. I surely didn't get mine because I'd contributed to *Galaxy*, for I've appeared less often there than Avram has. My point was not that Amis sent his questionnaires only to *Galaxy* writers, but that *Galaxy* and Ballantine appear to have operated something like an organized campaign to get *replies* to Amis, hence the skew on the data. If this true — and I certainly can't guarantee that it is — the fault for the skew lies not with those who did reply, but with those who didn't; and it can't at all be said to lie with the questioner.

AVRAM DAVIDSON

You Cur, Sur,

I have dealt with your perfidy in re: me on the adjacent pp., and will now go on to other items.

Please ... someone ... anyone ... What means "Zonky?" I've asked Harlan Ellison, and all he says is "Now, don't get *broygus* with me, kid; don't get *broygus* with *me*.

I wish to announce that my churlish remarks about Randy Garrett were written in a moment of despair, and that sf's own Amorous Theologian has since reduced his indebtedness to

This Establishment by a full 20%. Anybody who will mimeo any amount of Anthony Boucher off the page & give full space to driveling inferiors is capable of anything. Even dropping two pages out of my so-called "odd" letter, you sonuvabitch.

ALGIS BUDRYS

Rogue Moon? What kind of title is that? Obviously, this is a low-bodice book about a Mississippi riverboat gambler with wavy hair and a cheroot stuck in the corner of his mouth. (The low-bodice is for hiding extra aces.) Whaddaya doing reviewing it in an sf fanzine? First commix and now this!

BETTY KUJAWA

A beautiful, beautiful, beautiful issue! The covers, front and back, are gosh-wow! Personally I still dig poetry in zines not at all — but this is your zine and not mine — would rather see them all put on *one page* and thereby have more space for other things. I don't mean to sound mean or anything — just ain't my cuppa tea and I hate to see the space used up that way.

I got a copy of *England Under Hitler* when we were staying in Chi two weeks back — the info in it I found deeply interesting (like to see this reported on at length in a zine someday) was that part about the mating of Nazi superior boys and girls and the babies reared in State Homes and how, says this author, it was discovered at war's end that these children were mainly feeble-minded or emotionally defective due to the impersonal state-run upbringing. I had often wondered the outcome and results of that breeding-farm plan of theirs.

BILLY JOE PLOTT

The cover by Ivie strikes me as being beautiful — yes, beautiful. There is something weirdly captivating about the ominous figure, the delicate shading, and the sharp lettering. It's the first piece of real G*H*O*O*D Ivie artwork that I've seen in a long time; it's much better than the crud he had in *Monster Parade*. Heck, it's downright unghodly to compare the two at all.

I like Ebert's verses. They are indeed "more than meets fan standards." Reminds me of Carl Sandburg, but then all free verse reminds me of Sandburg, who just happens to be one of my favorites.

Ah, I'm glad to see you voted for *Amazing* for the Hugo. Old Gernsback's descendent is where I cut my first stf teeth outside of Winston juveniles. I've stood faithfully by and proudly watched the Ziff-Davis era climb the ladder to respectability after an all-too lengthy stint in the quagmire of crudity.

READER BEWARE

BY COL. AVRAM DAVIDSON

In Xero 5 there appeared a four-page essay by Colonel Avram Davidson, the essay entitled "He Swooped on his Victims and Bit them on the Nose." As happens on occasion in the assembly of such magazines as this, a leaf was omitted from several copies. Colonel Davidson's own copy was one such, the missing leaf being, by sheerest (and most innocent) coincidence, from the Colonel's very essay. His comments upon this unhappiness follow ...

Once upon a time there was a man named
        Lick* Lupoff.
He had long fangs and two vestigial, but
        visible, horns.
He was E V I L.

Finding that, outside fannish circles,
People tend to look askance at fangs
        &/or horns,
Dupoff took Steps:
What with a concealing prosthesis and a
        hair-piece,
Dupoff looked Almost Human.

But he was, of course,
Still E V I L.
He was ... utterly evil ...

Presently he met Avram Davidson.
Avram Davidson was GOOD.
He was also simple-minded.

So, when Lick Dupoff asked him
        to write eppis**
For Dupoff's fanzine, Xeno***,
He, Avram, beard dripping with

*From "Lycanthrope"

**From epic opus

***From xenophobe

the Milk of Human
Kindness, complied, and
Wrote a long, long, long, good,
      good, good piece.

On receiving this 1., 1., 1., g., g., g., p.,
Lick Dupoff screamed with fiendish and
Inhuman Glee.

He bared his fangs.
He shewed his horns.

Reader, do you know what he next did?
You, with your pure mind, will scarce credit
What the monster, Dupoff, did next.

He printed page 40, with the beginning
Of simple, lovable, Avram Davidson's eppis;
And he printed page 43, with the end
Of gentle, sweet Avram Davidson's eppis;

But pp 41 & 42, containing the corpus
Thereof —
These he did not print; instead
He just laughed like a sonofabitch-gahdam
Fiend … I have given them [he said]

A herring with a head

And a tail

But no body

Ah hah hah hah hah hah hah heh heh ho ho ho haw!!!

Pause, Reader, and Meditate. Beware
The Fiend DUPOFF,
For he bitath like a Serpent, yea,
He stingeth like an Adder.

FIEND DUPOFF, bhob Stewart

MY LAST ANNISH
DEDICATED TO METROPOLITAN MIMEO

ROG EBERT

That's my last Annish framed on the wall,
Looking as if it were Gestetnered. I call
That ish a wonder, now: Ted White's hands
Cranked busily a day, and there it stands.
Won't you have a seat? I said
"Annish" by design, for it was never read
By BNFs like you, or any of fandom;
Its sense of wonder seems almost random,
But to myself it's sercon (and since I'm shy,
Allowed no one to read it, but I)
And worried that they would ask me, if they dared,
How such repro was accomplished, since I fared
So poorly on previous issues. Well, was not
My mimeo only; White's mercenary rot
Brought those five colors to the page; perhaps
Ted himself said, "The Atom illo laps
Over the logo," or, "Ink
Can never reproduce crayola; Ebert stinks
As does his crude stencilling": such stuff
was his concern, I thought, and cause enough
For paying him a ten-spot. He laid
It in his wallet; his mimeo — how shall I say? — is too soon paid,
Too easily bought; he likes whatever
He is paid to print, his zines go everywhere.
VOID, crud, all 'tis one! My zine at its best,
Or the trash of Berkeley rabble from the west,
The Hugo at a Worldcon in smoke filled room
Presented at the banquet, the bem costume,
Worn at the ball — all and each
he used to draw from fen approving speech,
Or LoCs, at least. He thanked us — yass! — but wrote
As if — I suppose — he someday hoped
To replace my gift of a paid-up 'zine

With columns in Downbeat. He must be keen
On jazz trifles. Even had you will
To crank and pub — (which I have not) — to get a bill
From such a one who says, "This crud
I print for you disgusts me; the thud
Is of your fanzine dully falling. " — and still will let
His mimeo by purchased so, and plainly set
On getting money for it, makes no excuse,
 — And even then the cash is spent for booze,
Never for stencils. Oh sir, he smiled, no doubt,
Whenever I paid him; but have dirty, bearded routs
With my money. This grew; I gave commands;
Then the blasts were hidden from me. There the Annish stands,
as if Gestetnered. Have you finished it? We'll greet
the fen below, then. I repeat,
The mimeo of your club is said to reproduce
Others' fanzines when it's not in use,
An ample sign that should I proffer
My fanzine, with a sound cash offer,
 — Though the noble sercon goal, I admit,
In pubbing, is my purpose — you would print
It on your machine. Uh, notice the bhob Stewart illo there,
As we leave; blasting off for Mars without fear,
In a four-color cover drawing I saw at a convention
And bought amidst the auction's tension.

THE MASTER SHALL NOT ABATE

BY BOB TUCKER, WRITING AS HOY PING PONG

WILSON TUCKER (1914-) sometimes wrote for the fan press as Hoy Ping Pong. He published a fanzine, The Planetoid, *in 1932, followed by many other amateur publications. His first novel,* The Chinese Doll *(1946), was a murder mystery, as were his next four. His first science fiction novel,* The City in the Sea, *did not appear until 1951. In all he wrote more than twenty novels, evenly divided between the two genres, as well as numerous short stories and nonfiction works. Critics have remarked that Tucker's novels are marked by an intimacy of viewpoint and a modesty of execution that makes them far more memorable, in the long run, than the more bombastic and sensationalistic works of many of his contemporaries.*

I approached the house with diffidence, acutely aware of the Personage who dwelled within. (The sound of a busily clacking typewriter reached my ears and I smiled knowingly, albeit diffidently.) It was a modest home as befitted the Personage — a charming little fourteen room bungalow set back from the street about an eighth of a mile, having a three-stall garage and a kidney-shaped swimming pool in the rear. Through the open garage doors I caught a glimpse of the automotive power stored there: a sedate Rolls-Royce for the Deity's wife, a speedy little Lancia for his own use as he dashed hither and yon between the studios, and a gold-plated motorscooter for his teenage daughter. It was all so charming, so simple, so diffident. My memory went back to the humble days in Weyawega when the Personage owned nothing but a rusty bicycle.

It was so heartwarming, so truly American.

I climbed the steps in rather timid fashion and rang the bell. Perhaps half an hour later I rang again, suspecting that no one had heard me. When the shadows lengthened and intuition told me that the afternoon was waning, I became a bit impatient and kicked the door in. The poor thing hung there on one hinge, diffidently. A harried young woman ran to the door and put her head through the new opening.

"Quick, quick!" she cried, "what do you want?"

"I have come to interview the Master."

"Oh, heavens, no!" she gasped. "He hasn't time for interviews. He is busy, busy, busy ... "

"But he will see *me*," was my urbane reply. "I represent the fan press, and besides, I knew him in Weyauwega when he possessed nothing but a rusty bicycle."

"Is this blackmail?" she demanded.

"Perish the thought, madam. I wish only an interview."

The harried young woman sped away from the door and ran to the foot of the staircase, shouting upwards: "Jim Harmon is here. He wants an interview."

I corrected her in a gentle manner. "The name is Pong, my good woman. From *white* China, of course." And with that I brushed past her and climbed the stairs to the Master's workshop.

I paused in the doorway, aghast.

The workshop was a bedlam of frenzied activity, crowded with milling people. The room itself contained nothing but a desk, a typewriter and a chair; the Great One Himself sat in the chair lustily banging the typewriter and I saw the desk quivering beneath the onslaught. (My breath caught in admiration as I watched his twelve fingers flying over the keyboard.) A callow youth stood nervously at one side of the desk feeding fresh paper into the machine, while on the opposite side another youth snatched the typewritten pages from the mill and passed them to a waiting girl. The girl hurriedly proofread each page and then assembled the completed pages into neat little piles. At intervals, the harried young woman who had admitted me would snatch up these pile, stuff them into envelopes and hand the packages to uniformed messengers — the messengers would then race down the stairs, leap to their waiting motorcycles and rush the manuscripts to the proper studio. I was watching a fiction factory at work and my admiration knew no bounds.

The Personage was clad in his favorite working clothes: a colorful sport shirt, slacks, and house slippers. I noticed dust on his glasses and realized with dismay that he'd not had time to take them off for their weekly rinsing. A long black cigarette holder drooped from one corner of the tired mouth and as I looked, the badgered secretary snatched a butt from the holder and quickly inserted a fresh, lighted cigarette. He puffed on without interruption.

After a moment he sensed the presence of a stranger in the room and glared at me without pausing in his work. "Whaddyawant?"

"My name is Pong," I reminded him, "and we knew each other in Weyauwewga when you owned nothing but a rusty bicycle. I once treated you to a steak dinner."

"Come/back/Tuesday," he snapped. "I/toss/coins/to/beggars/only/on/Tuesdays."

"I am not a beggar, sir. I collect picturesque sentences."

"Such/as/what?" he barked, the busy fingers never stopping.

"Such as this," and I quoted a recent acquisition: "The LASFS Christmas party was a rouse, with plain eggnog, and the police, and gift trading and all the rest of the wonderful things that had come to mean Christmas."

"Didn't/go," he cried. "Too/busy, work/piling/up, no/time/for/frivolity/or/the/police."

"Of course you didn't, Great One. That's merely a sentence I discovered in the fan press. I collect such odd statements."

"What's/that/got/to/do/with/me?" he demanded.

"Oh, Sir, I have a precious quote from your Very Own Lips."

"What/izzat?" (And the boy snatched another page from his machine.)

And again I quoted a line found in the fan press: "I intend to write the book next month."

"So?" he hissed, as a new sheet was inserted in the typewriter.

"You meant to say next year, didn't you, Master?"

"I/said/next/month/and/I/meant/next/month!"

"But sir, surely there is some mistake. I appreciate your industry, of course, but the published letter recounted many other activities: the half dozen new television scripts you were planning, the movie scenario you were polishing, the several short stories you were revising for anthology publication, the novelettes you were writing for the science fiction magazines, and the galley proofs you were readying for the printer. And *then* you said you planned to write a certain book next month. I felt certain it was a slip of the tongue."

"Well/dammit/I/did/write/the/book…that/was/threemonths/ago. Two/more/books/since/then!"

"A book a month?" I inquired in amazement. "In addition to all your other work?"

"Whattaboutit?" he snapped, working like a demon.

"Sir, aren't you just a teensy-weensy bit concerned about … (and I hung my head to conceal the blush) … about quality?"

"Quality/schmality!" was the cold rejoinder that cut me to the quick. "I'm/busy/busy/busy … "

At that moment (to my horror) I espied a dreadful sight. The harried secretary had dropped to all fours beyond the desk and was removing the Great Man's slipper and sock from one foot. She placed a yellow pencil between his toes and a sheet of clean paper beneath the pencil. The foot began to move!

"Sir," I cried out in protest, "what are you doing down there?"

"Writing/my/*Rogue*/column/stupid!"

In a state of fright not unmixed with awe I moved nearer to

desk to study this human dynamo. Beads of sweat stood out on his wrinkled brow and ran down his gaunt cheeks; there was a certain wild look of — something — in his tired eyes; his lips quivered with agony and even the veins of his neck betrayed a great secret emotion. Clearly the man was in some terrible difficulty.

"Master," I whispered, "what is the matter? Tell me!"

"I/wish/I/could/stop/for/a/minute," he breathed huskily. "I've/got/to/go/to/the/john!"

"Please, sir, stop and go. Surely this masterpiece in your typewriter can wait."

"No/no/no," he cried. "Deadline/deadline/deadline ... "

I peered closely to see what he was doing, and my breath caught. The Master was composing volume six (BulgCarf) of the next edition of the Encyclopedia Americana.

THE *NAUTILUS*, THE *ALBATROSS*, THE *COLUMBIAN*

LIN CARTER

Most authors seem to enjoy a vigorous, if brief, resurgence of popularity shortly after death, no doubt due to their names suddenly becoming topical again. (This is happening to Eugene O'Neill right now.)

Then, as if by dying they identified themselves and their work with an outmoded, passé generation, they fade out of view and become neglected, seldom mentioned, no longer "important." (This is happening to George Bernard Shaw right now.)

Sometimes they remain generally forgotten for a considerable period of time, and their achievements, however once significant, are passed over and consigned to general oblivion. (This is happening to James Branch Cabell right now.)

But sometimes — due to a variety of different causes — they return to the full light of popular and critical attention, and suddenly become of far greater importance than ever before. And this is what has happened to Jules Verne.

Jules Verne was born in 1828. A restless and inattentive schoolboy, he entered a bohemian life in Paris once free of school. At 28 he settled down, married, became a stockbroker, and left his wilder ways behind to become a typical bourgeois. But he was not fated for this kind of life. His wife encouraged his imaginative literary bent, and at 35 his first book, *Cinq semaines en ballon*, was published.

This book — *Five Weeks in a Balloon* — started one of the most amazing literary careers ever launched. His publisher labeled the work a "Voyage Extraordinaire" — and to live up to it, Verne began putting his heroes through every imaginable sort of trip, under the sea, off on a comet, around the world by land and air, via

LIN CARTER (1930-1988) contributed essays, reviews, parodies, humorous verse, and even drawings to Xero. Remarkably prolific, he soon emerged from his fannish cocoon as one of the most productive writers and editors in the history of science fiction and fantasy. A master of pastiche, he wrote scores of novels in the varied traditions of Edgar Rice Burroughs, Robert E. Howard, "Kenneth Robeson" (Lester Dent), and A. E. van Vogt, as well as critical works on J. R. R. Tolkien, H. P. Lovecraft, and, more broadly, the art of fantasy.

JELLYFISH MAN, Dan Adkins

balloon, airship, giant sealiner, space vehicle, mechanical steam-powered elephant, and a wonderful, wacky amphibious machine called *The Terror* that was a combination automobile-airplane-speedboat-submarine.

The odd thing is that Verne wanted to be a serious writer. *Five Weeks in a Balloon* had its origin in a serious non-fiction treatise on the future of balloon-travel, dealing especially with its possibilities in the exploration of Africa, which in those far-off and innocent days was still a Dark Continent, no doubt liberally filled with Lost Egyptian Cities, dinosauric survivals, colonies of Atlantis, and other delightful conceptions that would endear the names of Rider Haggard and Edgar Rice Burroughs to the heart of the world.

Verne's first publisher, however, persuaded him to present his theories in fictional form. *Five Weeks* was so well received that Verne followed it a year later with *A Journey to the Center of the Earth*. And from there, there was no stopping him. He became a one-man literary factory, and in the following forty years he produced seventy books. Books of all sorts — scientific romances, boys' adventure books, historical romances (including one about the American Civil War), an *Illustrated Geographical History of France*, "straight" travel-adventure stories, humorous works, plays, article, short stories, a history of world exploration, an occasional Gothic piece (testifying to his life-long admiration of Poe), American frontier stories — in short, just about every kind of story conceivable.

His popularity was more than immense — it was gigantic. At times he challenged the stupendous fame of his friend, Alexandre Dumas. When he died in in 1905, however, his vast following died with him, and his international audience dwindled. Many of his works had never been translated into English, and of those that had, only a few survived with unimpaired appeal. By the mid-point of this century, his rather dubious claim to immortality was resting on the uncertain basis of having his *20,000 Leagues Under the Sea* included as a standard item in the Scribner's Illustrated Classics series.

Then — the revolution! From a forgotten author virtually

impossible to find in English, Verne was catapulted to the position of a writer (dead over 50 years) who was more popular and topical than many best-selling novelists still living. He mushroomed all over theatre marques and paperback stands and began making millions for those publishers and producers who had wisely decided to hitch their wagons on the star of Verne.

Why — and how? I have been at some pains to find out where all this started, and the closest I can come to the answer is to say: Walt Disney.

In the early '50s, you may remember, Disney was turning from the all-cartoon feature, which had become prohibitively expensive, to the live-action feature. However, to preserve his association with the classics of childhood, most of his early live-action films were taken from standard childrens' books such as *Rob Roy, Robin Hood* and *Treasure Island*. I suspect it was *Treasure Island* that convinced Disney he was on the right track. That film — it was a lovely piece of work, with an inspired casting choice of Robert Newton as Long John Silver — made a pile of money for Disney, and became one of his biggest hits up to that time.

At any rate, in 1955 Disney released his Technicolor, all-live-action version of *20,000 Leagues Under the Sea*, an excellent science fiction extravaganza which preserved much of the authentic Verne flavour, and featured a fine cast headed by James Mason, as the brooding and enigmatic Captain Nemo, with Kirk Douglas as Ned Land, and Peter Lorre in an unexpected comic role that came close to stealing the picture.

As is usual with Disney, the book was released widely as a publicity tie-in with the picture. *20,000 Leagues* deluged the newsstands of the nation, and the book was lifted to a new level of popularity from which it has not yet (six years later) decline. Last year the Heritage Club, a deluxe publisher of boxed gift books, presented a gorgeous edition of Verne's hoary masterpiece, as one of their offerings. It was pleasant and exhilirating to find Verne on a publishing list in the austere company of Dostoevsky, Milton, Virgil and Boccacio!

And only one year later — on October 7, 1956 — came a new picture that *really* made theatrical history. The Disney feature had been a fine commercial success, and had received an Academy Award for set decoration, but Michael Todd's *Around the World in 80 Days* proved even more screen-worthy. This masterly film, one of the screen's outstanding examples of pure, unadulterated *entertainment*, broke boxoffice records, played for years at reserved-seat houses, won a brace of Oscars (including Best Picture of the Year) and made a fortune. It was the first story-picture in Todd-AO, and the first "cameo" picture to include scores and scores of guest stars in bit parts. Virtually everybody in Hollywood who could still walk was in it, as well as herds of foreign stars like Fernandel, Cantinflas, José Greco, and Martine Carol.

Naturally, book tie-ins followed. *Around the World* became available in a wide variety of paperback and hardcover editions — and the flood began!

In the next couple years, other Verne titles were resurrected from library shelves and paperbacked. *Hector Servadac* (*Off on a Comet*), *The Purchase of the North Pole*, *From the Earth to the Moon*, *The Mysterious Island*, *Around the Moon*, and so on ...

Hardcover houses also got into the act. A.A. Wyn, Inc. and the Associated Booksellers began bringing to light inexpensive editions of previously hard-to-find Verne novels like *A Floating City* (about a giant sea-liner), *The City on the Niger*, *Five Weeks in a Balloon*, *The Begum's Fortune* ...

Nor were the movie moguls slow to follow the Disneys and Todds. A so-so version of *From the Earth to the Moon* was released, with Joseph Cotton and George Sanders, to moderate success. It retained the colorful period flavour of the novel, and elicited amusement by presenting a spaceship with oak-paneled lounge decorated with brass oil lamps and red leather cushions.

A charming version of *A Journey to the Center of the Earth*, with James Mason, Arlene Dahl, and Pat Boone, came out hard on its heels. This delightful picture was played with tongue-in-cheek seriousness as a straight boys' adventure book, with splendid

FANTASTIC BUNNY RABBIT,
Steve Stiles

sets and fine color photography. It was one of the best of the Verne pictures, and indicated the sophisticated entertainment the movies could draw from Verne's prodigious storehouse of books.

A foreign-made color version of *Michael Strogoff*, starring Curt Jurgens, had a healthy run (and of course the paperback houses filled newsstands across the country with *Michael Strogoff: Courier to the Czar*; *A Journey to the Center of the Earth*; *From the Earth to the Moon*.)

By the time this article is printed, a distinguished companion will have been added to that famous fleet of vehicles that included Verne's super-submarine, the *Nautilus* (whose fame was not impaired when a real-life atomic submarine of the same name explored the Polar regions a few years back), and the famous projectile in *From the Earth to the Moon* (one can only wish the Russians had christened their Lunik the *Columbiad*, in honor of Verne's machine which circumnavigated the moon long before Lunik). The new vehicle will be the *Albatross*, the super flying-machine in *Robur the Conqueror*. For a new color movie, starring Vincent Price as the dynamic engineer, Robur, will soon be released. This movie combines two Verne books, *Master of the World* and *Robur the Conqueror* into one story, and Ace Books has already released a paperback edition of the two stories.

Also thrilling the screens of the nation about the time of this article is a Czech-made film called *The Fabulous World of Jules Verne*, which will be followed in months to come by a movie version of *The Mysterious Island* (with James Mason recreating his role of Captain Nemo), and a Disney film starring Hayley Mills, adapted from another Verne book.

The Fabulous World of Jules Verne is described by the list of screen credits as being adapted from Verne's story *A Dangerous Invention*. There is no such — the Czech-made film is an original, a clever pastiche of several bits and scraps from popular Verne books. The film uses a new screen process that lends the illusion of animated steel-engravings to everything in the scene, thus giving a "period" aspect suitable for a Verne movie.

The forthcoming Disney film will be *The Castaways*, with Hayley Mills, Charles Laughton, Maurice Chevalier, and others. It is taken from the story *Captain Grant's Children*.

At the moment, and for some time to come, there would seem to be no letup in the popularity of Jules Verne. In the last seven years, eight movies have been made from his books. That would be an extraordinary record for any contemporary writer to attempt to match. About 15 of his books are widely available from paperback and hardcover houses, with many more to come.

How nice it would be, to have in print those of Verne's many books most intriguing and rare. Books like *Le Sphinx de glaces* (*The Ice-Sphinx*), Verne's sequel and completion to Poe's fragmentary novel, *Arthur Gordon Pym*! Or *The Steam-House*, with its mechanical steam-powered iron elephant ... or *Keraban the Inflexible* ... *The Green Ray* ... *The Invasion of the Sea* ... *The Floating Island* ... *The Lighthouse at the End of the World* ... *The Eternal Adam* ... *The Giant Raft* ... *The Cryptogram* ... *The Archipelago of Fire* ...

And what a ripe harvest stills await movie-makers among Verne's as yet untouched titles: A mad, Todd-style comedy could be produced from *Five Weeks in a Balloon*, in which a small party of Englishmen explore Darkest Africa in a large balloon, get involved with cannibals and drop down to hunt animals, and have one merry series of hair-breadth escapes from Zanzibar to the Atlantic. Or *The Chase of the Gold Meteor*, one of Verne's eight posthumous books published between 1907 and 1911, and the only one of them to be translated into English. Or *The Adventures of Captain Hatteras*. Or *A Floating City*, in which the super giant sea-liner battles across the Atlantic on her maiden voyage, through storms, waterspouts, icebergs ...

Let's hope the movie men keep on with Verne. Perhaps someday they will even get around to Olaf Stapledon and E.E. Smith.

I hope I'm here to see it.

EPISTOLARY INTERCOURSE

EPISTOLARY INTERCOURSE #6

CONDUCTED BY PAT LUPOFF

BOB SHEA

Your typo in the first line of "Reader Beware!" making the name of the villain "Lick Lupoff" instead of "Lick Dupoff" as the author obviously intended is yet another coal heaped on the head of much-put-upon Avram Davidson. Indeed Lick Dupoff is evil.

WALT WILLIS

Tucker's article alone is a classic, the best thing he's done in years. I liked the editorial too and Avram Davidson is a perpetual joy. The comics material is rather lost on me because they didn't have them when I was a kid, but I know a similar material about the Magnet and the Gem and the Nelson Lee would be just as

interesting and nostalgic to me as this stuff evidently is to you people. In fact there is, I believe, a fandom around these old boys' papers.

GUY TERWILLIGER

Xero is hitting a nice stride — from the early comic centered zine has grown into a massive tome of interesting material. The much appreciated articles on comics, the wonderful cartoons, the serious-without-being-serious-sercon articles right down to the fannish type writing all blend together to make the best fanzine in fandom.

Collins' "The Fantastic Paperback" makes me wish all the more that I had the courage to go ahead and open a paperback bookshop here in Boise. The idea in fascinating to me ever since I went into in San Francisco this summer. I have to be rational, though, and remember that Boise doesn't seem able to support even a magazine-tobacco shop combination. Yet it would be nice to see some of these books that Collins mentions without having to order them sight unseen. Rather than our newsstands increasing in size, they are dwindling into nothing. What few there are carry so few zines that you might as well stay at home. In fairness, though, they do carry the sf zines.

Pong's satire on the master makes me wish wistful when the "great one" had more time for our goings on. Perhaps someday he will tire of the mad pace and drift back.

ETHEL LINDSAY

It is nice to see you in the editorial chair, Pat, and I hope you manage to find a mansion to suit you. I have lately bought a (second-hand) filling cabinet, and have found this invaluable. At last all my zines are filed in proper order, the correspondence all together, the various bits and pieces really in a sensible manner. Will Scot and Haver material in their own compartments I can at last put my hand on anything I want without trouble.

Avram Davidson is a hoot.

EI 6, bhob Stewart

JAMES BLISH

Now, Richard Kyle. Maybe this Amis discussion is wearing out and you (Lupoffs) should call it closed, the way British magazines do when the editors detect the participants starting a second round without having been aware of the first; that certainly happened, and repeatedly with the *Starship Trooper* hassle, and is certain to happen over *Tsias Land*. If you need a place to start cutting I suggest here ...

Excellency in an index is a judgment of whether or not it covers the material in the book, not of whether the material itself is adequate. Kyle is not the first person to scream because Amis' index doesn't list certain names often enough to satisfy him, but this is not what an index is for. (A minor point, evoked by puzzlement over Kyle's oddly punctuated phrase "the 'excellent' index James Blish speaks of").

On matters of more substance, I find I can agree with Kyle on only one point, that being that some important writers were neglected by Amis. My letter which follows in your [last issue] says as much. This was almost inevitable and doesn't greatly disturb me; were I to write such a book, the authors I would emphasize and/or ignore would comprise a sharply different list and perhaps it wouldn't satisfy Mr. Kyle any better. It would not, for instance, pay any more attention to Olaf Stapledon than Mr. Kyle finds in Amis; I consider Stapledon a bow-legged philosopher and arthritic writer of no interest or importance whatsoever; whereas I might have gone on at some length about M.P. Sheil, whose style Sprague de Camp finds as impossible as I find Stapledon's (or Merritt's). What ought to be borne in mind here is that Amis has almost wholly thrown aside the standard genealogy of science fiction and concerned himself with the phenomenon as primarily an American one with its focus in the history of the magazines; hence the only book authors of any previous era he finds it necessary to mention are those who appeared in the earliest magazines and hence formed other writers' impressions of what was wanted — there being, of course, Wells and Verne, *not* Sheil or Stapledon or Hugh Benson, who are a hell of a lot less important than even so minor a writer as A. Hyatt Verrill in the formation of modern science fiction. If you cling to the standard family tree, going all the way back to Lucian of Samasata and all that crap, then of course Amis' approach is going to seem unfair and scrappy; but I think it is quite defensible. Is there any influential s-f writer who has ever read *any* of these antiquities? If not, then why bother to name them? Can any writer in the audience name a science fiction by Voltaire, or show a single example of its having influenced 20th-century s-f in any way? I doubt it, and obviously, so does Amis.

I think this may explain why Kyle, and some others, call the book badly researched, etc.; they are looking for data excluded by Amis' scheme (which is coherent and logical, whether you like it or not; no man is required to document a point he doesn't think worth making). I would like to see some of these critics of Amis come up with a list of errors. I could find very few, and these small, as I indicated in my review. If Mr. Kyle has had any better luck, let's see the specifications.

Next we have criticism *ad hominem*, which in this instance asserts that those who praise Amis' book are simply licking his eminent boots. (I leave out the part of the argument which says that those who damn the book are also licking his boots, as being a little too subtle for the likes of me.) I reject this as a personal inconvenience because it would force me to assume that the kind things Mr. Kyle has said about me were also designed to be boot-licking, whereas I prefer to believe that he meant them. But there is no real need to be that personal about it, for long experience with *ad hominem* criticism has shown that it never gets the critic to any real understanding of the work; he is too busy reviewing the author and the readers. What profit has Mr. Kyle got out of it? Well, the customary ones: First, "The literary reputation science fiction deserves – in the measure it deserves — will be determined by time and truth, not by any man, no matter what his name;" this is what Mr. Amis calls a "piety," which is something less than a truism. Second, a demand that s-f take a "good, direct look at itself and its history" and show "proper respect for the men who made it;" this is of course the antithesis of the piety; the head that could contain them both without finding them at war with each other has my admiration, but not my envy.

I for one refuse to be scolded for lack of piety toward any figure, any more than I accept scolding for too much piety toward Amis. This applies mostly to Kyle's remarks about JWC, Jr., though it might equally well apply to his estimate of Stapledon or Wells. Like Mr. Kyle, I was reading sf in the early '30s and constantly thereafter, and I know what Campbell accomplished; I was one of the beneficiaries, as I have often said in public and in print. I am also one of the beneficiaries, as is Mr. Kyle, of Hugo Gernsback. But I am not going to don horse blinders and assert that Mr. Gernsback's recent utterances deserve any serious attention; and were Mr. Amis to say that JWC, Jr. lately has become a crank (he does *not* so say, though Mr. Kyle marks the word "crank" as though he were quoting somebody), no considerations of reverence or gratitude would prevent me from agreeing though both gratitude and reverence exist.

I remember what John Campbell did, and honor him for it, but Mr. Kyle hasn't said what it was. He says John "created the modern magazine science fiction story." This is a fraction of a fact. John created some modern magazine sf stories, and fostered many others; but he had lots of help. Horace Gold created, in part, another kind of modern sf story; but again, he made perhaps 85% of the noise and about 3.5% of the work. This is the natural relationship between those who edit and those who write, as you may see by consulting any anthology in any field of writing whatsoever. What constitutes "proper respect" can't be judged except operationally, by what one finds one can respect each time the subject comes up; there is *no* operational definition of "proper." It was proper of writers to respect their editors at the time that their editors were useful to them, perhaps; and maybe it is not proper for a writer to show respect to the editors who are now actively pushing notions that prevent the writers from writing, even though the same sets of writers and editors (so far as the names are concerned) seem to be involved. If this is a sensible way of looking at the matter, then I can't see that reverence has much to do with it. And mind you, I was talking exclusively about what is called the "creative" editor, who sometimes does actively help and influence a writer or a whole field; those who are simply parasites on writers are always in the large majority, and collect even larger slices of the check; and the one may quickly turn into the other — and invariably does.

So one's opinion of current editorial work is far from irrelevant. It is the only way one can form a current opinion. The rest is reverence, which I leave to bystanders.

Finally (honest!) I have what I suspect may be an *ad hominem* argument of my own, or at least an anti-populist heresy, which is: It is silly to wax angry or pious over a hobby, as Mr. Kyle and Mr. Beale do. Does Mr. Kyle write stf? Or Mr. Beale motion pictures? If not, of what use is all this self-righteous passion? The practitioner has to be conditionally involved or he can't practice, no matter how minor the art (such as Mr. Kyle's "westerns as an art-form"); but the fan of teensy-weensy crafts like stf or cigar-band collecting would be saner than practioners, at least to the extent that he can avoid turning into a cloud of live steam over matters of no moment.

No, Mr. Kyle, sf is not Melville, and John Campbell is not the Albert Schweitzer of our field. We have no such, nor are we ever likely to get them.

DON'T CALL US, WE'LL CALL YOU

DONALD E. WESTLAKE

DONALD E. WESTLAKE (1933-) was regarded as a rising star in both the world of mystery fiction and that of science fiction when he offered his now famous essay "Don't Call Us, We'll Call You" to Xero. His decision to abandon science fiction and pursue a life of (literary) crime was clearly a good one. He is the author of a long series of humorous mysteries about the incompetent mobster Dortmunder, several tougher novels about the hit-man Parker (written as Richard Stark), a series featuring ex-cop Mitch Tobin (written as Tucker Coe), several non-genre novels including the painfully hilarious A Likely Story (1984), and a number of screenplays. One of the latter, an adaptation of Jim Thompson's The Grifters (1990), won Westlake an Oscar. Now closing in on 100 books (unless he passed that mark while the scorekeeper's back was turned) Westlake continues to be as productive and as excellent as ever, with no end in sight. Oh, what science fiction lost when Westlake made his choice!

About a year ago, Henry Morrison asked Randy Garrett and me to speak at an ESFA meeting over in Jersey. The last echoes of the science fiction boom had faded away, the alarming dimensions of the resulting crater were becoming increasingly noticeable, and the people at ESFA thought it would be interesting to know what a couple of writers in the field intended to do next. Garrett was there as the old pro, I, as the recent entry into professional science fiction writing. Despite the disparity of our standings in the field, our personalities, our backgrounds and our financial conditions, we both wound up by giving precisely the same answer: "I am a professional writer. My entire income comes from writing. If science fiction can't support me, I'll write in some other field."

That was a year ago. Today, I am a full time mystery writer, working on my fifth mystery novel. (The first had already been published at the time of the ESFA meeting), and the last time I saw Randy Garrett (a week ago) he was working on a biography, for decent money.

Isaac Asimov is writing good science fact these days. Lester del Rey is writing bad science fact. Bradbury and all the little Bradburys (Matheson, Beaumont, et al.) are writing bad big-time fantasy for television and *Playboy*. Arthur C. Clarke is writing popular science fact. Sheckley is writing paperback mysteries. Judith Merril is anthologizing. De Camp and a lot of others aren't doing much of anything. God knows what Budrys is doing. The list of living *ex-*science fiction writers approaches infinity.

The field can't support us. It can't support even the big boys, the established names, and it sure as hell can't support anybody new. But what's worse, it can't even interest us.

It's time for credentials, before going into this thing any deeper. If I'm going to talk as a professional writer who isn't doing anything in science fiction and who claims that he might have done something worthwhile if it were worth his while to do so, I ought to show my identity card. Therefore:

Science Fiction. I have sold thirteen stories, two of which have not yet been published and none of which are any damn good. I have sold to *Universe, Original, Future, Super, Analog, Amazing, If,* and *Galaxy.* A fourteenth story was sold to *Fantastic Universe,* which proceeded to drop dead before they could publish it. Both John Campbell and Cele Goldsmith have asked me to write sequels to novelettes of mine they had bought (I haven't written either,

EDDIE JONES was a British fan and sometime professional artist. Unlike his contemporary Arthur Thomson whose works were often stylized or semi-abstract, Jones worked in a detailed, realistic manner that gave even his fantastic drawings a noteworthy believability.

and won't). In a desk drawer I have twenty-odd thousand words of a science fiction novel, which *is* good, but which I'm not going to finish because it isn't worth my while.

Avalon pays three hundred and fifty dollars for a book, and I wouldn't support such piracy either by writing for them or buying their wares. John Campbell isn't the hero, so it can't be serialized in *Analog*. If finished, it would run a lot longer than forty-five thousand words, so that leaves out Ace. There's no gratuitous sex, so that excludes Galaxy/Beacon (or would if they were still being published). It isn't a silly satire about a world controlled by advertising agencies or insurance companies or the A&P, so it can't be serialized in *Galaxy Magazine*. It's in sensible English, so *Amazing* is out. It isn't about the horrors of Atomic War, so no mainstream hardcover house would look twice at it. I'd like to write it anyway for my own amusement (you know, like a real writer-type), but unpublished manuscripts unfortunately have a low enjoyment quota, at least for me. So the hell with it.

I have three other stories sitting around the house and all I have to do is rewrite them the way the various editors want, and they are sold. To hell with them too.

Mystery. I have sold twenty-five short stories a couple of which are pretty good. They've appeared in *Manhunt*, *Mystery Digest*, *Alfred Hitchcock's Mystery Magazine*, *Guilty*, *Tightrope*, *77 Sunset Strip* (a one-shot, though they didn't mean it that way), *Ed McBain's Mystery Book*, and *The Saint*. One was reprinted in *Best Detective Stories of 1959*, four more are shortly to be anthologized here and there, and one is maybe (at the time of this writing, I'm not sure yet) going to be bought for television.

I have sold three mystery novels to Random House, a fourth (aimed paperback) is currently being considered by Dell, and the fifth is in the writing. The first, *The Mercenaries*, won a second-place Edgar from the Mystery Writers of America for best first novel of the year. Anthony Boucher called the second, in the *Times*, "a considerable novel," giving it a very long and very pleasant review.

I am not sitting around bragging, I'm simply trying to make

something clear: I can write. I can write well. I am capable of first-class work. But the only thing I've ever written in science fiction that I am at all proud of is a novel I'll never finish because there is economically, stylistically, and philosophically no place for it.

Do you know what I'm talking about? *I cannot sell good science fiction.* All right, the field can't support me, so what? I don't spend all my time writing mysteries. I could still, it would be financially feasible for me to, write an occasional science fiction story, five or six a year, or maybe cut the budget a little and write a novel. But it doesn't *interest* me, the requirements of the field are such that I couldn't write anything that would interest *me*, so how could I presume to interest *you*? All of the *ex*-science fiction writers could still write in the field part time, but they don't. I guess it doesn't interest them either.

In *Xero 4* a letter-writer bitched about the *deus ex psionica* ending of *Out Like a Light*, the second Kenneth Malone serial by Randy Garrett and Larry Harris, in *Analog*. I know Randy and Larry, so let me tell you something: They had a relatively good ending for that story, one that would have satisfied your letter-writer's conditions for believability. John Campbell made them rewrite the ending, to make Kenneth Malone a psuperman, a John Campbell hero. Sixty thousand words at three cents a word is eighteen hundred dollars. Plus the virtually inevitable "An Lab" bonus (serial chapters always place first or second, or almost always) of three to six hundred dollars.

Randy and Larry disliked Campbell's ending, but couldn't talk him out of it. Had they decided not to prostitute themselves on a bed of gold (the letter-writer's phrase) , they would been throwing away not only the time they'd spent on the serial, but also nine to twelve hundred dollars in real money for *each* of them. At that point, I'd have rewritten the damn thing, too, and the hell with integrity. But I'm not ever going to get to that point; I'm not writing the stuff any more.

Now let me tell you a very sad and a very funny story. A while back, Randy Garrett was staying at my place. We worked in the same room, and we were both writing stories aimed at *Analog*.

Enjoying ourselves in the process, we both included private jokes for the other guy's benefit, and one thing I did was make a minor character, an Air Force Colonel who showed up in the last three pages of the story, the spitting image of John Campbell, betting Randy that Campbell would never notice it. I described the guy as looking like Campbell, talking like Campbell, and thinking like Campbell.

We brought our respective stories in at the same time, handed them to the great man, and both went back the next week because he wanted revisions on both stories. I forget what he wanted Randy to change in his story, but I'll never in the world forget what he wanted done with mine: He wanted me to make the Colonel the lead character. I did it. Eighteen thousand words. Four hundred and fifty dollars.

(P.S.: That's the story he wanted a sequel to. He really liked that Colonel.)

(P.P.S.: It was a better story the first time, when it was only fourteen thousand words. If I was going to rewrite, I wanted more money, so I padded four thousand unnecessary words into it. It makes for duller reading but frankly, my dear, I don't give a damn.)

More recently, when Frederik Pohl took over *Galaxy*, my agent suggested that I aim a story at him, as he was in a mood to build an inventory of his own. So I researched. I read the introductions to all the Pohl-edited *Star Science Fiction* series, and I reread the first and last sentence of every Frederik Pohl story I had around the house (which was a lot, since I have all but six issues of *Galaxy* up till this year, when I stopped buying it), and then I wrote a Frederik Pohl story. "The Spy in the Elevator."

A Pohl title and a Pohl story, and a very silly insipid story it was, but by that time I was getting cynical. Pohl bought it. It was my next-to-last science fiction story. It would have been the last, but a few months later my agent got me an assignment from Cele Goldsmith to do a cover story for *Amazing*. I'd never tried to match a story to a pre-drawn cover before, so I took the assignment, figuring I ought to get some enjoyment out of the novelty of the thing. And there I stopped. So far as I can see now I'll never write another word of science fiction again. (After this article, assuming the editors at least have sense enough to read the fanzines for the temper of the readership, which judging from their competence otherwise isn't necessarily true, I don't suppose anything of mine would be too welcome on their desks anyway. I've never burned a bridge with more joy.)

Campbell is an egomaniac. Mills of *F&SF* is a journeyman incompetent. Cele Goldsmith is a third grade teacher and I think she wonders what in the world she's doing over at *Amazing*. (Know I do.) As for Pohl, who can tell? *Galaxy* is still heavily laden with Gold's inventory, and when Pohl edited *Star* he had the advantages of no deadline and a better pay rate than anybody else in the field, so it's difficult to say what *Galaxy* will look like next year, except that Kingsley Amis will probably like it.

I will not end with a panacea. I have none. A lot of professional science fiction writers have moved on to other fields in the last few years, and a lot more haven't bothered to take their place. You may have wondered why, and since I'm one of them I thought I'd tell you, speaking only for myself. I don't know whether I speak for any of the others or not, but I suspect so. (The guy who beat me out for the first place Edgar, by the way, was Jack Vance, another escapee.)

I don't know why science fiction is so lousy. I suspect there are a lot of reasons. But I can at least hint at one reason which has special reference to *you*. At the ESFA meeting I mentioned earlier, Sam Moskowitz mentioned a story from *Weird Tales*, some time in the thirties. All the members had read it, and remembered it. A little later, Randy Garrett mentioned a story from the previous month's *Analog*. Two members present had read it.

THE WILD ONES

DON THOMPSON

DON THOMPSON (1935-1994), along with his then-fiancée, later wife, Maggie Curtis, founded Comic Art, *along with* Alter Ego *and* Xero, *one of the three "original" comics-oriented fan magazines. Thompson was co-editor of two books that grew from* Xero, All in Color for a Dime *and* The Comic-Book Book. *The Thompsons appeared at a World Science Fiction Convention costumed as the comics characters Ibis the Invincible and Princess Taia, a perfect embodiment of their prototypes. Thompson worked for many years as a reporter for the Cleveland Press. After that publication folded, the Thompsons created* Comic Buyers Guide, *by far the most important publication in the industry, a weekly bible for professionals, magazine dealers, fans and collectors.*

Superman is a sissy.

Oh, sure, he can withstand A-bombs, jump from Earth to another solar system without kicking Earth out of orbit, melt metal with heat vision, look through walls with x-ray vision, travel into past or future (sometimes being corporeally present, sometimes invisible and intangible — but always ineffective) and do all sorts of wondrous things.

But he can't grow larger than the solar system or smaller than an atom. He can't fight a duel with comets as weapons, ski on stars, raise the dead, stop time or talk with God.

But the Spectre could. And did.

The Spectre could have given Superman cards and spades and still beaten him soundly, while simultaneously trouncing Batman, Captain Marvel and all the rest. The Spectre was one comics character who really *was* omnipotent. He could, quite literally, do *anything*. Nothing could kill him, because he was already dead. He was an honest-to-goodness ghost, with the most amazing range of powers of any comic book hero.

The Spectre, like Superman, was a creation of the fertile mind of Jerry Siegel, whose byline appeared on all the stories. The artist who took credit for drawing the strip was Bernard Baily, who apparently was proud of his work because he signed it both at the beginning and at the end of each story. Baily also was credited with the early adventures of Hourman, back when Hourman took dope to be superhuman.

Siegel, apparently flushed with the success of Superman, lavished still more powers on the Spectre. Too many powers, as it turned out. For a while, it's fascinating to follow the adventures of a hero who can do anything, but only for a while. After that, it gets kind of boring.

About the only thing the Spectre never did was get a comic of his own. The Spectre appeared in *More Fun Comics #52* (Feb. 40) to 106 (late 45) inclusive and was a member of the Justice Society of America in *All-Star Comics* for quite a while.

Possibly because of his omnipotence, he was relegated to the back of the book after a while. A hero who can do anything and is totally invincible doesn't create much suspense. Besides, he was frightening.

The Spectre was the ghost of Jim Corrigan, a "hard-fisted" police detective who was clobbered by crooks who had kidnapped his fiancée, dumped into a barrel, encased — still alive — in concrete, and chucked into the river. You can't get much deader than that.

Jim's spirit rose from the barrel and headed heavenward, with only a momentary pang about leaving earth and his fiancée, Clarice Winston. He was rather looking forward to eternal rest, but a voice (obviously God, although never explicitly stated to be Him) told him that he could not have his eternal rest until he had wiped out all crime on earth. All of it. A pretty tall order, but he was promised special abilities.

He returned to the river where his body lay and discovered that he did not need to breathe, that he could walk on water, levitate or disappear at will, grow or shrink to whatever size he wished, and walk through walls. Armed with these weapons, and many more he didn't yet know about, he set out to rescue Clarice from the gangsters who had killed him.

This was where the first installment of the two-part origin story (#52-53, February and March 1940) ended.

The second began, with a *very* brief synopsis (52 words), exactly one panel later. The last panel of the first installment showed Jim walking into the wall of a warehouse. The first panel of the second chapter showed him emerging, halfway through the wall, in the room where "Gat" Bensons's gangsters were menacing Clarice.

The poor damned hoods never had a chance. Their bullets either bounced off him or went through him with no effect, whichever he wished. One by one he called them to him and had them look into his eyes, where they apparently looked either upon Death incarnate or the very pits of Hell itself. They either died or went mad on the spot.

However, one of the shots fired during this brief melee hit Clarice, and she was dying. Corrigan touched the wound and the wound closed, healed and vanished as if it had never been.

Since Clarice had fainted he was able to explain away the death or insanity of the baddies quite easily — especially since he then distracted her attention by breaking their engagement. He felt, with some justification, that a ghost was no sort of husband for a fine girl like Clarice. Not knowing his reasoning — or even that he was a ghost — Clarice refused to let him go and this led to the stock comic book situation of the heroine chasing the reluctant hero with matrimony as her object. But there were a couple of differences. Corrigan was more than willing to marry her but felt his lack of mortality (not necessarily *im*mortality; with his powers, it isn't inconceivable that he could have wiped out crime and got what was always referred to as his eternal rest) prevented this, I'm not sure why; also, Clarice was in love with *him*, not his alter ego, the Spectre. Believe me, nobody but the most ardent necrophile could have loved the "grim ghost."

For some reason, it was necessary for Jim to make a costume for the Spectre the hard way, sewing it laboriously by hand (a strange talent to be possessed by a hard-fisted police detective, no?) when he could have created it out of moonbeams, spider webs, or cool night air with a perfunctory thought.

Possibly his lack of skill as a tailor accounted for the bagginess of the green shorts which he wore over a skin so deathly white that it looked almost as if he were wearing snowy tights. Green gloves, cloak and hood and floppy green boots completed the costume. The face of the Spectre was the same deathly white, with dark, shadowed eyes and a grim, tight-lipped mouth. He was quite imposing, more than slightly frightening.

In order to assume the identity of the Spectre, Corrigan needed no convenient phone booth, no facile alibi to explain his absence from the scene. He could go right on about his business, talking, eating, sleeping, fighting crime while the Spectre, like a supernatural amoeba, split invisibly off from his body and took on a corporeal form of his own. The two halves of Corrigan's personality could exist simultaneously and independently, so the problem of protecting a secret identity never arose.

Naturally, Corrigan the cop was assigned to catch the Spectre, who naturally got the bulk of the blame for the rash of supernatural crime which popped up about that time. Corrigan did catch himself, too, but of course no one could hold the Spectre after Corrigan "caught" him.

Naturally, too, the Spectre had nothing to do with these crimes. They were caused by necromancers, wizards and ghosts without Spectre's moral fibre. Zar, for example. Zar was a wizard who had the same powers as the Spectre (though presumably from the devil, not God) but who had been dead longer and was consequently more experienced in using them. The Spectre chased him from dimension to dimension, was trapped for a spell in Zar's paralysis ray and came out second in a comet-hurling duel.

In a more or less typical story (*More Fun #61*), a rash of newspaper headlines praising the Spectre arouse the wrath of the police chief, who orders Corrigan to arrest the Spectre. Then a phone call comes in; one of Center City's biggest promoters has been threatened by the Spectre. Corrigan and the chief go to the man's house and see him turn to gold before their eyes. A witness rushes into police headquarters, says he knows who is responsible for the "golden curse" death threats (which all wealthy men are getting now) and then turns to gold before he can name the villain.

"Corrigan departs from headquarters a very bewildered chap indeed" and finds himself confronted by a feeble social outcast who thrusts free samples of chewing gum upon him. Noticing a car trailing him, Jim plays a hunch about the gum and and turns himself into gold. Two men jump from the car, pick him up (yes, I know a six-foot man of gold would weigh more than two men could lift, but they did) and put him into the car, drive to a bridge and toss him in the river. The Spectre pops out of the water a moment later and follows them, foiling another assassination attempt by turning the gun to worms. When one of the hoods calls the boss to report the worms, the Spectre shrinks, enters the phone, and races through the wires, only to be stymied when the boss hangs up. Returning to the hideout, the Spectre reveals himself to the hoods, just as *they* turn into gold statues.

That evening, Corrigan goes to visit Clarice and meets Gustave Gilroy, who knows a scientist who is trying to change the atomic structure of objects. Corrigan calls upon the scientist and is lassoed around the neck and hanged by a booby trap while a voice booms out "Thus perish those who oppose the Spectre." Corrigan alters his body so it becomes one-dimensional and drops free of the noose, slips through the wall and grabs the scientist. The scientist is unable to tell him who hired him because he doesn't know, so the Spectre bombards him with L-rays, which cleanse his mind of all evil. Says the scientist: "I see the error of my ways! From now on I will lead an honest existence!" (These L-rays, incidentally, were a bomb of letter "L's" which came out of the Spectre's eyes.)

He returns to Clarice's home to find that she is going to surrender herself to the bogus Spectre, who has threatened her father. She meets a green-robed figure on the docks and is struggling with him when the real Spectre shows up — but the Spectre suddenly disappears, caught by "an occult occurence" (this happened in several stories, with no explanation and varying results) which flung him an hour back in time as Jim Corrigan. With the extra time on his hands, he arrests the Spectre and turns him over to the police chief, after which the Spectre vanishes and goes back to the docks to nail Gustave (now called Gustaf, oddly) Gilroy, who was the man masquerading as the Spectre. Gilroy confesses, then commits suicide by turning himself to gold. The story ends with the chief ordering Corrigan to continue pursuing the Spectre,

ROCKET GODDESS,
Eddie Jones

despite the fact that he has been cleared.

The theme of classical gods has long been used in comic series. Captain Marvel obtained his powers from six "gods" (such as Solomon, an odd god you'll agree) and the Bouncer was known as a personal descendant of a Greek god. But gods are one thing and God is another, and the Spectre used to talk with God. Actually and literally, not just the one time Jim Harmon mentioned in his Justice Society article, but many times. In fact, whenever the Spectre came up against a foe who was worthy of his mettle, such as the aforementioned Zar, he generally got his tail in a crack and had to ask for extra powers, which were always granted. He kept all of these powers, too.

Those with deep religious convictions might be a bit annoyed to find God credited with a rather shoddy trick designed to keep the Spectre working for him. In one instance, just as Clarice is about to be killed, the Spectre is called away by God. Clarice has a bullet heading toward her skull and will be a goner by the time Spec returns. God, it seems, has reconsidered, decided that Spec is getting a raw deal, and is offering him a choice of taking his eternal rest now or going on to wipe out all crime. Of course, should he decide to take up the harp, that's the end of Clarice. Since staying in Heaven would doom the girl (who presumably has not led a blameless life, else he would have been assured that she would join him in Heaven), he chooses to return to Earth and finish off crime. It was a stacked deck.

However, much later on, God made up for this (sort of like with Job, I guess) by restoring Jim Corrigan to life without removing any of his powers. This happened after a supposedly funny character named Percival Popp (the super cop) appeared on the scene.

The level of humor exemplified by this big-nosed, buck-toothed and bespectacled little runt is pretty well indicated by his name. He had unevenly crew cut and rather wild hair which varied from red to brown to black, and protruding eyes. He wanted to be a detective and plagued Corrigan by following him about, interfering in his cases and generally making a pest of himself. While searching for evidence, Percy was about to dive off the pier at the very spot where Corrigan's concrete-encrusted corpse lay on the river bottom. A quick request to God for assistance to prevent discovery brought the ultimate — Corrigan was restored to life in his own body (thoughtfully freed from the concrete first) without losing his identity and powers as the Spectre.

The Spectre himself could bring people back from the dead and cure the incurable. Unfortunately, Popp was one malignant growth he couldn't lick. Percival Popp (the super cop) began dominating the stories and sharing the billing and the whole series degenerated into slapstick — badly done slapstick. The Spectre no longer disposed of his enemies in such gruesome fashion, although his powers remained the same. Not that the Spectre's powers weren't spectacular enough even when they weren't gruesome. He could, as shown in the "golden curse" story, trace phone calls by shrinking himself to molecular size and following the impulse through the telephone wires, exiting at the receiver of the caller's phone — unless the caller hung up too soon. (This trick has been given to the revived version of the Atom). If the phone trick didn't get the information he wanted, he could use mental telepathy or call on God. I suppose he could have cast runes if he'd wanted to bother.

Some times after Percival came along, the Spectre and Jim Corrigan parted company. Corrigan entered the service to fight the Nazis and Japs while Spec stayed behind to fight crime, working with Percy in a state of invisibility.

Corrigan never returned. Eventually the whole series just sort of dwindled away and, when *More Fun Comics* became strictly humorous (to use the word loosely), the Spectre finally achieved his long-sought eternal rest.

More Fun Comics had a checkered career. The earliest issue I have seen contained the origin of the Spectre, and that was #52. Other characters in that 64-page issue were "Wing Brady" by Tom Hickey, a pretty poor Foreign Legion strip; "Biff Bronson" by Al Sulman and Koppy, which featured a brawny hero and his fat friend who, in this issue, fought off an army of robots (it was actually a serial, but I'm sure Biff and Dan, his fat friend, won in the end); "Radio Squad," a police strip originated by Siegel and Shuster, now written by Siegel and drawn by Martin Wheeler; "Lieut. Bob Neal of Sub 662," a Navy strip by B. Hirsch and Russ Lehman which was no better than "Wing Brady"; "King Carter" by Paul J. Lauretta was a mediocre adventure strip; "Detective Sergeant Carey" by Joe Donohoe, a mystery strip, was a lacklustre job; "Sergeant O'Malley of the Red Coat Patrol" was a routine Canadian Mounties story drawn by Jack Lehti, who later did "Crimson Avenger" and currently does the religious comic strip "Tales From The Great Book"; and Bart Tumey's "Bulldog Martin" was a cops and robbers story with the added fillip of an invisibility potion.

None of these strips, all of which were holdovers from *More Fun*'s pre-costume hero days, lasted very long once the super guys, Spectre their vanguard, began their invasion of the pages of *More Fun*. Biff Bronson did have enough of a following to make the first issue or two of *All-Star* (he was out when the Justice Society was formed in #3), and *More Fun* was popular enough to be a monthly. In issue #55 Dr. Fate was added, and six months later the lineup still included Detective Sergeant Carey, Lieut. Bob Neal, Radio Squad (now drawn by Chad), Biff Bronson, and Sergeant O'Malley. Congo Bill, a jungle strip by George Papp which lasted until just a few months ago (with several metamorphoses), and Captain Desmo (an airplane strip by "Win") had been added.

More Fun eventually served as the birthplace of Green Arrow, Aquaman, and Johnny Quick, and featured the adventures of Superboy. When, with issue #106, *More Fun* regressed into a theoretically humorous publication featuring Genius Jones [by Alfred Bester(!) and Stan Kaye], and Henry Boltinoff's "Dover and Clover," Superboy, Aquaman, Johnny Quick and Green Arrow moved over to *Adventure Comics*. The Spectre and Doctor Fate were dropped.

Doctor Fate sprang upon the scene without benefit of an origin story. He was a wizard of incredibly ancient origin and virtually unlimited powers. He said that he had been placed on Earth by the elder gods long before the time of man. He spoke familiarly of ancient Egypt and Chaldea and admitted imprisoning an evil wizard many, many thousands of years before. He now dwelt in a doorless and windowless tower in "witch haunted Salem," surrounded by musty tomes, weapons and devices both of advanced science and advanced necromancy. He exited from his tower by walking through walls or by using some machine.

A girl named Inza, whose presence in his life was never explained, wandered at will about the world and called on Dr. Fate whenever, as she frequently was, she was in difficulty. She usually got in trouble as a result of some slumbering wizard's awakening or some bush league Merlin stumbling across the Book of Thoth. Things like that happened all the time.

Dr. Fate was clad in blue (or, on the cover, purple) tights with yellow boots, shorts, gloves and cape. On his chest was a large golden medallion of unspecified purpose, strung on a cord about his neck. His face was completely smooth except for two eye-holes. This helmet was later altered, unfortunately, but this was the original costume.

Dr. Fate had achieved complete control of energy and any blows or bullets directed at him were turned into power for him. He could emit rays of energy which were capable of knocking over buildings or thoroughly disposing of unsavory characters. He also had a crystal ball and various spells at his command. He could fly, too.

Doctor Fate was obviously the creation of someone who had read a great deal of H. P. Lovecraft. The hints of elder gods and vanished civilizations, of wizardry which was actually a form of science far beyond what we have attained and "witch haunted Salem," which reminds one somehow of Arkham, all point to a familiarity with Lovecraft's mythos. Some of the Doctor Fate stories were written by Gardner F. Fox; I do not know who drew them.

A better than average Doctor Fate story (#55 and #56 of *More Fun*) dealt with the evil Wotan (apparently unrelated to Norse mythology,) this Wotan had a green skin, a Mephisthophelean face, wore red tights with a high, stiff, flaring collar and a green floor-length cape. He opened his campaign against Doctor Fate by

making a puppet of a normal man by means of a glowing crystal globe and ordering him to kill the girl, Inza. The dupe is strangling her when Fate arrives, rescues the girl, frees the man from Wotan's spell and saves them both from a fire started by the angry Wotan. The story is then interrupted for precisely four panels, while Doctor Fate explains that he has the power to control energy and can convert it into matter and vice versa. This, friends, is the origin story of Doctor Fate; it was his first appearance. He then called upon Wotan with Inza and was set upon by gorillas. Fate subdues one gorilla, and another has set upon Inza and Doctor Fate transfers his strength to her body. Wotan, taking advantage of his momentary weakness, tries to stab him, but is not quick enough. Doctor Fate has a reserve store of energy and is able to withstand Wotan while Inza overpowers the gorillas. Wotan then turns on Inza and surrounds her with flames of energy just as strong as Fate's. Fate counters by clouting Wotan with a roundhouse right ("Sometimes I think a good fight accomplishes more than all the learning in the world") and throws him out the window which, we now learn, is many stories above the street.

The next issue's story opens with Fate and Inza going to the land of the dead to make sure Wotan is there. He forces the boatman to take them across the Styx where they pass through the seven gates to the regions of dead souls (the gates are iron, copper silver, gold, "the unknown grey metal," alabaster and emerald, in that order) and climb the stair of judgment to meet the gods of old. At the top of the stair is Wisdom, who rules the world. Fate and Inza stand atop the staircase, shielded by Fate's cloak, in a blinding light while Wisdom tells them that Wotan lives and says: "The fate of the world depends on you who are called Fate! Wotan *must be stopped!*"

Fate and Inza quickly return to the upper world, where they find that the mad Wotan has discovered how to increase the electric and magnetic flow between the poles of the earth and "can explode the earth just as an extra load on an electric wire blows a fuse. Doctor Fate arrives in time to counter the machinery of Wotan and beats him soundly with his fists, and chains him to the earth "as Prometheus was chained to a rock." Fate and Inza relax and enjoy the beauties of the earth while "Wotan — in

SPACESHIP FIST, Steve Stiles

a magical trance — is encased for eternity in an air bubble and hidden beneath the earth he would have destroyed." Somewhat later, he was freed by another of Doctor Fate's opponents and was eventually destroyed by Doctor Fate.

Doctor Fate apparently became a very popular strip because he soon began taking over *More Fun*'s lead spot and cover from the Spectre. And then came the big change in Doctor Fate.

After he had been established as an ancient wizard who never removed his helmet, during the first few stories, he suddenly pulled a complete switch. He started by showing his face to Inza, when she was mooning over some young lover (sort of as a consolation prize, I gathered). My reaction on first looking in Doctor Fate's face was one of disappointment. He didn't look like anything special.

And, starting with the next issue of *More Fun* (*#67*), he wasn't. You recall that bit about his being thousands of years old? The writer of the series conveniently forgot. After several issues, they finally got around to doing his origin.

In the Valley of Ur, "in the year 1920 or thereabouts," an Egyptologist named Sven Nelson, with his young son Kent, has come to learn who built the pyramids. He has a theory that people from another planet built them; he doesn't think the Egyptians knew enough to do the job.

While his father studies a strange language engraved on the walls, young Kent Nelson explores the ruins. He finds a man standing entombed in an open casket and, following telepathed directions, turns a lever and frees the man from suspended animation.

The man, whose name is Nabu the Wise, is close to half a million years old and "was born on the planet Cilia as she swing in her orbit passed (sic) the earth." *His* people built the pyramids. He and Kent discover that Sven Nelson, Kent's father, is dead of poison gas prepared to kill any who learned the secret of the chamber. They bury Sven and Nabu says, "I will try to repay you for your loss by teaching you the secrets of the universe," which he does. He then gives young Kent the costume and the name of Doctor Fate and disappears without a word of explanation from anybody. Since these stories appeared in the very early '40s, Doctor Fate had suddenly gone from being millenia old to being barely 20. The Lovecraftian aura was shed with the years.

After this, the series went rapidly downhill. The beautifully mysterious face covering was sawn off just before the eyes, revealing the Doctor's nose and mouth and concealing only his hair, forehead, and the area about his eyes. His powers were even more sawn off.

Starting with the idea that he was only invulnerable from outside harm and still needed air, the writer or writers soon developed this idea to the point where Fate was depressingly mortal. If you cut off his air, Dr. Fate would lose consciousness, so gas or drown him. (Okay, so far.) Now, if you strangle a person you cut off his air, too, so they could strangle him into unconsciousness. (Well ...) A good blow in the solar plexus will knock the air out of a guy too, so... (Oh, the hell with it!)

So what happened to his super powers? Well, he could still fly and he was still immune to bullets, but that's all. And he stopped chasing wizards and concentrated on petty thugs. And he started making ridiculous back chat with the thugs as he fought with them — with bare fists, not magic ("What are you, the joker?" *sock* "Ouch! I feel like the deuce!" replies the crook — crooks usually got the best of the verbal interchange, though Fate naturally triumphed physically). And he decided to justify his name by actually becoming a doctor. He got through medical school in one heck of a hurry and became an interne within half a page. And he used modern medicine, too, completely dropping the wizard bit.

And so he became less of a super hero and more possible (loosely speaking) and more vulnerable. And more monotonous. So, when More Fun retooled for comedy, they didn't bother to transfer Dr. Fate over to Adventure, as they did Superboy, Johnny Quick, and Aquaman. They also cancelled his membership in the Justice Society. And the AMA probably pulled his medical license ...

serves him right, too...

Doctor Fate and the Spectre are gone forever; the names and some of the attributes of each could be revived in modern code-approved comic books, but the spirit and the essential qualities would not be present. Any version which could be approved by the Comic Code would have to be so emasculated that only the name would link the modern version with those flamboyant, overblown, often ridiculous and yet, somehow, magnificent creations of two decades ago.

Doctor Fate and the Spectre were, of course, too super to last, even in an age of flamboyant comic book superheroes. But the first few stories about these characters have a spirit, a driving force and and imagination that is mind-shaking. Nowhere in science fiction, even in the cosmic settings of Doc Smith's Lensmen stories, or in the stories of Captain Future, do you find such lavish backdrops for the action. Even fantasy can't match them, for fantasy generally is held down, limited in its flights of imagination. This is a good and necessary thing; if anything is possible, there can be no doubts about the triumph of Good over Evil — the author has an infinite number of rabbits ready to leap out of the hat.

But, just because we are used to reading fiction with rules, stories where not quite everything can happen, it is a new, startling and, for a time, fascinating thing to find stories in which there are no limits, where every card is wild and can be whatever the dealer says it is.

To the best of my knowledge, the only comic book characters who enjoyed this freedom from all rules, all logic, all restraint were Doctor Fate and the Spectre.

They could do anything they wanted, anything their creators could conceive.

They were the wild ones.

Epistolary Intercourse #7

Conducted by Pat Lupoff

Harry Warner, Jr.

Donald E. Westlake says some telling things about the mess that stf is in, but he unconsciously reveals some equally enlightening things about himself. For instance, he doesn't seem to have suspected the probable truth about the episode when he put Campbell into a story. Whether or not JWC realized what happened, Campbell undoubtedly recognized that here was a real, living character that was drawn from life, not the cardboard hero that pulp writers normally draw out of plotto. Of course it's absurd to complain that one can't sell good science fiction: if the prozines won't buy it, no sane person would deny that it shows up regularly in book form.

I read the Tolkien article, but the more I read about Tolkien, the less inclined I am to read his stories. I predict a revolution against them within the next two or three years paralleling the one that occurred against Lovecraft in the late 1940s, simply from sure surfeit of material on the topic.

I doubt that I ever read a comic featuring the Spectre, but the review of his activities was pleasant and I shall pounce if I ever should run across a cache of the things at some public auction.

Steve Stiles

Donald Westlake — whom I've never heard of — produced some of the most substantial and realistic reasons for not writing sf that I've ever seen. His piece also had a tremendous sense of organization about it. I was pleased to see that he covered not only the monetary reasons for not writing it, but artistic ones, too. I was growing a bit sick of the "Well, ya gotta *eat!*" school of thought. It's a hell of a shame that a field with limitless possibilities for themes is tied down by three or four incapable — and in cases, unimaginative – big shots. By the way, what story was it that the lead character was patterned after Campbell?

COLONEL AVRAM DAVIDSON

Dear Abu-Ken and Um-al-Ken:

Greetings and Genuflections, and a Health unto his navel: or, as say in our native Doric, a *gezint ahf zyne pippick*. Lo, this is the first time I've seen snow in November in many a year. When I was a boy and there were wolves in Westchester, snow used to frequently fall in November, my uncle, Dai Beigel, snoring like a porpoise in the parlor after a surfeit of turkey, and frost rimming all the window panes...

But I perceive you are perturbed, even *con*turbed, it does you credit, and I will hasten to answer: Why (you wish to know: and rightly too), after all my good resolutions of regular work-schedules and no larking around till after finishing that novel with which my name is legally linked to that of Harlan Ellison, and, after having given over a night and a day to the PhillyCon, am I now writing to *Xero* (*ah gezint*, etc.) instead of working? Well you may ask. Because, sir, because my collaborator, instead of delivering over to me the ms of Chapter Two, in order that I might continue with Chapter Three, and *sic sempre et passim*, has vanished off the face of the earth and into a blinding snowstorm. Rumor that he was seen entering an opium den just off of Mott Street, and kept by a Malay of the most evial reputation, will I trust, prove to be utterly mistaken, and himself the mere victim of a cruel misconstruction. I am much more disturbed by the fact that, in the year 1879, a Harlan Feibelman walked into a snowstorm in East St. Louis (Mo.) and was never seen again. You will, with your keen mind, have already attained the kernel in the nuts, viz: *Is someone collecting snowstorms?* What has science to say about all this?

I now come to a matter which has caused me a semi-sleepless afternoon, vide-licit Steve Stills' vertical cartoon strip by name "Lin Carter's Fantastic Bunny Rabbit" (it will never catch on with the syndicates, Lin & Steve): Why are rabbits called *bunny*? Bulwinckle says of this only, "A pet or familiar name for rabbits, conies, or squirrels." That's a big help. If anyone can tell me why rabbits are called *bunny* I'll tell him why cats are called *pussy*.

Guy Terwiller, out there in Boise, Idaho wists all the more that he had the courage to open a paperback bookstore in Boise. Guy, come closer so that I won't have to talk so loud, and I'll tell you my sadsad story. Many years ago I had a brilliant idea: having read the Bemelmans story of the restaurant which served only cutlets, but from all *kinds* cutlets, I had the brilliant idea to open a bookshop that would sell only paperback books. And for my locale I had in mind San Francisco, notoriously bookstore-prone, or Intellectual Berkeley-by-the-Bay, seat of U of C. So I wrote to my friend Stan Anger, who lived in IB.b.t.B., asking him to look around and tell me what he thought, and offering a partnership. Stan looked around. He looked around steadily. He looked around thoroughly, and finally wrote that such a bookstore had no chance, no chance at all, and certainly none in SF Bay Area ...

You still with me, Guy? Well, so I stayed put, and opened not, because Stan was a keen observer of the economic scene and a great reader of reports to consumers and he knew how many threads per square inch and what it meant that carloadings were up on the Union Pacific, etc. And so, three or four months later, a cat named Lawrence Ferlinghetti who probably doesn't know a carloading from a condom, opened in San Francisco, the City Lights Bookshop, first all-paperback bookstore in the gahdamn *world*: and then he opened another, and then ...

And that's how I escaped being the Millionaire Paperback Bookshop King, Guy, and if you want to open, so open.

My network of agents has just reported that Harlan Ellison did not, after all, remain in the opium den of evial reputation just off of Mott Street; he was only buying a bag of litchi nuts which they deal in, wholesale, there, opium denning not being what it used to be. Where did he go after that, instead of here with the ms? Why to a milkbar in the upper west 40s, where he consummated a deal for the sale of a collection of his science fiction stories to Gold Medal Books (you listening, Don Westlake?), an outfit which wouldn't buy a collection of *my* science fiction stories if I threw in both the Windward *and* Leeward Islands for lagniappe. Listen, so long as my collaborator's happy? Huh? You know what I mean? Maybe now we can finish our contracted novel.

What, Don? Er ... uh ... no. It's *not* science fiction.

James Blish refers to "the way British magazines do when" they want to close a correspondence that's been going on too long. They do it like this:

"This correspondence must now cease."

RICHARD KYLE

Mr. Westlake's "Don't Call Us ... " seems a little too vindictive. Granted that his comments about the financial rewards of sf writing are all too true, but why does he have to be so bitter? He's not the only writer who thought the editor was a complete idiot for spoiling the writer's masterpiece. To end all this I'll mention that de Camp, far from "not doing much of anything," is writing some excellent historical novels and has somehow managed to leave the sf writing field without feeling personally insulted by it.

JACK CHALKER

Although I have received *Xero Comics*, this was the first *Xero* itself that I have seen, and I'm going to do something that I almost never do – write a letter of comment.

"Don't Call Us, We'll Call You:" Well at least somebody's come out and said it. It's all true, of course, that's almost universal knowledge. I'm glad to see it finally down in print with all its horror and tragedy — "Why an Entire Field of Literature is Rotten Lousy" by Donald E. Westlake. Listen — I *liked* Jack Vance, Bob Bloch (curiously not mentioned among the escapees although he's a prime example) and all the others. It hurts when you remember that each one has had old sf kick him in the teeth. Point: Couldn't Westlake be sued for libel for some of his remarks? Particularly by Campbell? Yes, I know he didn't say an untrue thing in the entire article and every one of your readers knows it – but does Campbell? Do any of them?

ETHEL LINDSAY

Was fascinated by the glimpses into *Analog*'s editorial office revealed by Don Westlake. I would say no one could possibly blame him for not writing sf, in fact it's a wonder anyone does!

I see Walt has decided he must tell you that strictly speaking the last cover is not very like him. Mind you, there was a resemblance, mostly about the eyes. If asked, I would say ... he is quite good looking. Is there any fan who is really handsome, I wonder? The British ones are fairly ordinary in their looks, Norman Shorrock being the one who comes closest to the classic mold. Most American fans seem to wear glasses, due no doubt to poring over sf and kindred material. But a truly handsome fan ... have we such a one?

What do you mean, no handsome fans? Why there's – ow!
– there's, er, well – no! – youch! Yow! – my own husband.
Okay, now, will you stop twisting my arm, Dick?
–P.L.

JOHN BAXTER

Many thanks for *Xero 7*. I sent off a couple of my zines in trade, but comparing them with your latest effort I wish it were possible to get them back from the post office. Fair shames me to see you people putting out such a nicely-reproduced, excellently-written stuff.

Your rediscovery of Lin Carter (by his absence from fmz since the demise of *Inside*, I assume he was lost). Carter is a scholar, perhaps the only one at present apparent in the fanpubbing field (Harry Warner, Jr. is a marginal contender for the title, but in fandom rather than sf). His work shows a deep knowledge of the genre in which he has specialized, and the way he uses that knowledge shows that, in addition to an encyclopedic memory, he has great intelligence and perception. He writes in an extremely literate style, never tedious nor yet oversimple. He has humor, a rare commodity among sercon fans. In short, he's a bloody treasure, and you two are the luckiest faneds in the world for having him on the contents page of *Xero*.

> *What have you done, Baxter? Carter is already among the most highly-paid of our staff writers, and now he'll swell bloody treasure headed want another raise, and we'll have to give him another ten percent or lose him to some higher-paying market like* Logic at Work *and I hope you're satisfied.*
> -P.L.

Westlake's piece is so reminiscent of the old days of fandom, when no gafiate felt he had actually departed until he had alienated everybody on his mailing list. Remember ... "and in conclusion, I'd like to say to all organized fandom, 'I hate your guts!'" (That's an actual quote, though I don't recall who wrote it.) It seems the pro field, or at least that part inhabited by Westlake, is getting equally petty, now that things are not as rosy as they were.

I just don't trust items like "Don't Call Us, We'll Call You." There's no objectivity to them, just a lot of angry epithets and character smearing which I find very distasteful, not to mention highly suspect. I have no illusions about John Campbell's ability as an editor (which is tenuous to say the least) but this is the first occasion on which I've seen him described as an "egomaniac," and until I've heard a few other qualified persons level this charge, I'll reserve judgment. Mills may be "incompetent," but again, I don't think much of Westlake's ability to gauge character, so no comment. Ditto Goldsmith and Pohl.

BOB LEMAN

As the new owner of a duplicating machine, I am most tremendously impressed by page 29, here. How did you get the solid black? I ask as one who seriously seeks instruction. In my last issue I essayed the duplication of a few simple illustrations, with, as you may remember, results that were most horrid. The machine itself is, I think, capable of duplicating well anything that's fed into it. I want to learn what to feed in.

Those ATomillos on page 29, last issue, were stenafaxed,

like all our ATomillos. The electronic stenciling technique not only spares the artist from the uncertainties of the stenciller's stylus, it also permits us of solids and/or shading techniques impossible with conventional equipment.

The purple bem on page 46 thish was a full-color Atom drawing (suitable for framing, which it will be). Bhob suggested that we have it 'faxed just to see what would happen; Chris Steinbrunner had it done for us, and — lo! — the machine did a tone conversion of the original colors!
—P.L.

HOW WESTLAKE'S SPY GOT INTO *GALAXY'S* ELEVATOR

FREDERIK POHL

FREDERIK POHL (1919-) was a member of the New York Futurian Society and a professional science writer and editor at the age of 19, putting his stamp on such gloriously lurid pulps as Super Science Stories *and* Astonishing Stories. *In later years he would edit the (relatively) more sedate* Galaxy, If, Worlds of Tomorrow, International Science Fiction, *and* Star Science Fiction. *He is a prolific novelist and short story writer, primarily working alone but also working in collaboration with the late Cyril Kornbluth on the classic* The Space Merchants *(1953), with Lester del Rey as "Edson McCann," and with Jack Williamson on several novels starting with* Undersea Quest *(1954). He has continued to produce important works for half a century, including the highly regarded* Man Plus *(1976),* Gateway *(1977), and* Black Star Rising *(1985).*

Well, I suppose I should thank you for sending me your fanzine with the curious Westlake piece in it. It's a pretty foolish piece of work, though.

Let me correct a couple of false statements and false implications. One false statement is that *Galaxy* is "heavily laden with Gold's inventory." At the time I took over the inventory was unusually low; at present, I have exactly two stories on hand that Horace bought — out of a total inventory of about half a million words.

As to Westlake's account of how I came to buy his story "The Spy in the Elevator," I have the correspondence before me. What happened was that Westlake's agent, Scott Meredith, sent me a story, "Call him Nemesis", which I wanted to buy, but for *If*, not *Galaxy*. Scott demurred, saying that Westlake was most anxious to crack *Galaxy*; couldn't I put it in *Galaxy*, even at a low rate? I didn't want to do do that, for reasons having to do with my attempt to make *If* a magazine with a character of its own; but I offered to do everything I could to buy a story of Westlake's for *Galaxy* if he cared to write one, up to and including working with him or revisions if necessary (something I seldom do, on principle; I don't believe in editorially dictated revisions in most cases.) Scott was happy; he turned up shortly thereafter with "The Spy in the Elevator," which I read, discovered it was harmless confetti, shrugged over and bought. It wasn't particularly good, but it wouldn't actually stink up the magazine, and there certainly was little hope of making any great improvements in it through revision. This was a few months before I restored *Galaxy*'s word rate to three cents, although I was paying that and more for good material; the advantage of not having a fixed minimum rate was that I could occasionally take on a story like this for bargain-basement rates and use the saving to pay somebody else for a better one at some other time.

This is the implication in Westlake's piece that most troubles me: His smug conviction that he did a Smart Thing in copying what he deems to be my own way of writing. In the first place, what madness is this that makes any writer think I want to pay someone else to write stories that I can write better than he can? If a writer comes up with a Pohl-type story and I like it, I'll of course buy it; but if what he thinks he is doing is cannily tricking me into a sure sale, he's mad. (A good way to check on the validity of this statement is to read *Galaxy* and see for yourself what kind of stories I publish.) In the second place, as Scott surely informed Westlake, the story was all but sold before it was written, so if ever he had a chance to write For Art, this was the chance.

If what turned out was "a silly insipid story" — as Westlake puts it — this may reveal something about the author himself, then, but I assure you it says nothing about the editorial policy of *Galaxy*.

To judge from your postscript, your views of *Galaxy* don't support Westlake's thesis either. I'm glad to know this. I think it would have been nice, though, if you'd said it in your magazine instead of privately to me.*

By the way, I hope I've made one thing clear. It isn't unfavorable comments that I object to. If Westlake, or you, or anybody reads *Galaxy* and thinks it stinks, and says so in print — God knows, I don't agree; but they're within their rights. What I dislike (and indeed fear, because of the effect it has on people who take it seriously, and govern their actions accordingly when they sit down to write a story for me) is the phoney "inside stuff."

I haven't much interest in what Westlake thinks or doesn't think — a man so unhappy within himself is uncomfortable to be around. Contrariwise, I have a great interest in next year's writers … many of whom are today's fans … many of whom may swallow this nonsense. If junk is published, it is easy (but unfair) to blame the editors. They are limited to what is written. The writers write the junk; if they haven't the guts to write what they think should be written, they might at least have the decency to refrain from screaming "rape." To write good science fiction requires a certain amount of gutsiness; those without it are probably better off in other fields, where the standards are lower anyway.

But it isn't true that everyone has fled. Westlake lists half a dozen or so "escapees" who don't write science fiction any more. Two of them — Clarke and Budrys — are in the current (Feb) *Galaxy*; two others — Merrill and del Rey — have been in the last couple issues, and will be again shortly. The good ones don't leave permanently. In spite of everything, they stick around; science fiction is where they can do their best writing, and to a good writer that means a lot. (Correction: Budrys is in the current *Galaxy* — as he was in the previous issue, and will be again shortly; Clarke is in April ... and was an issue or two ago in *If*.)

What I said was the customary disclaimer about the view of the author (Westlake) not necessarily being the "official" views of Xero or its editors. I said that Poul Anderson's "The Day After Doomsday" was a dandy story. I still think so. I voted for it on my Hugo ballot. I also thought Clarke's two stories were dogs.
-R.L.

DOING NOTHING DEFINED

L. SPRAGUE DE CAMP

Donald E. Westlake says: "de Camp and a lot of others aren't doing much of anything." If Mr. Westlake means that the stuff I write doesn't mean much of anything, he is entitled to his opinion. Sometimes I am tempted to agree with that estimate. However, if he means that I haven't been writing and selling since I quit SF, he is misinformed.

The last SF story I wrote was "Aristotle and the Gun," finished 11/9/56 and published in *ASF* for 2/58. Since then I have written and sold 33 articles (including some noncommercial pieces) and 12 books. The articles comprise: 5 published in SF and fantasy magazines, 10 in *Science Digest*, 2 in *Science World*, 1 in *Travel*, 3 in learned periodicals like *Technology & Culture*, 7 in Scithers' *Amra* (for fun), and 5 for miscellaneous outlets like encyclopedias.

The books break down as 1 textbook, 2 non-fiction books for the general market (1 out, 1 finishing), 3 historical novels (2 out, 1 to be pub Dec. 1 [now all out — RL], 1 fantasy novel (with Bjorn Nyberg), 2 small NF juveniles (1 out, 1 coming soon), and 3 large juveniles (1 out, 1 out but not under my name, and 1 being edited).

I think that makes my point, that I have at least not been idle, without bringing in reprints (cloth and paper) of earlier SF and fantasy novels, foreign translations, appearances in anthologies, radio scripts, writings in the technical and public relations fields, magazine reprints of stories, publication of stories and articles written before "A&TG", books contracted for and articles commissioned but not yet written, articles bought but not used, book reviews, published letters, and other fugitive pieces.

L. SPRAGUE DE CAMP (1907-2000) was tall, courtly, and erudite, and was one of the most imposing personalities in the science fiction world. A trained engineer who had attended both Cal Tech and MIT, he served in the United States Navy in the World War II and wrote radio scripts for the Voice of America between 1948 and 1956. Despite his reserved mien he was an astonishingly prolific and versatile author, writing science fiction, fantasy, historical fiction, biographies of H. P. Lovecraft and Robert E. Howard, books on the history of science and technology, the Scopes trial, archaeology and mythology. Among his nearly countless works, the most popular with many of his fans are the humorous fantasies that he wrote in collaboration with the late Fletcher Pratt.

PAINFUL PARTS

AVRAM DAVIDSON

And now is when I wished I had some of that lovely liquor left largely undrunk (though it was drunk largely — can one imagine the immense quantity of it, that fans should leave lashings of it uningested) at Kolchak's Kastle, that time at the PhillyCon; a drink, I say, I wish I had here in hand to fortify me for Don Westlake's "Don't Call Us, We'll Call You," parts of which are painfully true. And parts of which are painfully not, though I hasten to deny any intent to invidiate Mr. Westlake's veracity. In my intercourse with him (purely of a social nature, harumpph) I discovered him invariably amiable, and his beard, moreover, is at least a marquis in the peerage of beards: of such a beard must the Onlie Begettor be a man of honor. However —

He quotes himself and Friar Garrett as having said, a year ago, presciently, "I am a professional writer. My entire income comes from writing. If science fiction can't support me, I'll write in some other field." In fulfillment of his/their prophecy, he now says, "Today I am a full-time mystery writer, working on my fifth mystery novel (the 1st had already been published at the time of the ESFA meeting) and ... Randy Garrett [is] working on a biography, for decent money." And goeth on to list Asimov, del Rey, Bradbury, Matheson, Beaumont, Clarke, Sheckley, Merrill, de Camp, and Budrys, all of whom are earning beef, beer, and bedstraw by writing for other than science fiction. Having quoted, I now comment.

I am also a professional writer. My entire income comes from writing.* I have always written in other fields as well, because science fiction has never, by itself, supported me. I doubt if it ever supported Asimov and Clarke, the former having been long a collegiate staff member, and the latter having written science-fact as far back as s-fiction. I do not believe Judith Merrill ever lived entirely on her science fiction stories, she has written too few of them, wrote detective stories a long while back, and has been anthologizing for about five years successively, not counting earlier anthologies (*Galaxy of Ghouls*, *Shot in the Dark*). Bradbury, before he moved into the big time, was living in Venice, California, a low-rent district favored by citizens whose entire income comes from writing their names on social security checks. Del Rey long ago began to do juveniles. Etcetera.

Horace Gold is seldom quoted save to be hooted down, but he is the wise man who said, and said often, "No writer should ever depend exclusively on science fiction to support himself. The field is simply not big enough." At the time there were writers seemingly proving him wrong. But the times were out of joint; subsequent events proved Horace right. The key to Don's complaint lies not in science fiction's not supporting him, but in his comment that "it can't even interest us." The fault, dear Donald, lies not in your (ex) market... It is no offense, surely, to say that you probably never were a science fiction writer, but a mystery writer who wandered into sf by error, and who sold 14 stories before discovering that "none of /them/ are any damn good," and that you belonged in a different field. Those fourteen were sold to nine different markets, only two of which — *Analog* and *Galaxy* — were tops. Nine from fourteen leaves five, so it seems from my never-strong "arithmetic" that no more than four could have appeared in any top market. You do not say over how long a period you wrote and sold sf, though I do note that of your mystery stories five have been or will be anthologized, whereas none of your sf has — further evidence, I'd say, that you have gotten out of the wrong field into the right one.

Randy Garrett, our readers will remember, was last seen writing a biography, "for decent money." The implication is that Goodman Garrett tired of sf and turned to nonfiction. Not so. RG is a man of wit, humor, laughter, learning, and capacity. There is much reason to believe he could be capable of supporting himself as a writer in any of many other fields. However, he learned some years ago that he could write the kind of stories John Campbell would buy and that John Campbell would buy them almost as fast as he could write them — or would write them, for Randy Goodfellow has for a long time been engaged in a large-scale scheme of research involving comparative whiskey-testing, with no other thought in mind but the benefit of mankind, and this necessarily consumes a lot of time (it also consumes a lot of whiskey, too, but no man whose liver has not already turned green, and petrified, can hold more whiskey with less visible effect). Thus, his craft, capable of navigating any seas you care to mention, has ridden safe at anchor in Port Campbell for so long that he almost seems afeared to venture past the breakwater; wrote the bio — of the current pope — because his agent has a tie-in with the publisher and recognized that Randy has a knowledge of Catholicism both wide and sympathetic — this last an important point in view of the Roman Catholic market.

PAPALMAN, Steve Stiles

Last week RG finished *Papal People Leader* (*his* joke) — did he start on another bio? Not on your scapular, he didn't. He started on another story for John Campbell. Perhaps the bio will bring such scads, floods, freshets and torrents of royalty as will float him off to sea again.

Perhaps not.

So far I have been obliged to disagree with Westlake. But I must agree with him on a point or two, which is why I miss that drink I mentioned earlier. On the one hand, if we wish sf to be, and to be regarded as, part of fiction, and not something separate and distinct, we should be glad that more and more of those who write sf write other things as well; we could argue that this will tend to prevent stagnation, inbreeding, provinciality, etc.; that at the same time sf writers are writing non sf, non sf writers are writing sf, which will restore "improbilia" (Ward Moore's happy word) to its position in the world of letters which it held prior to Hugo Gernsback's having ghettoized (P. Schuyler Miller's verb) it by starting *Amazing*.

We *could*, I say, argue this. But would we believe it?

Summa, and sof-pasuk, Don Westlake ends with a "reason" "why science fiction is so lousy" — that ESFA members recollected a *Weird Tales* story from the thirties and had read it, while only two had even *read* a story from the previous month's *Analog*. I submit that this is not a reason, but a symptom. And this, of course, leaves us back where we were before. Magazine sf has seldom, if ever, been sicker. Paperback sf flourished (even if it seems to Donald W. impossible to market his novel; by the names of the two publishers cited, I'd guess he's barely scratched the market) — and, happy happy happy the science fiction fanzine seems remarkably healthy.

Of course, if writing for fanzines won't support me ...

*Written, of course, before the Colonel assumed the editorial helm of F&SF.

-R.L.

DONALD A. WOLLHEIM (1914-1990) was the "grand old man" of the New York Futurian Society, circa 1940. He was a married man in his mid-twenties when most of the other Futurians were mere teenagers. He edited pulp magazines (Stirring Science Stories, Cosmic Stories, Out of this World Adventures) *as well as many important anthologies.* The Pocket Book of Science Fiction *(1943) is generally regarded as the first paperback science fiction anthology, bringing science fiction to a large readership that did not follow the pulp magazines.* Portable Novels of Science *(1945) was the first important hardcover science fiction anthology, also notable for its inclusion of the work of H.P. Lovecraft. Wollheim also wrote at least 16 novels under his own name or that of David Grinnell. He was the guiding editor of Ace Books for many years, promoting the careers of such young writers as Robert Silverberg, Samuel R. Delany, Ursula Le Guin, and Roger Zelazny. After leaving Ace he founded DAW books, along with his wife, Elsie. The company still exists, under the control of the Wollheims' daughter, Betsie.*

NOR HAS HE INQUIRED

BY DONALD WOLLHEIM

Donald Westlake's essay is of interest to me, and strikes an honest note of free-speaking clarity in the sf writing business. I disagree with his summary dismissal of Ace, merely mentioning it in connection with one novel he hasn't finished and never will finish. Perhaps the sum of roughly two cents a word, slightly more, isn't enough to warrant his aiming at the Ace market — but he ought at least to mention it.

Nor has he inquired as to whether or not Ace can use longer lengths (we can) or shorter lengths (we can). I don't offhand recall who his agent is [Scott Meredith -rl.] but I don't recall having had Westlake ever submitted my way.

However, now that Avram is taking over at *F&SF*, maybe the outlook there will change. I agree in general that Mills' editorship was somewhat less than inspiring.

THE CALIPH OF AUBURN

BY H. P. NORTON

Dissect Noodle, fantasy is part of our literature, and depends upon the folklore and traditional beliefs passed on from each generation to its successor. Who has not sat up rather late upon a cold, stormy night and dreamed sleepless dreams of imaginary terrors — conjured up before his fancy by some popular mystery novelist? Who, indeed, has not experienced the thrill of having a splendid ghost story read to him by some noted actor — or being artistically interpreted for him, through the recordings of some of the greatest composers of the ages? Only the utterly lost can claim that the realms of the mysterious do not appeal to them!

Symphonic fantasy has never been so clearly or so skillfully translated into modern prose as it has been in the tales of the late poet, Clark Ashton Smith. And may I not be too bold in stating that his death came as a great blow, not only to the connoisseur of the macabre, but to the general reader who was familiar with his writing as well.

The prose tales of Clark Ashton Smith have a haunting effect upon the reader, whoever he might be. Although the spectral element dominates all, also woven in we find the powers of web-like enchantment and gothic wonder which form so much a part of the major work of the author of *The Wine of Wizardry*, whom Smith both knew and emulated.

But the world of Clark Ashton Smith was a world of his own creation — a world of delicate fantasy, opium-tinted mystification, and Oriental splendor. And to this creative dreamer belong the laurels accorded to many of the more respected fantasists of our generation. Although he was a thorough romanticist, and an attractive verbosity expressed itself in his style of writing, Smith had a keen admiration for the classics, particularly those centered around the legends and myths of early Greece and Rome, and thus, his best work can be found utilizing themes of ancient sorceries

H. P. NORTON (unknown) was a tall, almost cadaverous individual who turned up at the Xero *editorial office with a passion for Clark Ashton Smith and an unquenchable desire to share his enthusiasm with anyone who would listen to him or read his essays about Smith. Once his paean to his idol had appeared in* Xero *he seemed to disappear. His death was reported several years later, although details were lacking.*

and elder worlds.

Testimony of this can be afforded verification by what is considered to be the most representative of his short stories — notably, "The Double Shadow," the events of which take place in a strangely Illyrian kingdom known as Poseidonis.

We are introduced to the hero, Pharpetron, apprenticed to the sorcerer Avyctes … "And in (his) master's marble house above the wide sea" he pens his tale "with hasty hand, scrawling an ink of wizard virtue on the gray, priceless antique parchment of dragons." Avyctes conjures up the demon Oumor, the nature of whose powers are not entirely known to him, and is devoured by its shade. His neophyte, who relates the tale, is likewise doomed to a similar death. We see, in this tale, a goodly portion of Smith's powers of imagery. As in Beckford's *Vathek*, we are confronted with a mummy, this one of "gaunt umber," whose presence is deemed necessary for the incantation. Although the theme of this tale is obviously a variation upon the Sorcerer's Apprentice legend, "The Double Shadow," skillfully wrought and draped in classical imagery, emerges as a masterpiece of story-telling.

The classical atmosphere prevails also in "The Dark Eidolon" where a civilization is destroyed beneath the hooves of colossal steeds who come "anon like a swift-risen storm" and later disappear into the very bowels of night.

With Clark Ashton Smith, the world of ancient Greece still hovers at our doorsteps, as it did to some extent, no doubt, with H.P. Lovecraft, his contemporary, the germ of whose "The Tree" owed itself to Smith's suggestion. It is quite remarkable indeed that both of these magnates were self-educated, and even more remarkable that they were held in awe by the more formally scholasticated members of their circle. I would not be going too far to say that their powers of creativity touched upon the sublime — and at time even surpassed it!

The genius of Clark Ashton Smith, however, I find to be more vitriolic — it imparts a greater knowledge and appreciation of life than does that of his contemporary. Lovecraft, in his writing, centers his tales towards death, graveyards, and the charnal — whereas Smith's landscapes are more robust and active. This does not mean to say that either is inferior — but Lovecraft cast discriminating eyes upon what he termed the futility of "pretentiousness" and "gaudy pomp" and Smith states in his *Spells and Philtres*, a bit cynically: "The modern intolerance toward 'the grand manner' springs too often in vulgar minds by all that savors of loftiness, exaltation, nobility, sublimity, and aristocracy."

Lovecraft also emulated "the grand manner" with certain reservations. In none of his tales does he cast aside his New England mannerisms and, to some extent, prejudices. His Huguenot acquaintance dissimilarly shows a lack of regional confinement, and his tales pour forth a sensuousness that Lovecraft could not project, and what is even more distinctive, the former can be nearly identifiable with a Gautier-like Gallic touch. In "The Maker of Gargoyles" Smith introduces two demons, one carnal and lecherous, and the other a ravager killing without intent or purpose. In "The Disinterment of Venus" a statue of that goddess, unearthed in a monastic garden, becomes imbued with voluptuous life. One cannot but notice the throwback upon the Pygmalion theme. In "The Enchantress of Sylaire" and "The White Sybil," we are confronted with beautiful sorceresses, realistically and enticingly described, boasting a delightful ancestry, whose strains bespeak of Hans Heinz Ewers and *The Arabian Nights*. Needless to say, in these, as in many others of Smith's tales, we are haunted betimes with the old Frenchman's "Ivory and Marble" overtones — the credo of the classical Gallic neorenaissance of the 1830's.

In many of Smith's tales, also, though not in all, we find the recurrent motif of poetic justice. It is indubitably of classic origin — but it has nonetheless been identified with romanticism. Take for example the melodramatic hero-villains of Lord Byron with their Schedonistic scowls — storming across four or five cantos, and welcoming their melodramatic taste — as if it would alleviate all the ill effects of their Joan Crawford-like delusions. Poetic justice is still more prominent in the simpler themes of the gothic romance. Hence — Ambrosio carried off by the devil — an appropriate punishment for his three-fold offenses: fratricide, matricide, and incestuous love; and the scheming Count Montorio, murdered by his sons at the instigation of his dispossessed brother — and the inevitable ruin of Ippolito in the same romance for his uninhibitive worldliness.

As a more characteristic instance, need we go further? We find in Dumas' celebrated The *Count of Monte Cristo* justice meted out somewhat strongly against the enemies of Edmond Dantes. In the indisputably gothic "Colossus of Ylourgne," the tables are turned on the evil Mathaire, and in "The Black Abbott of Pthuum" white magic triumphs over unholy forces. No less than the legend of Lot's wife could have influenced the theme of "The Devotee of Evil" where the central character is turned into an ebon statue as punishment for his unhallowed curiosity. And in a similar manner, the unapprenticed conjurer meets his fate in the earlier "Treader in the Dust."

Dark contrast is provided by such tales as "Genius Loci" and "The Hunters from Beyond" where the innocent fall prey to dark forces — although mind, someone like the Reverend Montague Summers might presume with a mere modicum of unctuousness: "They could have avoided it if they wanted to!"

The taste for moral fable also introduces itself in Smith's tales. It might be interesting to note, that although he writes of runic or exotic "other worlds," Smith still maintains a forthright interest in those qualities which form so much a part of human behavior. I might cite, particularly, reference to his short sketch "The Last Incantation," included in his second omnibus volume *Lost Worlds* (1944). The aged warlock, Malygris, invokes the spirit of his childhood sweetheart, Nylissa, but when her shade stands before him, he recognizes not his youthful love. Addressing the viper with whose aid he had summoned her, Malygris reproaches it for flaws and imperfections which he beheld in the ghostly representative of his lost Nylissa. But the serpent, looking upon him, replies, "No necromantic spell could recall for you your own lost youth or the fervent and guileless heart that loved Nylissa — or the ardent eyes that beheld her then." This reproach could well be applied to ourselves who, in later years, lack the spontaneity and candidness which form the most prolific and, ofttimes, richest attribute of youth in directing itself toward objects of appreciation.

Tales like "The Enchantress of Sylaire" and "The Holiness of Azedarac" also possess that moral quality. In the former, the hero tosses aside the magic mirror designated to reveal the supposed inherent evil of the enchantress. This reminds us to depend upon experience rather than hearsay in forming judgments upon others. In the latter the monk, Ambrose, learns that the obvious evil of Azedarac was potent for many centuries while he lived — and when he died, it was his lot to be raised to the full rites and honors of his church. A bit farfetched? I should think not — when one reviews the terrific extravagance and ceremony accorded at the recent death of an individual who was, while he lived, one of the most depraved and lawless monsters of the present century!

The modern "graveyard school" which permeated the better quality pulps in the first half of the century — I refer particularly to *Weird Tales* — had also drawn Smith's genius into its scope. The ghoul theme, through this periodical, had ascended to a more direct prominence, and was rescued somewhat from its ill-deserved oblivion.

The legend of the ghoul, referred to copiously by Summers in his meticulous *The Vampire: His Kith and Kin*, is primarily an Oriental one. It is dealt with in the pages of *the Arabian Nights*, and references to it can also be cited in such works as Beckford's *Vathek*, and in the metaphysical verse of Poe. The two latter ideal with the supernatural aspects of this legend, which centers itself about an inhuman creature who feeds upon corpses to survive, but its ubiquitous appetite does at times extend itself to the living. However, it might be particularly noteworthy to mention that the ghoul's psychological aspects were dissected in noxious detail by the Marquis de Sade, episodes of whose *Juliette* draw from actual case histories revolving around human ghouls and their atrocious mania. No less an imagination than that of E.T.A. Hoffmann, became science-pressed with the ghoul theme as to develop a tale about it, which he included in his *The Serapion Bretheren*.

However, it was not until the beginning of this century that the subject had once more arisen in literary circles. I refer, of course, to the sardonic pen of Ambrose Bierce, whose tales, permeating with "tombstone gibe," indirectly run the subject dry. But it was about this time also, that the conventional ghoul was spun forth by E.L. White, in his somewhat crudely wrought, though grotesquely powerful, "Amina." Twenty years later, the tradition was broadened in the pages of *Weird Tales*.

Thus the literature of the ghoul boasts a fine register of contemporary tales, the most notable of which are: "The Loved Dead," by C.M. Eddy; "The Chadbourne Episode," by Henry S. Whithead; "Clay," by C. Hall Thompson; "The House of the Worm," by Merle Prout; "The Outsider," "Pickman's Model," "The Rats in the Walls," and "The Hound," by H.P. Lovecraft; "The Horror in the Burial Ground," by Hazel Heald; "The Pacer," by Messrs. Derleth-Schorer; "Far Below," by Robert Barbour Johnson; "The Grinning Ghoul," by Robert Bloch; "The Graveyard Rats," by Henry Kuttner; "The Ghoul," and "The Nameless Offspring," by Clark Ashton Smith.

Of Smith's two tales, "The Nameless Offspring," by far is the more effective. Surmounted with an atmosphere of haunting terror and dread, and leading off with a quotation from the hideous Nekronomikon itself — "The Nameless Offspring" is a creepy tale of gothic horrors, taking place in modern Britain, at the manor house of Sir John Tremoth, where his lady's mind snaps because of a fatal experience of "the nameless offspring" upon the scene is expertly introduced by subtle hints and doubts — and it is quite notable that in this tale, the ghoul betrays no exclusive dependence upon an Oriental ancestry. Thus we are not confronted baldly with a graphic image of this eldritch monster as we are in "Amina" and "The Chadbourne Episode" — for the two latter tales depend upon the portrait for their effectiveness, without dedicating any space to shade — and in the final denouement, when we are cognizant of the nature of the "nameless offspring," we find ourselves comfortably thrilled, and left without any ill-feelings in the pit of our stomachs.

As a sort of tribute to this friend H.P. Lovecraft, Smith penned a Poe-esque epitaph in the form of a tale called "Who Are the Living?", which has since been retitled as "The Epiphany of Death." This tale exhibits a sombre power, which characterizes the better part of Smith's later work. A man strolling among the tombs with a companion is surprised to find the body of his friend decompose before his eyes, and maggots feasting upon his decaying flesh. Believing he is alive still, he appears to behold the victim's lips atremble, as if he would speak, but nay — it was in truth only this movement of the conqueror worm as he sallied forth from the mouth of the corpse. A most sardonic epitaph indeed — in commemorating the death of Lovecraft and that fine era of weird gothicism, which died with its master. Or did it?

Much of Smith's work, as we have seen, avows acute appreciation which is easily distinguishable from mere imitation. Truly, in his clear, flowing prose, and in his gifted, forthright imagination, he can boast no peer. It is interesting to note his encompassing knowledge of Baudelaire, Beckford, Poe, Homer, Sterling, Gautier, Maturin, and Fort — and of his keen recognition of their powers. And it is also noteworthy to record his histrionic ability to merge the best points of their styles, without descending to unconscious "cropping."

However, I find that his greatest tribute was meted out to Baudelaire, whom he translated copiously from the original French, and to Beckford, whose extravagant spirit haunted Smith's imagination most profusely. No greater proof of this need be cited than his magnitudinous completion of the regency eccentric's "Third Episode of Vathek" which sparkles cleverly with the familiar Oriental wit and corridors of onyx. The halls of Eblis swim before us once more — and once again the reader is called into that portentous subterrestrial kingdom of the damned, where victims are heralded through its portals by bats' wings flapping demonically at the gibbous moon. Smith's terrible abbeys of baneful decadence remind us of Fonthill, and the luxurious breath of Araby lures us again and again into the spell-binding magic of his prose. Is it not befitting that we dub him, with sincere and regal appreciation of his artistic genius, Caliph of Auburn — as he would have dubbed his precursor, less genuinely perhaps, Caliph of Fonthill? No doubt, when Smith met his death, his spirit fled Eastward — though we, of the Occident, still possess his soul.

The best of Smith's tales have been collected in four volumes:

Out of Space and Time (1942), *Lost Worlds* (1944), *Genius Loci* (1948), and *The Abominations of Yondo* (1960). A fifth, *Tales of Science and Sorcery*, remains in the offing. I await its arrival with impatience. His poetry, typified by "The Hashish Eater," reminds us in its all encompassing sensitivity and charm of that of Shelley. And his artistic accomplishment also bespeak of infinite, higher spheres than our own.

The death of Clark Ashton Smith followed that of the much admired and assiduously reviewed Hemingway. And if time effaces Smith's writing from our heritage, it will blot out a school of thought simulating sensitivity, in favor of a purely contemporary one which knows only selfishness and bits of information carted away upon wearying travels — whose god is war, and slums of foreign metropoli providing the only outlet for its carrion tainted brain-spawn.

When students of literature one hundred years hence will be forced to read the contemporary titan, they will yawn, as if to say: "Voici un homme qui puisse ennui!" And when a fortunate one lights upon a rare volume of Clark Ashton Smith's memorable tales which will, like as not, be mowed down by canting hacks, he will cry out to the very heavens in the thankfulness of ecstasy: "Voici un homme qui fasse enchanted."

For thou, with elysium key, unfetter'd the souls
Of many — And now, the night shade of thy fancy
Echoes alone, with renewed vigour,
Your peerless visions to the attending stars!

EPISTOLARY INTERCOURSE #8
CONDUCTED BY PAT LUPOFF

H. VINCENT LYNCH

I take typer in hand primarily to rise to Col. Davidson's challenge, i.e. "If anyone can tell me why rabbits are called *Bunny* I'll tell him why cats are called *Pussy*." I developed an etymological theory on both origins that was no less brilliant for being completely wrong, then chanced to discuss the matter with a friend (Col. Davidson's query turns out to be the season's best cocktail-party conversation stopper). Said friend, Herb Cheyette of CBS' legal department, went off and brooded about it, and perchance got the entire CBS research department brooding about it, then sent me a letter of which the following is an excerpt:

"Apropos of our conversation Saturday night, there is a philologic axiom made popular by Sir Walter Scott in *Ivanhoe* that the English name for live animals are Anglo-Saxon, i.e., ox, cow, pig, sheep, deer, but the names for meat on the table were all French, i.e., venison, pork, mutton, steak, indicating that the Normans left the care of the animals to the natives but permitted them to eat very few.

"Young cats and dogs, while not eaten, were both Norman and Anglo-Saxon household pets. *Kitten* is derived from the French, but *puss* is an ancient word probably of Indo-European origin which occurs in English, Icelandic, Norwegian, Lithuanian, the Casgar dialect in Afghanistan, and South Tamil. Despite its lineage, *puss* is supposed to be onomatopoeic, resembling the hiss of a cat. For a dog, the Anglo-Saxon word was *whelp* (see also: mongrel and cur), and the *puppy* derived from the French *poupee* meaning doll and loosely applied to the young of animals.

"Unlike the words previously mentioned, *rabbit* is Walloon in origin, the Anglo-Saxon being *cony*. Presumably *rabbit* was brought over by the Normans. All this leading up to the fact that no scholar has been able to find a satisfactory derivation for *bunny* except to note that it was originally *bun* and first appeared in

English in 1587."

Whew! A veritable CBS report — I can practically hear Cronkite delivering it. Getting back to my own researches, while Herb was exploring Iceland I was doing my own tracking and got *pussy* as far as the onomatopeia theory and *bunny* to and beyond *bun*. That is, the original meaning of bun seems to have been any rounded protruberance, such as a blister, or the well-known baked item or — the short stumpy tail of a rabbit.

Herb's scholars seen to be a cautious, conservative lot. I for one buy the onomatopoeic explanation of pussy completely and I go along with this "tail" explanation of bunny, too. Scorn 'em if you will, Mon Colonel, they call cats pussy because that's what they call each other, especially when they're mad, and they call rabbits bunny because of their buns of tails.

FREDERIK POHL

Thanks for printing my comments and for sending me the current *Xero*; I don't suppose you meant to set me off again, but the letter from Jack Chalker gives me pain. It isn't Chalker's fault, of course. He hears "inside stuff" from a pro, so naturally he takes it as gospel. But it isn't gospel. In fact, what it is, it's hot air.

It simply is not true that the reason that bad science fiction appears is that good science fiction cannot be sold. There is no truth in it at all. Good science fiction *always* sells. (I'm not talking about average-competent yardgoods, although it is probably true there too.)

What is true ... but quite irrelevant ... is that some writers find they can make a faster buck by writing junk than writing good stuff. Sometimes this is because they have learned to push an editor's buttons. Sometimes it is because they are kidding themselves, and what they think is good stuff is really junk too, just a different kind of junk.

However, any writer who has the talent to write well, and the integrity to do so instead of bellyaching about the obstacles in his path, will inevitably get his stories into print.

He may not make a quick sale, or realize as large an immediate cash return as the hack. Some of what are now considered important contributions to science fiction took a while to get published. Ray Bradbury wrote reams of stories before he was selling at all consistently. Jim Blish's *A Case of Conscience* went through three editors before *If* had the wit to buy it. Some of my own favorite stories wound up in the penny-a-word magazines, and *The Space Merchants* was turned down by seven sf book publishers before Ballantine took it on.

But ... Bradbury went on to become about the highest-paid sf writer in history, by sticking to what *he* thought he should write; *A Case of Conscience* got a Hugo; *The Space Merchants* had some twenty-odd editions, including more than a dozen foreign languages. I mention these particular cases because I happen to have some personal knowledge of them; there are many others. The point is that virtue does triumph. The fast buck is not necessarily the best buck. The truly pathetic — and exasperating — thing about the "inside stuff" peddled by Westlake and others is that it is based on a fallacy: Any writer who writes deliberately bad stories cheats not only his readers but his own bank account, because the good stories will still be earning him money when the trash has long been a distasteful memory.

It is true, of course, that a lot of editors are difficult people to deal with. (So are a lot of writers — and for that matter, a lot of fans.) It is even true that they print a good many bad stories. But they are not allowed to send out their magazines with blank pages. They have as a class printed every good science fiction story that has ever been written, either in a magazine or in a book, and, you know, you really can't do any better than that. If the really good stories aren't enough to fill the publishing schedule, then they have to print some which are not really good; if more good stories were written, fewer bad stories would be published; and if more good stories are not written the one and only place where the blame can be laid is on the writers themselves.

Conceivably some of the editors could be a little more active about seeking out good stories. Some of them have sometimes seemed a little torpid. But that is one hell of a long way from saying that they all actively *refuse* to publish good stuff because they like the bad stuff better.

The proof of this is very simple; it rests on the statement I made above. Every really good science fiction story that has ever been written has made its way into print. I have made this statement a number of times over a period of years, within the hearing of just about every pro alive, and no one has yet to come up with the exception that would disprove it. If anyone does, I will at once do two things. First I will abjectly beg his pardon. Second, I will buy the story for *Galaxy* ...

P.S ... By the way, I can add a couple to the list of the "refugees" from science fiction who have come back into the fold — for *Galaxy* and *If*, anyway. Jack Vance has a very good short novel in the August issue of *Galaxy*. Ray Bradbury is in October. Judith Merril probably also October, or within an issue or two thereafter. I forget who else was on the list, but I have a Heinlein serial for *If*, a Hal Clement complete short novel also for *If* — in fact, by about the end of the year both magazines should be shaping up just about the way I want them. Meanwhile I admit that some of the stories are less than perfect.

BETTY KUJAWA

Two weeks ago tomorrow *Xero*, *Bug Eye*, and *Warhoon* all arrived at 3:15 — four minutes later we got the worst storm in the history of our town – tornadoes by the bagful — havoc, destruction ... I was without electricity for the next twenty-three *long* hours — all about us chaos, utter chaos ... *is* there any connection? I was looking (eeeeek) at that (shudder) colorful color cover of *Xero* when all hell broke loose ... hmmmm.

Next time either put a warning on the envelope or include dark glasses — my eyes aren't what they used to be.

RICHARD KYLE

I was happy to meet all those chaps in the "Introducing" section of "Absolute Xero." This fellow Kyle *sounds* remarkably talented and mysterious. A writer, under a dark and hidden name, of many tales of violence and death. A contributor of letters to such widely diverse publications as *Xero*, *SFT*, and *Discord*. A creaking ancient, buyer of the first Superman story ever published, who yet retains the strength and hot vigor to batter at the cupola of one of the ivory towers of science fiction. Gad, what a figure!

On the square, though, this is the first time anyone ever wrote even a thumbnail sketch of me — and it is a curious experience. It's strange how much more interesting people sound than they really are. Or maybe it depends on how you put it, as Philip Wylie demonstrated in *Finley Wren*.

The yarn Westlake was apparently talking about seems to have appeared in the May *Analog*. And if it *is* the story, Westlake reveals his utter lack of story sense. He must proceed wholly by instinct when he writes. It seems evident from the internal evidence that Westlake wrote the story — in the original version — entirely from the viewpoint of Jeremy, a private soldier with weak bowels, who crawls, whines, whimpers, and cold-sweats his way through the whole novelette. Now Campbell *has* to sell *some* magazines. Who is going to be interested in a "hero" like this? Westlake, maybe. So Campbell took the one strong character in the story and had him turned into the hero. It isn't artistic, maybe, but by God it is commercial. Westlake says the original version was the best. Well. From the standpoint of form, it was, probably; but from the standpoint of readability the original version was vastly inferior, if things were the way they look to be.

(And I also suspect, by the way, that if Campbell could get an author or two who could write what Campbell wants — as Heinlein did in the '40s — *Analog* would be one of the best sf magazine ever printed. I think I had an insight into what he is aiming for a couple of issues back, and I can see his problem. Have you ever seen the woodcuts, and such, artists made years back of the strange beasts explorers had encountered on their expeditions? The artists had not been there; they had only the explorers' descriptions to go on, for the most part, and they could only draw from those, using their own knowledge of similar seeming animals. Elephants were turned into the damnedest, unlikeliest looking things. Gorillas became animated mountains with saber-tooth tusks. All that sort of thing. I think that's what Campbell's writers have been doing with his ideas. And coupled with the fact that Campbell himself has probably gotten only a quick squint at the critter he wants drawn up, the results have not been too admirable.

(But as a consequence of this insight into *Analog* and Westlake's woodenheaded behavior, I have considerably more respect for Campbell's current work — and a hell of a lot more sympathy.)

By God, Norton on Smith was charming. The first few paragraphs threw me, but he soon came through in proper manner. Much of the charm, I'm afraid, is in Norton's prose, but it's still there, regardless of the cause.

Davidson on everything topped "EI" handily. I'd rather read his letters than almost anybody's stories. Did he ever try selling letters? They might have gone.

ETHEL LINDSAY

Bhob's work stenciling reminds me that I must congratulate you upon the beautiful production throughout *Xero*. I do like to

FAST WORKER MAN,
Steve Stiles

see such care taken — believe me, it *is* worth it: your fanzine stands head and shoulders above the majority in this respect.

The discussion of the Westlake article had the usual effect upon me. When I read something like that I think: "Now that's true!" Then I read a rebuttal and I get annoyed that I had not thought out these things for myself. Oh well, I suppose it is a good thing to be able to see both sides of a question, but sometimes I wonder I don't overdo it.

HARRY WARNER, JR.

I have put a fondness for the tales of Clark Ashton Smith down as a sin of youth. His fiction got remarkably bad as I encountered more and more good writing in mundane literature. But there was a time when I thought so highly of him that I picked one of his stories ("City of Singing Flame") when *Startling Stories* picked a bunch of fans to choose reprints. I tried my best to suspend belief in Smith's verbosity and clumsiness as I read this article, but I didn't have much luck. Lovecraft for all his equally large faults can be re-read because he left something of himself in the stories. When you return to the Smith stories you find not a man but a dictionary.

BOB BRINEY

Each issue of *Xero* is more impressive than the last. I hope that I have done whatever will ensure me a copy of numbers nine and ten — letters, money, human sacrifice, the complete works of Sax Rohmer???

At one time I had vast enthusiasm for Clark Ashton Smith's stories and poetry (I memorized "The Hashish Eater" — all 583 lines of it — and used to recite it at people …), and still derive much pleasure from re-reading many of them. I had found Norton's dissertation of CAS generally enjoyable, but rather absurdly adulatory in places: " … his powers of creativity touched upon the sublime – and at times even surpassed it!" Indeed! Even Derleth's jacket blurbs don't go quite this far. The best of Smith's stories, including most of those mentioned by Norton, were written in the

1930s. From the time of the publication of *Out of Space and Time* until his death, Smith wrote no prose worthy of attention, and much of his later poetry, though technically impeccable, suffers by comparison with his early flights of fancy.

One of the qualities of Smith's prose which is not mentioned explicitly in Norton's essay is the strain of sardonic humor which occasionally shows itself, as in "The Weird of Avoosi Wuthoqqan" and "The Voyage of King Eurovan" and in the endings of several other stories.

ROBERT SMITH

Xero has a pretty swingin' letter-column, due no doubt to the presence of Avram Davidson and his absolutely fantastic method of commenting. (I wonder how many non-fan readers of *F&SF* would *believe* that this is the gentleman who edits their favorite prozine …) I would like a collection of Avram's letters so's when I'm feeling low and ready to curl up into a ball I could grab 'em and laugh my way into insanity. Wonderful! Being torn to shreds by the good Colonel would probably linger with one forever, but what an experience!

JOHN BAXTER

Well now, that is what I call a *cover*! None of this half-hearted eye-catching — it jumps out and gives you a knee in the visual groin. I don't know how much trouble that thing has caused me, what with people stopping me in the street and asking "What the hell *is* that thing?" the whole office staff arriving one morning in dark glasses … yes, very vexaticus, but worth it, I suppose, just to have anything so startling in the collection. I'm currently in monastic-like seclusion, preparing myself for the cover of *Xero* 9. If you should see my obituary in *Fanac* some time after September next, you'll know that a diet of locust and wild honey and stopping up the seven bodily orifices with sweet-smelling herbs is not proof against bhob Stewart's fiendish color sense.

Why do you go to such great lengths to stress that *Xero* will fold after the tenth issue? I counted at least three mentions of this depressing fact in the first couple of pages, which is three too many. It always helps when writing a loc to think that, in some way, you're assisting the editor by commenting. Even if it's only rah-rah egoboo, there's always the chance that this will inspire him to greater heights and the next issue will be as good, if not better than the one you're writing about. But with *Xero* … it's just one foot after another and the grave at the end. Reminds me of a determinedly cheerful tea party at the Eventide Homes.

"Strange, slightly different-drummered use of the English language" says Dick, being mighty careful not to commit himself as to whether he thinks H.P. Norton's article is good or bad. Well, take my word for it — it's a stinker. That's pretty blunt, I guess, and if this trespasses on your editorial taste, sorry. It is all very well to take liberties with English — with *any* language — in a letter or in a conversation, but when one is writing for publication, it would seem to be essential that a writer at least take some notice of the rules under which he is creating. Norton doesn't. His grammar and syntax, his punctuation … urk! And some of those phrases are incredible. "As a more characteristic instance … With Clark Ashton Smith, the world of ancient Greece still hovers … Baudelaire, whom he translated … the modern graveyard school which permeated … " This may represent "strange, different-drummered" prose to you, but in my opinion it is nothing more than the published maunderings of a writer on nodding acquaintances only with the elementary rules of grammar, punctuation, and writing in general. You have a perfect right to publish such work if you feel the theme and the writer's knowledge (which is, I concede, apparently considerable) justify his shaky command of language, but to attempt to explain, even glorify, his ineptness is not entirely logical.

DON WESTLAKE

Sorry to have taken so long to answer. Frankly, I wasn't sure whether I should answer or not. My agent advised me to stop, and since he has done more for me in writing career than almost anyone else I can think of, and since he is a knowledgeable man in this business, his advice carried a lot of weight. On the other hand, you people had been kind enough to send along *Xero 8*, which did contain comments and questions which shouldn't be left up in the air. So this letter will be the last chapter on the subject and I'll try to make it inoffensive. The people I offend, it seems, don't tell *me* about it; they call my agent.

Point number one: I have never tried to imitate anyone's writing *style*. Frederik Pohl's or anybody else's, and I hardly think I could even if I tried. I have tried, however, to aim at editorial interests. In Mr. Pohl's case, I had to go on the stories he had written rather than the stories he had bought, for obvious reasons. (By the time he wrote the letter which appeared in *Xero 8*, he still had two stories in inventory that Gold had bought.) If the implication that I was doing a pastiche was contained in my article, it was unintentional. The point of my "phony inside stuff" was that I was aiming at the market *and nothing more*. In other words, the story I had written had no merits other than as an example of aiming at a particular market. And so, a lousy story.

Which brings me to Avram Davidson's suggestion that I'm not a science fiction writer at all, but wandered into the field by mistake. This idea had never occurred to me before, but now that it has been suggested, I must admit it might be true. I gave up Perry Mason for science fiction when I was fourteen, and read science fiction voluminously for the next six years, before the Air Force took me at twenty. In 1958, when I started the drive to become a self-supporting writer, it was to science fiction that I returned, compiling a library of about five hundred magazines, being *Galaxy* and *F&SF* complete, *Astounding* back to 1948, and a batch of secondary magazines, and it was only after having waded through all this that I decided to branch out into the mystery field and see what I could do there. My first sale, in 1953, when I was nineteen, was to *Universe Science Fiction*. My sales in 1958 and 1959 were about half and half, mystery and science fiction. All of this might sound like the beginnings of a career as a science fiction writer, but obviously the appearances are deceiving.

Let's pursue Avram Davidson's idea. The first stories I sold in both the mystery and science fiction fields were nothing spectacular – the mysteries to *Hitchcock* were the drab droll dreck used as ballast in that magazine, the science fiction was summed up by Mr. Pohl's comments on "Spy" — but gradually I think I improved. In mysteries anyway. As my "slanting for the market" became less conscious and worrisome, I could concentrate more on the story itself, and so the stories began to have more meat on their bones. I imagine that this is normal development of a writer in any field; first conscious agitating, "aiming" at the market, gradual mastery of the conventions and taboos and interests and typings in that market, and so gradual freeing of the concentration for the story itself.

This process happened to me in the mystery field, but it didn't happen in science fiction. I never got beyond stage one. When the chance came to send a story to *Galaxy* with guaranteed sympathetic attention, I honestly didn't know what to do with it. If I muffed it, I come close to closing a market. I was still in stage one; *slant* the story. That was in 1961, and I still hadn't found a firm footing in the field.

On those few occasions when I thought I'd taken a small step forward, I was immediately returned to Start, either by a No Sale or a slant-oriented revision. The Campbell story about the Colonel is a fine instance. (It was in the May issue of *Analog*, to answer the questions.) In the original the Colonel showed up at the end of the story. There was no secret organization of psupermen in the Air Force. The point of view never deviated from Jeremy. It was a story about a *person*. God knows it was no masterpiece, but it was a *story*. (In this connection, Harry Warner, Jr.'s idea that the Colonel was a "real, living characterization," just ain' so. *Analog* is full of Secret Societies with Strange Powers, and the Colonel under one name or another, runs them all. You will find this same character in spy stories. He's the chief of Counter-Intelligence, the hero phones him in Washington every once in a while, and his name is Mac.) At any rate, I for one am more interested in a *person*, who suddenly and shatteringly learns he is a teleport, who doesn't want to be a teleport, and who more than half suspects he's lost his mind, who struggles through the problems thus created – aggravated by the fact that he can neither control nor repeat the initial teleportation — and works things out to some sort of solution or compromise with the world, than I am in all the Secret Societies and Mystical Powers in the Orient. But the writing and rewriting of the story kept me vigorously marching in place, back there at stage one.

So you see, Mr. Davidson may be right. I had read more science fiction than mystery. I was more interested in science fiction, and had sold my first story to a science fiction magazine. But it was in the mystery field that I could adapt myself to the requirements of the market and then go on to stories — and books — that fulfilled for me, *more* than the simple requirements of the market. In science fiction, once I had fulfilled the requirements of the market, I never had any elbow room left. Using that Colonel story again, once that man and his Secret Society took over the story, it became impossible to do anything with Jeremy, my teleportee. Instead of his taking his own risks, fighting his own way through to triumph and defeat, the story became a Mystical Inner Circle affair. Jeremy still struggled, but he was no longer his own man. His every move was planned and anticipated by the Secret Society, and the whole story became the recounting of an initiation into the club. All it lacked was a badge with a decoder on the back, for spelling out Ralston. Phooey.

Could I have fulfilled the market requirements with that story, and still have written a story interesting to *me?* No. Is that a flaw in my writing ability? Maybe. I have not thought so, but maybe it is. If so, it's a flaw that seems to bother me only in science fiction.

Point number three: At a certain risk, I must point out that at least one sentence in Frederik Pohl's letter is balderdash. This is the crack about "other markets" having "lower standards" than the science fiction magazines. He must be referring to those non-science fiction editors so obtuse as to buy stories and/or books from me. Among these editors are Lee Wright, a Senior Editor at Random House, generally accepted as being the top mystery editor in the United States, and possibly in the world. Bucklin Moon of Pocket Books, who is no slouch. The good people at T.V. Boardman in England, Gallimard in France, Mondadori in Italy, and so on and so on, who have bought various foreign rights to my books. Hans Stefan Santesson, William Manners, and Ed McBain, who have bought short stories from me in the mystery field. The people at Dell, who have bought reprint rights to my mystery novels. If in Frederik Pohl's world these people have "lower standards" than the six science fiction magazines which have not yet joined their sisters in silence, then either Mr. Pohl or myself is living in a parallel universe.

Point number four (and last): My article, in twenty-five hundred ill-chosen words, attempted to say one thing: *science fiction is neither an artistic nor a commercial field.* Avram Davidson suggested I was in the wrong pew. L. Sprague de Camp objected to my cavalier ignoring of his non-science fiction output. Frederik Pohl complained about my "'phoney' inside stuff." Though I'd stated that I'd never written a science fiction novel, Donald Wollheim wondered why he hadn't seen anything submitted from me. The letter without a name thought I was too vindictive. John Baxter thought I was too petty. But until one of these people *directly* disagrees with this statement — *science fiction is neither an artistic nor a commercial field* — they haven't said a damn thing.

RICHARD KYLE

Until I saw James Blish's letter in *Xero 7*, I didn't really understand what "Semi-literate" meant. For although Blish can write, he cannot read.

Item: " ... [Kyle] asserts that those who praise Amis' book are simply licking eminent boots. (I leave out the part of the argument which says those who damn the book are also licking his boots as being too subtle for likes of me.)" I didn't say that at all. I said the *extremes* of emotion (the "shouts of praise and screams of outrage") this trivial and inadequate little book produced were not warranted by the book itself, which should have died a silent death, but were produced — in the main — by the name and status of the author. As poor relations excessively praise and damn the rich — out of a sense of their own inferiority — so, I thought, much of science fiction praised and damned *New Maps*. Nothing very subtle there. And I *excluded* Blish from this group: "It is beyond me, though, why James Blish, *who is certainly no poor relation* ... " It must be tough when you can't read.

Item: Blish objects to my "demand that sf ... 'show the proper respect for the man who made it'" (evidently thinking I was referring to Campbell. Well, I didn't say that either. I said "the *men* who made it," and it appears in my copy of *Xero*. Nor did I "demand" they be esteemed for their accomplishments; I said I thought it was time they were. And I do think so. What would science fiction be like if there had *never* been an *Astounding Science Fiction*, if there had *never* been an Olaf Stapledon, if there had *never* been a Robert A. Heinlein? These men are absolutely critical to the development of science fiction (as, say, writers like Henry Kuttner and A.E. van Vogt and M.P. Sheil are not, no matter what the quality of their individual stories may be) and they should be remembered along with Verne and Wells and Gernsback. No good book can exclude them, no matter what its point of view may be.

Item: " ... [Amis] does *not* so say [that Campbell is a crank], tough Mr. Kyle marks the word 'crank' as though he were quoting somebody ... " Amis doesn't, eh? Page 130 of the Ballantine edition: One imagines [new young writers from 'ordinary' fiction] ... above all, kicking out the cranks who seem bent on getting science fiction a bad name — John Campbell, the editor of *Astounding* ... " Blish could have learned this if he had used the "excellent" index he has spoken of. (My quotes around *excellent* seem to trouble Blish. They're there to show his praise of the book extends even beyond the text to the good, but in view of the length of the book, not exceptional index.) But, of course, the man doesn't read. He doesn't even read the books he reviews, let alone the letters he criticizes.

Item: "No, Mr. Kyle ... " Blish says, addressing me directly. Not only doesn't he read the books he reviews and the letters he criticizes, he doesn't read his own letters, either. For right at the top of this letter he writes: "Maybe this Amis discussion is wearing out and you (Lupoffs) should call it closed ... If you need a place to start I suggest here ... " I guess Blish doesn't read *any*thing.

Item: "No, Mr. Kyle, sf is not Melville ... " I never said it was, of course.

Item: " ... and John Campbell is not the Albert Schweitzer of our field." You know, all along, I never did really think he was. I didn't even mention Schweitzer name, matter of fact.

I'd send Blish a *McGuffey's Reader* to help him out — but I'm afraid he'd try to hunt up McGuffey to give him his reader back.

It sure must be tough, though, not being able to read. All the things you miss, Dick and Jane stories. And Fireman Joe stories. And Winnie the Pooh. And Raggedy Ann. It sure must be tough.

ANDY ZERBE

I have just read *Xero 8* and I think it is the best fanzine I have read yet, but I'll probably change my mind when I get around to reading more fanzines.

COL. DAVIDSON,
bhob Stewart

DICKIE'S DIARY

CONFESSIONS OF A SMALL-TIME DUPER BUG

RICHARD A. LUPOFF
APRIL 15, 1962

"Vicolor!" exclaimed Walter Breen, holding his copy of *Xero 8* open to page 33, jabbing his forefinger triumphantly at a small area about an inch over Alfred Bester's left hand, and at another on a line with Avram Davidson's yarmulke but some inches to the left thereof. I suppose I should explain that Walter was pointing to spots near pictures of Alfred and Avram, on bhob Stewart's first "Writers at Work" page, not at the gentlemen themselves. As a matter of cold fact, I have no idea where Alfred Bester was at that time; Avram Davidson was nearby I know because Walter, Pat and I, and numerous other fans were in Avram's apartment attending a surprise party given by the Colonel's lady in honor of his approaching birthday.

But back to Walter and the Vicolor ... Walter was pointing to two areas on page 33 where ink of one color shaded gradually into another. It was quite hard to detect, as that particular page had been run in black ink on green paper, then rerun with an overlay in that lovely purplish shade Gestetner calls burgundy, and finally rerun again with a different overlay, this time using both green and red ink in a process comparable to Vicolor. Walter mistook it for Shelby's process and I, in my cups as it is my custom to be at Avram Davidson's Birthday Parties, unthinkingly confirmed Walter's deduction.

I'm sorry, Walter, I was too quick to agree. It wasn't Vicolor at all, it was a process that I

invented myself, and that is so far nameless. I propose to call it Rextripe because it gives the effect of striped ink on a Rex Rotary or similar mimeo. It won't work on a pad machine, but then you wouldn't need it on a pad machine: you could use Vicolor.

Say, is everybody out there still with me? I have a feeling that a lot of readers don't dig Vicolor, no less Rextripe, and explaining the new process in terms of the older one is pretty futile if that's true.

Okay, let's back up some and talk about mimeographs and color processes. Back about ten years ago Shelby Vick got tired of monochromatic mimeography. Shelby had a conventional mimeograph, i.e., a pad machine. It worked this way: a hollow drum is the heart of the mimeo; a cloth pad is stretched tight around the drum, and a stencil is fastened over the pad. Normally, ink is placed inside the drum. It passes through perforations in the surface of the drum, soaking the pad, and passing in turn through the typing or illos cut on the stencil, to be deposited on paper as the drum revolves.

By conventional means you can run only one color at a time; to change colors you clean out the drum, change pads, and re-ink. With Vicolor you don't ink from the inside of the drum through the pad: you "paint" the ink on the outside of the pad. And you can paint stripes, polka dots, or any other pattern of colors you like, and when you run off your pages the ink will be deposited in the exact pattern of your "painting" … or, to be really precise, in its mirror image.

Vicolor is inapplicable to the Rex. There is no drum, no pad. Instead, there are four hard-surfaced rollers. Two large ones — about four inches in diameter and slightly longer than a stencil is wide — are mounted one above the other, with a gap of about an inch separating them. The smaller rollers are mounted parallel to the large ones so that the four rollers, seen end-on, form a diamond shape.

(Actually there is a fifth roller, the impression roller, located below the path of the moving paper and used to hold it against the stencil, but this is not involved in the Rextripe process.)

Next, a silk screen is wrapped around the cylinders. The stencil is mounted on the outside of the screen. On the hand-inked model (and this is crucial: Rextripe will not work on a machine with automatic inking) there is a gap between the ends of the silk screen. Inking is accomplished by applying paste ink directly onto the top roller, through the gap in the silk screen. A few turns distribute the ink onto the four rollers; when you start your actual run, the ink passes through the silk screen, through the stencil, and onto the paper.

Now, here is why Vicolor is impossible on the Rex: Whereas the entire mechanism of the drum/pad machine rotates on a common axis, with a given point on drum, pad, and stencil being permanently associated ... on the Rex each cylinder rotates on *its own* axis while the screen and stencil revolve about all four cylinders. No "patterned" inking is possible ... with one exception: vertical stripes.

You can see why this is so by visualizing the operation of that four-cylinder system. No horizontal pattern because the motion of the rollers and the screen would swiftly smear out any horizontal stripes of ink placed on the roller. But since there is no horizontal smearing* bands of ink placed side-by-side on the exposed roller will be spread in parallel vertical stripes as the rollers and screen are turned. The result, when a stencil is run, is vertical bands of color on the final page. The bands can be any width from a practical minimum of an inch or so up to the full width of the page, and as many colors as there are bands.

For a sample of Rextriping, see the Rriss cartoon facing. That cartoon, by the way, has been the cause of some controversy in this house. Andy did it for us last year, intending it to be used as the cover of a Cultzine. Pat and I were high on the waiting list at that time — about third or fourth, I think — but some pretty rank goings on were under way in the Cult, and the USPOD was investigating, and between revulsion at some of the publications and a frank desire to remain uninvolved in an indecent mail case (which never came about, by the way) we dropped.

Since then the cartoon has languished. *I* just don't think it's particularly funny; bhob thinks it is, and that it says Something Significant to boot. Using it this way it earns its keep as a sample, whether it's a worthy cartoon or not.

This, by the way, is only my second attempt at Rextriping ("Writers at Work" in *Xero 8* was my first), and my first using a "faxed stencil." Rextripe seems an easily learned process, requiring little or no practice before "live" use. It is not patented. In fact, I'll be both flattered and fascinated to see the results if anyone else tries it, and I'll be most interested to see the results, hear of any problems in its use, etc.

I also mentioned, earlier, that Rextriping is possible only with a hand-inked machine. I have a feeling that it may be possible with a Rex equipped for automatic inking if the auto-inking mechanism is temporarily disabled. There aren't too many Rexes (Rexi?) around fandom — Bob Pavlat has one I know, and LASFS has another — but someone might be willing to try it. I'll ask Pat to print any such True Duper Experiences in EI next time. As for the other screen-type mimeos, there are quite a few Gesteteners around, and at least one Roneo that I know of. If you can just get that ink deposited, you can use Rextripe on any screen mimeo. How many can get the ink deposited?

> *This is not strictly true. The two small rollers have some horizontal motion in addition to their axial rotation; in fact they are sometimes called waver rollers for this reason. However, the horizontal "waver" is so little that it results in no significant changes in a run of 200 copies with re-inking after the first hundred. This "waver" is the reason for not attempting extremely narrow bands of color.*

-RL.

BOOKS

LIN CARTER

COL. DAVIDSON DEPARTMENT

OR ALL THE SEA WITH OYSTERS, AVRAM DAVIDSON; BERKLEY, N.Y., 1962.
176 PP., 50 CENTS

Now as this just happens to be the (thus far) only and firstest book Col. A. Davidson (U.S.M.C., Ret.) has written, it is just naturally a good collection because he crammed all his goodies to date therein.

You will recall the title story from *Galaxy*, 1957, the fortean one about coathangers copulating in closets and bicycles multiplying ... and stories like "My Boy Friend's Name is Jello" and "The Golem" from *F&SF*. The latter is one of the most skillful little things I have ever seen in fantasy: a comic treatment of the golem theme, mingling elements of science fiction and gothic horror in a sort of framework of yiddish humor. It sounds very difficult to write, but it is a pure delight to read.

Also among the sixteen stories here is the short novelette "Help! I Am Dr. Morris Goldpepper," also from *Galaxy*, 1958, which struck me then and stikes me now as very possibly the gawdam funniest story I have ever read in a science fiction magazine.

Also present are stories of "straight" science fiction, straight gothic pieces in a blackwoodian vein, literary curios like the one called "King's Evil," a period piece from the Regency period written in the style of the era.

In a word, there is something here for just about every taste in fantasy. Avram Davidson's fiction has always seemed to me outstanding among the more recent crop of writers in the field ... it is written with skill, style and charm with a certain warm touch of gentleness, quiet humor and — humility? — that is missing from most writers, at least in our field.

As a stylist, the Colonel bears comparison with Sheckley, Bradbury and Sturgeon. In that comparison, I feel he stands out as the least self-consciously arty and poetic, the only one with self-control, the best plotter, and the one least given to Unfettered Purpleness.

BURROUGHS GALORE

THE MONSTER MEN, EDGAR RICE BURROUGHS; CANAVERAL PRESS, N.Y., 1962. 188 PP., $2.75, ILLUSTRATED

Does everybody know by now that the Burroughs estate carelessly and foolishly failed to renew copyrights on the first couple dozen ERB titles, when the 27-year limit came around, thus releasing into public domain lots of goodies? Guess so.

The first set of reprints, illustrated by the distinguished (but highly unsuitable for Burroughs) contemporary American artist, Mahlon Blaine, are now available. These comprise *A Fighting Man of Mars*, *The Moon Maid* (retitled *The Moon Men*), and *The Monster Men*.

Reset in clear, large type; rebound in pressed paper a la Gnome Press; with rather attractive jackets also by Blaine — they are good editions of rare items and truly fine bargains at their low price.

I shall review only *The Monster Men*, principally because it is the only one of the set I have purchased (principally because it was the only one of the set I had not read before). This is a curio involving a Frankenstein plot, laid on the jungle isles in and around Borneo, involving:

1. A Mad Scientist who wants to Create Life
2. The Beautiful Scientist's Daughter
3. An Evil Associate
4. The most Handsome, Noble and Pure Monster in the History of the Frankenstein Stories.

Somehow or other, in a typical ERB plot, all hell breaks loose and everybody goes around chasing each other. The Monster chases the Girl who is carried off by a Chimpanzee and the Mad Doctor and the Pirate and More Monsters and the Evil Associate are also chasing or being chased for 188 pages, and everybody has a High Old Time, except maybe the Pirates and also the Head-Hunters (I forgot about them. Sorry.), who get it in The Neck.

By page 188, all sorts of things have happened.

1. The Mad Doctor has realized How Evil it was to try to Create Life
2. The Monster and The Girl are In Love
3. The Other Monsters have decided to Get Away From It All and go live in the Jungle with the Chimpanzees
4. The Pirates, the Head-Hunters and the Evil Associates have got it in The Neck

If I seem to be making fun of all this, I don't really mean to, but I hardly think ERB wrote it seriously. I like this sort of thing, it is light literary entertainment and Burroughs was the complete master of that sort of thing.

And it has a clever, refreshing, very unexpected Twist Ending that I was unprepared for and which left me gasping!

... Well, anyway, breathing heavily.

HARLAN THROUGH THE LOOKING GLASS

ELLISON WONDERLAND, HARLAN ELLISON; PAPERBACK LIBRARY; N.Y., 1962.
191 PP., 50 CENTS

This is a catch-all, or grab-bag, of Ellison's short stuff — sixteen stories in all — dating from 1956 to 1962. There are *Unknown*ish things like "Gnomebody" here; straight sf like "Commuter's Problem;" Sturgeony things like "Do-It-Yourself" — a pretty good average overall science fiction collection.

Ellison's best to date has been the novel *Man with Nine Lives* backed up, in Ace, with a selection of his shorts. That novel was one of the most exciting pieces of sf in recent years — taut, vivid, imaginative, a sort of second string Al Bester, but very good stuff.

These short stories, tho' ... I somehow get the feeling they were written with the Absolute Bare Minimum of talent, imagination and skill he thought he could get away with. They are skimpy (skeletal is a better word), often "cute," frequently displaying a sad tendency to turn off flashy writing and jazzy narrative instead of solid craftsmanship.

The end result is disappointing ... and why the hell are all these pocketbooks costing 50 cents now?

DREAMS AND FANCIES

H.P. LOVECRAFT; ARKHAM HOUSE, SAUK CITY (WISC.), 1962. 174 PP., $3.50

Alone of the specialty houses that blossomed just after World War II, Arkham House continues year after year to remain in good solvent condition, still publishing important books of high literary merit, beautifully printed, bound and jacketed with extremely fine taste.

This one, however, is a sport or curio (that's the third time I've used that word in these reviews ... must find another word) of little general interest, appealing only to collectors of the "Everything There Is," or Forrest J. Ackerman, brand.

It consists of several delightful Lovecraft letters about his wild and woolly dreams, together with a half-dozen stories written around the dreams.

Among the stories (which are largely from his early Dunsanian period) are some of my particular favorites, such as "The Doom That Came To Sarnath" (1919), "Celephais" (1920), and the novel — perhaps the most successful of all his novels — "The Shadow

Out Of Time" (1934).

While it is easy to understand why Arkham House wishes to keep the Lovecraft name before the public, and has a natural desire to continue making money off his work by reprinting it, it's hard to see why this book was published. How much nicer it would have been if they had re-issued *Shadow*, or other book-length novels such as *Herbert West, Reanimator* (1921-22) or *Charles Dexter Ward* (1927-28) in individual volumes all their own.

However, it does have a simply gorgeous jacket by Frank Taylor.

SOME WILL NOT DIE

ALGIS BUDRYS; REGENCY, EVANSTON (ILL.), 1962. 159 PP., 50 CENTS.

This is (to me) an utterly pointless rewrite of AJ's 1954 novel *False Night*, written during his apprenticeship and not particularly, I am sad to say, improved upon in the new version.

It is difficult to believe that the same man who wrote *Rogue Moon*, truly an sf masterpiece, could write this story. Dull, wearying, episodic, heavy-handed, predictable ... well, I don't know. Sometimes I wonder.

Now that AJ is heading Regency Books he seems to be, not unlike his distinguished predecessor H. Ellison, observing the time-honored custom among editors, commonly known as "Buy Yer Own Stuff and Screw 'Em All" gambit.

And this is another pocketbook that makes me wonder why they are all costing 50 cents now.

ARMAGEDDON 2419 A.D.

PHILIP FRANCIS NOWLAN; AVALON BOOKS, N.Y., 1962. 224 PP. $2.95

This is the hoary original of the Buck Rogers strip (a fact, surprisingly, not mentioned anywhere on or in the book). Despite the rather apologetic preface (of the "Quaint old relic, ain't it, boy?" sort), I find it neither quaint nor amusing ... but a tough, tight, fairly well-told (for its period) story, very much deserving of this hardcover permanency in its own right ... regardless of its value and interest as a historical or associational item.

Anthony Rogers (sic), excavating in 1927 for radioactive minerals, is overcome by the radiation and conks out, his body perfectly preserved for 492 years. He awakens in 2419 to find America a savage wilderness, long ago overrun and conquered by Yellow Hordes of the Han Empire who rule from their air-cities aloft.

The modern Americans are green-clad foresters, guerrillas armed with advanced technological weaponry turned out by subterranean factories, fighting a war-of-attrition with sabotage thrown in, to get back their land from the Degenerate Mongoloids.

Nowlan's narrative style is smooth and even, and he achieves a certain tension and excitement. His unfortunate tendency to stop the story dead every other page, every time somebody picks up a radiophone, and spend two paragraphs giving you technical details ... well, it's the only mark of "age" I can find in the book, and was standard operating procedure in the Gernsbackian (or Pre-Heinleinian) Era, and the author can hardly be criticized for using it.

Incidentally, a fact also not noted anywhere in, on, or outside the book: This is actually both the Buck Rogers novellas, *Armageddon 2419 A.D.* and *The Airlords of Han*, combined in one volume.

UNTITLED, bhob Stewart

Reprinting these two famous Nowlan stories is a Good Thing

and I think it were real nice of Good Ole Avalon Books to do so and at such a realistic price, too. Now, if we could just persuade them to reprint Nowlan's other big story, "Space Guard" from *ASF*, May, 1940...

ALL THE TRAPS OF EARTH & OTHER STORIES

CLIFFORD D. SIMAK; DOUBLEDAY, GARDEN CITY (N.Y.); 1962. 287 PP., $3.95

You know, I'm REALLY not in a bad mood today. Even though I have already in this column knifed H. Ellison, skewered A. Budrys, poignarded Arkham House — and am about to take the old scalpel to Cliff Simak for publishing this book, when he should have known better. Actually, I'm in a tip-top mood today, merry as a lark on the wing, bubbling over with brotherly love and fondness for Little Children, Home, Mother, The Flag, The Good Book, and Carl Sandburg.

But, Good People, Cliff Simak has sprung a gasket or something. Maybe it's because Doubleday has put out three collections of his shorts in as many years, or something, and the blood is rushing to his head.

Anyway: the title novelette in this collection is so long, so bad, so dull, so lacking in human interest, so emotion-soaked, so boring, so badly overwritten, that it gives the whole book a bad flavor, and sicklies o'er the entire collection with the pale cast of crud.

The rest of the stories seem to be typical mediocre Simak.

Gee I wish he would write another book like *City*. I bet he wishes he could, too.

RETURN TO OTHERNESS

HENRY KUTTNER; BALLANTINE, N.Y., 1962. 240 PP., 50 CENTS

It strikes me as sort of sad, to realize that Hank Kuttner is having more books published after his tragically early death, than he did during his lifetime. He was one of the very few s-f/fantasy writers we cannot very well do without — a prolific and brilliant, highly talented, creative and original man with immense variety and skill in his craft. God bless him, I wish he'd lived fifty more years.

This collection of only eight stories contains a Hogben story and "The Proud Robot" ... the very best of all the wonderful Gallagher stories, as well as "The Ego Machine" (apparently a previously unprinted story), not to mention "Gallagher Plus."

Jesus, he was a good writer. Hardly a bad page in the book. Tight, smooth craftsmanship in every story, and the wacky, irreverent Kuttner flavor throughout.

For this one I don't mind paying 50 cents. Get it and agree.

THE MASK OF FU MANCHU

SAX ROHMER; PYRAMID, N.Y., 1962. 191 PP., 40 CENTS

I think it is peachy keen the way the boys at Pyramid are bringing the Sax Rohmer stuff out again in paperback, book by book in series-order too.

This old-timer (1932), a fine Oriental-Gothic chiller in which the Wicked Doctor makes like the Veiled Prophet of Khorassan and almost raises the Yellow Hordes in a *jihad* against the West is the sort of scalp-tingling spook opera we enjoyed in our teens, and you can't hardly get that kind anymore.

Nayland Smith is back again, the poor old guy, weary and worn to a frazzle chasing the Doctor all over hell and gone, frustrating his Evil Plans and struggling against his sinister hordes of Dacoits, Thuggee-stranglers, poison flowers, spiders and what all, and getting grayer and more pooped in every book.

You'll like it. Hey! This one is only 40 cents — are the boys at Pyramid trying to spoil us?

TERROR

ROBERT BLOCH; BELMONT, N.Y., 1962. 157 PP., 50 CENTS

Speaking of Thuggee! R. Hassenpfeffer Block, or Bloch, or something — easily the most prolific Dirty Pro around these days (seven books in less than two years, count 'em, S-E-V-E-N) — has a little murder mystery here with people getting knocked off in a gory way all over, and a Stolen Hindu Idol of Kali the Black Goddess of Death and Murder and Income Tax Evasion, & a couple Gorgeous Dolls, and well you know ...

Oh, by the way; this is by the author of *Psycho*. Just thought I'd mention it in case you didn't know ...

(50 cents again ... maybe I'll start going to the Public Library or something...)

THE HOUSE ON THE BORDERLAND

WILLIAM HOPE HODGSON; ACE BOOKS, N.Y., 1962. 159 PP., 35 CENTS

Well, this is just one of the modern masterpieces of gothic fiction, a real chiller, an authentic classic of the field, and (although not Hodgson's best, for which I nominate the magnificent *The Night Land*) beautifully told, wonderful reading. Ace is to be congratulated for bringing this out, and let's see *Ghost Pirates* and *The Boats of the Glen Carig* too, huh Don?

This is the tenth Arkham House book in paperback, and that's okay with me because they are good books and everybody ought to be able to get them. 35 cents ... fantastic!

WITCH HOUSE

EVANGELINE WALTON; MONARCH BOOKS, DERBY (CONN.), 1962. 159 PP., 35 CENTS

This is the eleventh, but it's a clinker. Wimmin can't write, or anyway this one can't.

... AND LET ME SAY AGAIN I DON'T LIKE PAYING NO LOUSEY FIFTY CENTS FOR NO LOUSEY PAPERBACK BOOKS!

THE MAKING OF A FANTASTIC PAPERBACK

CHARLES M. COLLINS

CHARLES M. COLLINS (unknown) parlayed his deep knowledge of fantasy, garnered through years as manager of a bookstore, into the editorship of at least one anthology. After his association with Xero *he fell out of contact with the fan community. Recent attempts to reach him have led to many persons named Charles M. Collins, but apparently not the "right" Charles M. Collins. If he happens to read* The Best of Xero*, he is requested to contact the publisher!*

Some months ago the editor-in-chief of a long-standing paperback publisher negotiated with me to edit a collection of supernatural fiction. The anthology was recently completed; it has been accepted, and is scheduled for publication at the end of this year. This is the story of the book: of its conception, evolution, and final materialization. Because it happened to me, it is a highly personal story, and simply a "behind-the-scenes" account of its development in the intricate network of some publisher's production mill.

Because it is a fantastic paperback, Dick Lupoff has been interested in its progress, and thinks that many readers of *Xero* may well share his interest. He asked me to start at the very beginning, outlining each phase of the book's growth from the time I first conceived of the project to its completion in the spring of this year. Now it seems rather difficult to ascertain a starting point. The genesis of the idea goes back through many pleasurable years as a devoted aficionado and private collector of fantastic literature and outré lore. To commence at some amorphous point in time, way back there, would mean penning a kind of personal memoir the content of which would generate a questionable amount of interest. Yet the concept of the anthology had its origin long before negotiations were made or contracts signed. I find too that the telling of this tale must include an appreciation of sorts — that it must embody some tribute to a person whose unwavering faith, friendship, and conviction in me through several dark and precarious years has enabled me to gain a foothold in a profession that is extremely meaningful to me, and motivates me to give my best and most resolute effort to whatever work I may be fortunate enough to contribute to that field.

The man of whom I speak is Michael de Forrest. He is presently editor-in-chief at Avon Books, and was one of the originators as well as one-time co-owner of America's first paperback bookshop.

I suppose I have haunted bookshops much as the alcoholic haunts gin mills. It was almost inevitable that I should discover the Pocket Book Bookshop, and rather auspicious that there in this first and now, alas, no longer existent bookshop began the evolution of my initial professional contribution to the field. The genuine feelings of warmth and welcome extended by the two proprietors far exceeded my patronage, and the shop was, consequently, soon to become one of my regular and favorite purlieus. At that time Mike had recently obtained a position in the sales department of Avon Books, while working evenings in the bookshop. At dusk, after a dreary day of work, or looking for work, I would often return to the Pocket Book Bookshop, and in the dark obscurity of the small alcove where stock was kept and purchases registered, over cans of beer and countless cigarettes, we talked — and there, no doubt, Mike learned of my interests in fantastic literature.

It was in the early days of 1958 that Mike first proposed an anthology of horror tales which I would edit for Avon. He was in an excellent position to play my ideas in the proper hands, and asked if I might be interested in such a project. I became intoxicated with enthusiasm that night as I envisioned the realization of a long-time dream and hitherto silent ambition. The concept, as all such neophyte visions are, was grandiose. I would put together a giant collection devoted to tales of lycanthropy. The package was called *Some Live by Blood Alone*, and contained several old favorites, some rare and obscure masterpieces, as well as a representative collection of supernatural fiction from the nineteenth and twentieth centuries. Secondly, it would bring back long out-of-print tales obtainable only in rare, high priced hardcover editions. Thirdly, it would present works by some of the most distinguished men in the genre who dabbled diabolically in the black arts and who shared a common predilection for the vampire, werewolf, and sundry blood-sucking creatures in a low-priced, mass market paperback.

Included were such gems as D. Scott-Moncrieff's "Schloss Wappenburg," Bram Stoker's "Dracula's Guest," and a horrific masterpiece by Hanns Heinz Ewers, "The Spider." The Ewers piece was later used in Donald Wollheim's paperback anthology *More Macabre* (1961). Several months after submission my presentation for *Some Live by Blood Alone* was rejected on the grounds that it was too much for the connoisseur and not enough for the mass market.

There is an amusing postscript concerning the ultimate fate of this collection. Once it was rejected by Avon, I decided to place my outline with another publisher. I handed the material over to my agent, and thereafter put it out of my mind. It was now going into the fall of 1958, and my agent had submitted the presentation to a relatively new paperback publisher at that time. Several months passed without a word from them concerning the anthology. Inquiries from my agent about it were given vague, noncommittal replies. Finally he was told that the entire idea had been rejected, but the material was being held in one of the editorial offices awaiting a signature on the rejection slip. Twice my agent attempted to have the presentation picked up, but both times returned empty handed. Then, early one crisp September morning, I received the rejection slip in the mail. It had, I must say, been most beautifully signed by the executive editor, only there was no accompanying manuscript. I read the rejection slip once more to discover that my eight-page presentation, which could have been enclosed for (in those days) just an additional three cents, was being returned to me via express. I immediately wrote to the executive editor explaining to him that the script had been submitted through my agent, that it had been called for twice, that my agent maintained a pick-up service for such rejections, and that the material should be sent back to my agent in the manner requested when the script was first submitted.

Lo! About two days later a huge van pulled up to my house, and from it was extracted my eight-page presentation along with a bill charging me with a minimum shipping fee of close to two dollars. On principle I refused the envelope. It was returned to the publisher who also refused it. Then ensued some correspondence with the express company trying to clear up the situation and attempting to regain my manuscript, but all this while, nary a word in reply to my letter from the executive editor. The express company stood firm and would not release the script until someone accepted the charges. I decided to let the matter drop, not really needing the presentation since I had a duplicate copy somewhere about the house. A year passed without pursuing any further publication plans. Then, under the impression that the original script had long been lost and forgotten, I once again heard from the express company. This time I was informed that the manuscript was being held in their office, but, during the year, had gathered fantastic storage fees. Would I kindly come down, pay the charges, and pick it up. Another letter from me followed once more explaining the situation, and still holding to principle. To this day I have not heard from them, nor have I received my manuscript. I can only think that it sits in some obscure corner, buried under innumerable useless and unclaimed articles, gathering the mold and mildew of time, but probably worth a fortune in storage fees.

Though *Some Live by Blood Alone* had been placed in that cerebral receptacle wherein rejected and dormant ideas either take on new shape or quietly die, Mike yet remained undaunted, and was still of the opinion that I could put together a collection worthy of Avon. It was in the early part of 1959 that he told me Avon was now in the market for a supernatural anthology, and asked whether I was still interested in the project. I accepted with glee, and immediately set to work. This time a new vision sprung to mind, but I decided to limit the anthology for the most part to stories by contemporaries. It was called *Masters of the Macabre*, and included were such familiars as Ray Bradbury, Robert E. Howard, and David H. Keller. Added to this I offered C.M. Eddy, Jr.'s necrophilic grisly "The Loved Dead," Guy Endore's grim science-fantasy masterpiece "The Day of the Dragon," the macabre horror of D. Scott-Moncrieff's cannibalistic "Not for the Squeamish," and the strange, grotesque, nightmare world of the contemporary Japanese writer Edogawa Rampo's [a pseudonym for Hirai Taro, based on the Japanese pronunciation of "Edgar Allan Poe" —ed.] "The Hell of Mirrors."

The presentation was finished, turned in, and like the former, rejected. This time, it seems, I had lost out to Groff Conklin who had also been approached by the hierarchy at Avon for a collection of supernatural horror. His anthology, *Br-r-r-!*, appeared in the latter part of 1959, and contained ten tales by well known contemporaries in the field, including Ray Bradbury and David H. Keller. In all modesty, and in full awareness of Mr. Conklin's many fine contributions to the field, I honestly believe that *Masters of the Macabre* was a more interesting compilation than *Br-r-r-!* insofar as the offbeat quality and variety the story content offered, as well as the wide range of versatile moderns gathered together in one paperback volume. This time, I did not pursue the idea any further, but buried all my material in an unmarked desk drawer filled with past rejections where to this day it rests in peace.

For the next couple of years there was an absence of weird tales from the new lists of Avon, though they continued to publish science fiction from time to time and they did reissue their 1947 collection of H.P. Lovecraft, *The Lurking Fear and Other Stories* under the title of *Cry Horror!* In 1961 Mike became editor-in-chief at Avon. One of his first ventures in the realm of fantasy-horror was to reprint in a beautiful package the Orion edition of Jan Potocki's obscure but brilliant *Decameron* of Gothic horrors, *Tales from the Saragossa Manuscript*. This met with some fine sales in the New York area largely due, I believe, to the tantalizing cover and thoroughly engrossing copy. Few devoted readers of the Gothic romance knew of Potocki's sinister masterpiece until Anthony Boucher acclaimed the hardcover Orion edition. It was rather phenomenal that paperback sales reached such a vast readership outside the circle of fantasy-mystery enthusiasts.

With his ascent to editor-in-chief, Mike found it necessary to terminate his interest in the Pocket Book Bookshop. He and his family moved to outer suburbia on Long Island, thus curtailing our convivial meetings wherein grand but unrealized visions were born. But in the fall of 1961 I heard from Mike again. This was the beginning of the first concrete plans for the book which is now well under way towards completion. This time, however, I had some reservations about the assignment. Mike wanted a collection of ghost stories somewhat similar in format to the new defunct television series *Great Ghost Stories*. Frankly, I was not very keen on the idea of a traditional ghost story anthology as my first contribution to the field. Moreover, I found that the results of a Halloween promotion display of fantastic literature I had designed in a paperback bookshop last year proved that weird-horror far outsells the ghostly tale. But despite my personal feelings, I realized this was a far better opportunity than I had ever had. I knew too that the only way I could properly express my appreciation for the interest and conviction Mike yet held for me was to take the assignment and put my best effort into it.

I returned to my books, and spent the next few months reading, reading, reading. Gradually I found myself replacing selected ghost stories with tales of terror, and once more a grand vision took shape. The presentation that resulted was *A Treasury of Great Ghost Stories* — from Charles Robert Maturin to John Keir Cross. It was an anthology spanning close to two hundred years of supernatural literature. It ranged from almost legendary tales set down at the peak of the Gothic era by recognized masters of the Schauer-Romantik to contemporary pieces of nightmare-psychological horror.

Few of the stories had been previously anthologized, even though many had achieved an almost classic stature. None, to my knowledge, had ever appeared in an American paperback edition, and all observed the major themes from lore and legend that have become basic in the field. The stories were selected from magazines and publishers dedicated to printing supernatural horror which had, for many generations, thrilled a countless number of readers. And finally I had an anthology three times as large as that which was required. Then, through an involved and unrelated chain of events, I met Haywood P. Norton.

The presentation had been submitted to Avon, the contracts had been signed, and I was in the process of cutting the collection down to the 60,000 word maximum set in the editorial department, but after meeting Haywood Norton, the anthology began to take on a new shape. He offered me the first English translation of a long short story by E.T.A. Hoffmann and volunteered his enormous library of supernatural fiction, including a vast number of *Weird Tales* magazines, for my perusal. I was delighted though deluged with the newfound sources. I discovered stories I definitely wanted to use, others I would hold for substitutes or alternates, if needed. In between I had to get out a number of letters requesting reprint rights.

Meanwhile, Haywood was giving me the Hoffmann

translations piecemeal as he finished each section. I saw from the start that it would present some problems. First of all the story was too long. Secondly, it was extremely Gothic, and, consequently, subject to the shortcomings of its period. The structure was uneven, the language somewhat verbose, the exposition far too long (the actual story did not begin until page 11), and some action and motivation was contradictory. Moreover, the translation was too close to the involved Germanic sentence construction, and finally it did not seem to be the type of story Mike originally outlined for the package. And yet it was a good story containing a power and grandeur and shock quality which I felt outweighed its shortcomings. The fact that it was similar in style to their already popular reprint of *Tales from the Saragossa Manuscript*, and that this translation would represent a first English-language appearance of a work by one of the most gifted innovators in the field, gave me the impetus to set to work it into a shape and form that could be included in my package. The final consideration was that "The Forest Warden," for that was its title, is an unusual tale coming from a writer we usually associate with a lightness of style, a bizarre whimsy, and a satiric humor interjected into the most macabre plot concepts. The fevered genius of E.T.A. Hoffmann becomes manifest in what Haywood considers the finest of all his somber performances.

The work was written during the siege of Bamburg by the troops of Napoleon. During that time, Hoffmann was subject to lengthy periods of depression, and often contemplated suicide.

The tale, originally appearing as "The Forest Warden," received limited circulation in a Bamburg periodical early in 1814, and was later modified as "Ignaz Denner" and included in Hoffmann's second collection of tales, the renowned *Nachtstucke* (*Twilight Sketches*).

This first unaltered version gave stimulus to the preoccupation with the problem of evil in the early works of Dostoyevsky, and was hailed by Pushkin as being "written with a raven's quill dipped in midnight blackness." Haywood's translation is based on the first (1814) version. It has been slightly edited and condensed in its final form. The story ran some 17,000 words. The anthology was already too long, and a number of fine stories were being removed to bring it down to size. If "The Forest Warden" was to be taken at all, I knew I would have to edit it down and tighten the structure. Thus I cut a long description of a raid which did not advance the plot in any way, and digressions such as an exposition of the judicial procedures in effect in Hoffmann's day. All of the scenes essential to the basic story were kept intact, including the horrific climax which, violating strong taboos of its day, was excised from later German editions.

The theme of "The Forest Warden" concerns a diabolical quest for the elixir of life. Within there is much that is wild and beautiful, more that is spectral and grotesque.

The actual work on "The Forest Warden" consisted of three drafts. The first was Haywood's. I did a second which was returned to Haywood for corrections and revisions. This was next passed on to my agent who offered suggestions to tighten the plot, and who pointed out many overlooked redundancies. Subsequently I did a third draft, polishing, and, with much regret, cutting some 4,000 words. The job took about a month and a half to complete. It was then ready for my package which was shaping up but which bore little resemblance to my original presentation.

Up until the end I found myself making changes in the contents, and rushing out letters to clear the rights to new 'finds.' Now it is in the hands of the editorial staff at Avon. I am told it has been accepted, and will bear my title, *Fright*, and will probably be out in November or December of this year. It has been a long, involved, and often tedious job — a job I thought I could put together in a month or so, but which actually occupied a good part of my spare time these past six months. The telling of this aspect remains to be set down.

Just what is the job of the compiler, what are the problems of his task, what is the procedure, and what is a presentation? This is what I can speak of, but from manuscript to bound volume still remains a dark and wondrous mystery to me — an event I find quite marvelous. I suppose I have gone about the business end of it as a complete novice, and what I now have to relate may be regarded as anything but professional — but at any rate this is the way I went about it.

First step was the reading and selection of material. This is the most enjoyable, most time-consuming, most frustrating, most important, and never-ending task. Up until the very end I found myself considering material to be added, and forever looking for something better to replace what I already had. Obviously whether or not the presentation's accepted rests on the material submitted. It is, at the same time, frustrating because so many good stories must be rejected for one reason or another, and working towards a deadline means a vast wealth of sources must go untapped. Limitations must also be observed. The anthology could not exceed a certain number of words lest it incur great additional production costs. The stories should fall under the general aim of the book suggested by the editor. The modern mass market audience must, I had learned from previous experience, be kept in mind.

Several months passed, and after continuous reading I had a selection of fourteen stories and a good number of substitutes. The next problem to present itself occurred when I made a word count. The anthology ran far beyond the 60,000 word maximum, and this was before "The Forest Warden." Cutting began. This was based first of all on the difficulty of tracking down several authors for reprint permission. Several fine public domain stories were scrapped because of an archaic style which I felt would detract from the mass market appeal. Several stories were omitted because I just could not obtain rights, and in the end it came down to deciding what I felt would be the better of two. The rejected piece was held in my backlog of alternates. I had eight tales left after trimming the collection down to 60,000 words, and this was still before "The Forest Warden."

Meanwhile the presentation had been written, and submitted outlining the original fourteen stories. The contract had been based on this presentation, and my duties were stated. I would have to clear the rights to all the stories, make a manuscript copy of all the tales used, and have this material in their office within six months time. My presentation consisted of a table of contents, an introduction to the anthology in which my aims were set down, a synopsis of the plot of each story with (in the case of a somewhat obscure author) a little biographical information, an approximate word count of each story, and finally information concerning the copyright status of every story excluding those in public domain.

Next came the clearance of rights. This was an involved business which often required voluminous correspondence to procure the rights to one story. Letters went out to the Library of Congress (they offered no help whatsoever), the Mystery Writers of America, the Author's League, as well as to publishers, agents, and individual authors. Gradually replies came in, but many necessitated further correspondence extending this aspect beyond the deadline.

Between letters, I worked on the second and third drafts of "The Forest Warden," and began the tedious job of typing up the stories as permissions came in. I wrote another introduction to the anthology and changed its title to *Fright* since it was no longer *A Treasury of Great Ghost Stories*. After finishing an introduction to "The Forest Warden," my package was complete, and was placed in the hands of Mike de Forrest, who now controlled its ultimate destiny. Yet even at that time there was still another problem to be faced: with the inclusion of the Hoffmann piece, notwithstanding the 4,000 words cut from it, the anthology would again exceed the word maximum. It was submitted anyway because I still entertained some doubts as to the reception of "The Forest Warden". It still might be considered rather wordy and dated by the uninitiated to fit into the package. It was time, I decided, to let Avon pass editorial judgment on the selected tales.

About three weeks later I heard from Mike. The anthology had been accepted, and I was told that the editorial department was quite enthusiastic about it. Better news yet was that the translation had also been accepted, though two other tales had to go to make room for it. The front, back, and inside copy had been written, and the cover was in preparation.

As it now stands, the anthology contains six long stories of supernatural horror. It will be called *Fright*, as far as I know, and includes Hoffmann's "The Forest Warden", as well as pieces by

Sheridan Le Fanu, Seabury Quinn, and H. P. Lovecraft. I feel satisfied with the stories selected, but have some regrets that only a small handful can be used from the vast amount of material available. *Fright* is still far from the grand vision of a treasury of terror — a great paperback omnibus of tales spanning several centuries of supernatural fiction.

I am grateful for the cooperation of the Mystery Writers of America and the Author's Guild in helping me trace writers and agents for my quest for reprint permission, and I must express a word of thanks to the many who offered suggestions, opened their libraries to me, and who kindly made available so much of the material I wanted to use. Among them are Haywood P. Norton, George Townsend, Lin Carter, Sidney E. Porcelain, August Derleth, Leo Margulies, Seabury Quinn, and, of course, Mike de Forrest for making this vision a reality.

Finally, I felt a certain duty and responsibility as editor to both the longtime fan and aficionado as well as to the wholly new mass market audience that has been created with the advent of the paperback. I do not, however, feel that *Fright* offers some very fine yet not frequently reprinted tales by the very great writers of weird fiction. The longtime fan will, no doubt, recognize some of the stories collected in *Fright*, but many will discover them for the first time. If they are discovered or re-discovered with a joy tinctured with a slight, elusive dread, then I shall feel richly rewarded in my capacity as compiler.

CAPTAIN BILLY'S WHIZ GANG

BY ROY THOMAS

A long, long time ago, during what is sometimes still called, affectionately if not accurately, the "Great War," a large publishing company was born. Of course, the troops who witnessed this blessed event were doubtless unaware of it at the time — all they saw was a mimeographed joke-and-cartoon paper put out by their captain, Wilford Fawcett, and entitled somewhat flamboyantly, *Captain Billy's Whiz Bang*.

But, as the song says, it was the start of something big.

After the war Fawcett continued this paper as a professional magazine, and an occasional copy still turns up in the used-magazine shops: digest-sized, saddle-stitched, not too different in appearance from the "Army Laffs" type magazines published to this very day. Since war does not really teach us any lessons, Fawcett even kept the title *Captain Billy's Whiz Bang*, a title which passed, in a small way, into the very fabric of our culture. If you doubt this, listen carefully to the lyric of the song "Trouble" from the Broadway musical/Hollywood movie *The Music Man*.

Captain Billy's Whiz Bang was the first venture of what was later to become Fawcett Publications, publishers of movie magazines, women's service magazines, et cetera, et cetera, et cetera — and *comic books*! If the underscoring and exclamation point leave any doubts in the reader's mind, it is with the latter type of publications that this article is concerned.

It seems that even twenty years of peacetime publishing did not diminish the erstwhile solder's veneration for his humble beginnings. For, upon entering the comic book field in 1940 at a time when the mushrooming success of Superman was making the fantastically-endowed costumed hero the ideal of American youth, Fawcett's first major underwear-character was Captain Marvel, the first of the innumerable comic book captains to appear, alias Billy Batson, appearing first in *Whiz Comics #1*. And

ROY THOMAS (1940-) helped jump-start modern comic book fandom in 1961 as co-founder (with Dr. Jerry Bails) of the fanzine Alter Ego. *By 1965 his work on that magazine, combined with letters to editors, led to a job offer in the comics industry, and he turned his back on a graduate fellowship in foreign relations at George Washington University to accept it. He became a writer and often editor in the field -- from 1965-80 exclusively for Marvel, from 1981-86 under contract to DC, and since the latter date as a freelancer for those two companies and others. Thomas was editor-in-chief of Marvel Comics from 1972-74, and has been particularly associated with major runs on such comics titles as* The Avengers, The X-Men, Conan the Barbarian, The Savage Sword of Conan, The Invaders, Dr. Strange, Daredevil, All-Star Squadron, *and* Infinity Inc. *He currently resides on a country spread in South Carolina with his wife Dann, and, while still keeping his hand in as a comics writer, spends most of his time editing a revived, historically-oriented edition of Alter Ego.*

does it take a gypsy mind-reader to tell that almost coincident with this he also started a magazine called *Slam-Bang Comics?* Then, having run out of titles reminiscent of his career as a military leader, Fawcett came up with, almost at the same time, a third comic book called *Master Comics.* Or had he?

Slam Bang Comics, with a bunch of nondescript characters headed by a hero named Diamond Jack, soon perished, but it would appear that the others were successes from the beginning, especially *Whiz* with Captain Marvel. At least National Comics thought so, for they immediately launched suit against Fawcett for creating a "direct imitation" of their Man of Steel. The suit lasted a dozen years without ever reaching the final trial stage and was eventually settled out of court with Fawcett's agreement to cease publication of comics featuring the members of the Marvel Family (something it was doubtless ready to do by 1953 anyhow) — but that's another comic-book article.

At any rate, during this period of slightly more than a dozen years, Fawcett was the #2 publisher of comics, right behind National in most ways and ahead in others. (*Captain Marvel Adventures*, for example, had a circulation in excess of 2,000,000 copies each month at its peak, versus *Superman*'s all-time high in the neighborhood of 1,500,000.) Of course, next to the Big Red Cheese and the other members of the Marvel Family (Junior and Mary, primarily, although there were others including Uncle Marvel, Hoppy the Marvel Bunny, Black Adam (a villain), Levram (another), the Lieutenants Marvel, and Steamboat Willy, De Harlem Marvel, the rest of the Fawcett characters have a tendency to sink into relative insignificance, but the fact remains that a few of them were pretty darned good, and the rest could at least hold their own with some of National's lesser features like Mr. Terrific and others. And so, ignoring for the most part the Marvels, let's take a look at some of the super-doers who composed the second string of *Captain Billy's Whiz Gang.*

Casting aside the fact that all of the features to be discussed would fall into the general category of super or costume-heroes, it would seem that, for purposes of identification, three distinct if occasionally overlapping groups can be differentiated.

First of these would be the category of "Crime Fighters." Virtually *all* of the *National* super-doers would have fit under the classification, which I distinguish from the second, that of "War-Heroes," costume heroes whose popularity and activities rested largely if not solely on their wartime doings. A third and relatively minor group would be that of the "Magicians," who are distinguishable from the other two not so much by purpose as by methods of action.

Most popular of the crime fighters not connected by nature to the war probably was Bulletman, who first appeared in *Nickel Comics #1*, dated May 17, 1940 (only a few months after the February 1940 debut of the Cheese himself). Yep, you read right: this mag cost a nickel, for which you got 36 pages (the same number you get today for 12 cents) on long-wearing paper with no advertising except one or two house-ads and a back-cover ad for *Mechanix Illustrated*, a house-ad itself as *MI* was, as it still is, a Fawcett Publication. Sounds dreamy, don't it?

The first issue of this primarily experimental comic, as I said, featured Bulletman, "scientific marvel of the age, whose super-powerful brain and perfectly-trained body enable him to overcome all physical obstacles in waging his tireless battles against the forces of evil," a description which could have fit any number of underwear boys in the early '40's.

His origin, done rather primitively both artistically and story-wise — for example, the captions were printed at the bottom of the panel about half the time and rarely belonged there logically — was pretty typical, too. Pat Barr, "fearless police sergeant," is ruthlessly gunned down by mobsters, leaving his young son Jim an orphan. The boy, waiting impatiently for the day when he can don a lawman's uniform, studies criminology and ballistics like a fiend, to the exclusion of more normal boyhood activities. He even works for a long time on "a crime cure" intended to cleanse the human body of all germs and thereby, in some mystic way, to rehabilitate even sworn criminals. ("Crime is a disease"?)

However, when Jim goes to take the entrance examination, he finds that years in the college laboratory have taken their

toll. The first panel on page 2 shows him jauntily entering the police department door; in the second he comes out, dejectedly mumbling:

"I've failed. Too short ... too skinny ... bad marksmanship ... This would have broken Dad's heart if he'd lived."

However, Jim's laboratory training stands him in good stead, for he is soon working as a civilian police laboratory criminologist, living up to his childhood nickname of "Bullet Barr" with his work in ballistics.

Meanwhile, of course, he has not abandoned his great desire to perfect a "crime-cure," and, thinking that at last he has developed one, he tries it on himself to test its effects. Predictably as hell, he wakes up the next morning with splitting pajamas due to remarkably accelerated growth and bulging muscles. He tosses his bed around and knocks a hole in the wall to celebrate. Then, lest his new stature attract undue notice, he goes out and buys a new wardrobe of oversized clothing and goes to work.

Naturally, nobody notices the fact that he has grown several inches in height and many beefy pounds in weight overnight. And, also naturally, this very morning a gangster is cornered at his impregnable hideout. A newspaper headline blaring "Do We Need a New Robin Hood?" sets his mental processes working and in no time at all, what with his accelerated brain power, he designs a bullet-shaped Gravity Regulator Helmet which enables him to fly. At the same time he "salvages a costume that will strike fear to evil-doers," so the book says — it looks pretty harmless to me, unless crooks are afraid of pin-headed crime fighters — and zooms off.

In no time at all Bulletman has captured the cornered killer and a few other assorted hoodlums and has achieved great fame. One newspaper even offers a $1000 reward for a photo of Bulletman, which Jim mails to them with instructions to send the money to the police pension fund. The newspaper does not print the picture, however, so Bulletman decides to investigate. What does he find? "Don't miss the next great issue of *Nickel Comics*," but I do miss it, and if anyone has *Nickel Comics* #2 and will tell me what Bulletman found, I will be mightily grateful. For kids in 1940, however, it wasn't much of a wait, considering the fact that the short-lived mag came out every other Friday (with never-realized plans to come out *every* Friday). Even biweekly, it was the greatest frequency any comic ever had, tied later for a short time by the hugely popular *Captain Marvel Adventures*.

Actually, after a somewhat mediocre beginning, Bulletman turned out to be a pretty good feature, especially when the art was taken over by Mac Raboy. Bulletman's costume, which originally consisted of a yellow neckerchief, a tight red shirt slit to the belt to show off his bulging chest, and yellow riding-pants plus boots … was modified somewhat (whether for the better or not I leave a moot point): the gravity helmet was improved so that it now attracted bullets harmlessly that would otherwise have struck the mighty but not impregnable Jim, as well as enabling him to fly. And, as happened so often in those days (and these), he picked up a partner in his Crusade Against Crime. This was his longtime girlfriend, Susan Kent, daughter of the police chief, natch — who became Bulletgirl soon after the feature began and continued in the series until its demise, giving the strip, I always thought, a strong resemblance to the old Hawkman feature in *Flash Comics*.

Later on — much later on — Bulletman and Bulletgirl were joined by a little boy in a costume party Bulletman suit, whom they humored in a few adventures … and even, for a time, by a Bulletdog, complete with Gravity Collar. But these were minor developments and mentioned only for the record.

When the apparently impractical dream of *Nickel Comics* folded, Bulletman survived by moving into *Master Comics*, where he soon proved popular enough to earn (as did an astonishingly large number of those early Fawcett heroes) his own comic, the first issue of *Bulletman*, appearing in 1941, only a year after that first swig of the supposed crime-cure. With its logo printed in silvery metallic ink, a beautiful Raboy cover and excellent interior artwork, this first issue is today a rarely seen mouthwatering collector's item.

In 1941 its sixty-eight pages cost exactly one thin dime, and you could have as many copies as you could lug home from the newsstand, as long as your dimes held out. Sob!

Like most superheroes of that day, Bulletman fought a large array of unusual criminals. In *Bulletman #1*, for example, the crime-buster battled a costumed crook named the Black Spider, a monkey-faced villain known as Dr. Mood, and a nameless but terrifying giant in excess of twenty feet tall. Also, in one later story foreshadowing the *Injustice Society* stories in *All-Star Comics*, he and Bulletgirl fought three of their old enemies who had combined into a "Revenge Syndicate." There was the Weeper, who always cried before killing his victims; the Black Rat, a super strong guy who in costume looked just like a rodent; and the Murder Prophet, who always foretold evil and then made his prophecies come true. These three, before pulling a crime, would always throw dice to see which of them would be the leader for that evening's crime, but the Flying Detectives brought them to an untimely end in a flaming building. Small loss.

Bulletman's switch into *Master Comics* came at an opportune time for that magazine. It, like *Nickel*, had started off in an experimental format. Priced at 15 cents, *Master* was billed as the "World's Biggest Comic Book" (sic) and, in one sense at least, it definitely was! Though its 52 pages were somewhat fewer than the ordinary 68 of that glorious day, the *size* of the pages was roughly the same as that of today's *Life* magazine. Back in those halcyon pre-WWII days not only Fawcett but Fiction House as well could put out tabloid-size comic books; but whereas the primeval jumbo-size *Jumbo Comics* had only one-color printing, *Master* was all in color for a dime-and-a-nickel ... shortly cut to a mere dime for the giant *Master*.

Begun as a monthly, *Master* featured for a short time a thoroughgoing Superman imitator called Master Man, who was consistently if immodestly billed as "the world's greatest hero." Originally as skinny kid as young "Bullet" Barr had been, he was given some magic capsules by a "wise old doctor" and grew up into the strongest man on earth. He wore a sort of page-boy costume, with blue shirt and right red pants, and built himself a lofty castle of solid rock on the highest mountain peak in the world. From there, it says here, he could see all the evil in the world and "race to destroy it instantly."

Therein lies an interesting point about these Fawcett heroes — very few of them could fly. Bulletman could, of course, but that was by means of a mechanical device, albeit a marvelous and compact one — the Gravity Helmet. But Master Man (in imitation of the earliest days of Superman and Captain Marvel) and the rest of Fawcett's non-Marvels could not. Master Man *could* run like the devil, though, and in the first seven-page story he outran raging winds, a speeding automobile, and a falling bomb. In virtually every way he was like D.C.'s Superman, so National sued *him, too*, for once perhaps with more justification than that of commercial greed, and Fawcett dropped him at once. I doubt that he had anything near the potential of Captain Marvel, anyway.

At about this time, *Master* became a regular-sized comic and, after featuring for a while a hero named Minute Man (to whom we shall come in due course), began to cover-feature the recently-created Captain Marvel Jr., with unsurpassed drawing by our friend Raboy. So Bulletman had to wait for his own comic to receive that particular type of glory. *Bulletman* lasted well into the middle '40s, much longer than most of Fawcett's non-Marvel magazines about a single character.

Mr. Scarlet, of the soon-to-follow *Wow Comics*, was as much an imitation of the early Batman as Master Man was of Superman. An attorney in his secret identity (when he worked, which was far from always), this mustached crime fighter wore a suit that contained enough red to wake up John Birch himself, though in later days some silver trimming was added; he had no real super powers, and like the early Batman also, used a gun when the occasion demanded. Of course he picked up a kid partner, Pinky, in *Wow #4*.

As was pointed out in a recent issue of *Comic Art*, Mr. Scarlet was featured often in several tales per issue of *Wow* during its early days, thus coming about as close to obtaining his own comic as a costume-hero can come without actually achieving this goal.

The inclusion of Mary Marvel as a regular feature drove him off the cover, however, and limited him to one story per issue. Due to the excellent coverage of the Crimson Crusader of Justice in the *Comic Art* article, I'll move on to characters who have received less attention.

Two costume-heroes worth mentioning briefly under the admittedly imprecise heading of "Crime Fighters" are the Devil's Dagger and the Hunchback. The former was another Batman type, but wore a black tux and half-mask, and top hat, and, by utilizing a lethal dagger as well as a not-infrequent pistol, was featured in the first few issues of the giant *Master*.

More interesting though not much longer-lived was the Hunchback, who in actuality was a rather handsome young man who donned a grotesque disguise to frighten criminals, whom he evidently assumed to be quite superstitious. (Remember Bulletman above? This all harks back, I suppose, to that crazy lost bat that fluttered in Bruce Wayne's window one moonless night...). The Hunchback wore a set of green tights, devoid of ornament, and he either donned a fright-wig or arranged his otherwise immaculate hair into the semblance of one, and carried a gnarled T-shaped crutch. With the crutch he battered criminals, vaulted walls, and on at least one occasion deflected a knife hurled at himself so that it was imbedded — fatally — in the throat of a criminal. In another story the Hunchback traced a criminal conspiracy, leaving corpses scattered in his wake, to the police commissioner himself. To dispose of the master criminal he merely seized him by the throat and, with detailed pictorial representation, I assure you, throttled the life out of him. A brutal, fascinating mutation of the costume-hero.

One character who could undoubtedly be mentioned under either this or the ensuing category of "War-Heroes" is the quite popular Captain Midnight. Originating in a Dell comic entitled *The Funnies* in the late '30s, he was a World War I aviator, a *real* captain code-named Midnight for a special mission. After the war he came out of retirement, not as a real costume-hero, but just as an adventurous aviator.

Soon the hero of a popular and long-lasting radio series as well as a movie serial, he was picked up by Fawcett in 1942 and revitalized into a costume-hero wearing a modified aviator's suit in red, a purple-blue helmet with goggles that doubled as a mask, and the symbol of a winged clock-face on his manly chest. Still accompanied by his Secret Squadron, and still basically an aviator, Cap cut quite a formidable figure, whether dealing with criminals, or, as he often did during the days of World War II, spies.

Fawcett revised his origin in the first issue of *Captain Midnight*. He started off with his own comic book, without first sharing the pages of a *Whiz/Wow/Master* type variety comic with other characters, as most Fawcett heroes did. In his alter ego (whoops) of Captain Albright, famed inventor, he had decided to retire from the rigors of crime fighting, doing good for his fellow man as a scientist instead. However, with the rise of the Axis menace, he decided once again to become Captain Midnight, using his inventive powers personally against the enemies of the nation. The first issue even features a cover depicting Captain Marvel himself welcoming Captain Midnight into the fold.

In the actual comeback story, Albright is kidnapped because of a new invention of his which the Nazis want to get their mail-clad hands on, but, left alone in a locked room, he changes into Captain Midnight and, climbing into the next room in typical daring manner, mops up the enemy agents.

One of the most fantastic and appealing things about the comic book character Captain Midnight was the web-like projections between his arms and his sides ... or rather, presumably, the arms and sides of his costume. Called gliderchutes, these enable him to parachute at will from planes or buildings without fear of injury. What I always wondered was, what happened to them when Cap wasn't using them? They just seemed to disappear: now you see 'em now you don't. But anyway, the thought of being able to glide around like a flying squirrel always fascinated me. Wheeeee...

After the war, *Captain Midnight* lasted longer than most of the Fawcett heroes having a basis in the war, probably due largely to the continuing popularity of his radio show. With the war over, the comic book followed ambivalent paths. Midnight had always fought criminals, and he continued to do so in an equal proportion of the stories. In place of the percentage formerly devoted to war, there was now a science fiction trend, with fantastic inventions, invaders from outer space, and all the rest of that crazy Buck Rogers stuff.

Even with the death of the comic, *Captain Midnight* has hardly been forgotten. A rarity and a sport in the comics industry, *Captain Midnight* was owned, not by a publisher, but by the Wander Company, the manufacturers of Ovaltine. Ovaltine had sponsored the long-lived *Captain Midnight* radio series, and Ovaltine now sponsored a new television series of Captain Midnight adventures. (If you haven't seen it as such, reruns are still occasionally telecast, under the name "Jet Jackson" in deference to Ovaltine's proprietary interest in the name "Captain Midnight.")

From the transitional figure of Captain Midnight it is only a short step (from red to green, to be exact) to another popular Fawcett hero, Spy Smasher. These two heroes were similar in a great many ways.

Actually, when he started out as a supporting hero in *Whiz #1*, Spy Smasher wore a more-or-less standard aviator's suit of brown, decorated with a red diamond on the chest (a symbol never explained in all the years it was used), and a brown helmet-and-goggles, the goggles again serving as a mask as did Captain Midnight's. As a gimmick in the early issues, Spy Smasher's face was usually hidden or simply colored in black so that his facial features — if you can call them that, considering the inferior artwork in the early tales — were unseen. The reader was challenged at the end of some stories to guess the secret identity of Spy Smasher. However, unlike the later Sparkman who used the same gimmick with *three* possible secret identitites, Spy Smasher had only *one* — that of Alan Armstrong, one of the apparently unending supply of millionaire playboys who during World War II aided the war effort as costume heroes.

Within a few issues, Spy Smasher's basic costume was changed from brown to the more colorful green (no explanation in the story), and it was obvious to all concerned — if indeed it had ever been a secret — that Alan Armstrong was the mystery man. Obvious to all except the ever-present fiancée and potential father-in-law and the other characters in the strip, that is. Also in 1941, but *before* the costume change, Spy Smasher gained his own magazine, which he kept for a few short issues. A new and much better artist was brought in and the stories rose above the pitiful (even for comic books) level of the 1940 *Whiz* stories.

Spy Smasher remained in *Whiz* until the end of the war, at which time, under the mistaken assumption that there were no more spies to be smashed, he abandoned his costume for a trenchcoat and became a private detective called Crime Smasher. He didn't last long enough for anybody to count the issues, but the sad downfall of Alan Armstrong illustrated a point particularly noticeable in these Fawcett "War-Heroes" (and those of their publishers, for that matter). Almost without exception these characters died off within a short time after the end of World War II. Even the mighty Captain Americn of the Timely group switched to a weird story comic for a short time and then disappeared altogether. It was as if the Holocaust in the 1940s produced the need for this type of heroes, and they appeared in abundance, but, with the end of hostilities, they had no worlds left to conquer (or defend). Fighting crooks alone, perhaps, did not generate as much excitement, so that the heroes that were military in nature began to die off.

Of course, this point can be stretched to excess, as by the end of the '40s *most* of the superheroes were dead or dying and the comic book business itself had fallen off considerably due to various factors, but still it's worth wondering about. *During* the war Spy Smasher, for instance, had fought a fabulous array of Jap and Nazi villains, most notable of whom was his virtual antithesis, a stout little German named America Smasher, but *after* the war — *nothing.*

Probably the most colorful of Fawcett's various warlords was Minute Man who, when danger called, wrapped an American flag around himself — at least, that's how his rather baggy costume always looked to me — and was fit as a fiddle and ready for war.

Even more than Spy Smasher, who had at least a gyrosub for flying to other continents in a hurry. You never heard of a gyrosub? It was a sort of combination tank/submarine/vtol aircraft. Now you know. Minute Man was a hero who fought spies and enemy agents on the home front. Though ostensibly a private in the U.S. Army (he went to CCS and made lieutenant later on) he always found the opportunity during any emergency to duck behind the nearest latrine and change into a slimmed-down version of Captain America. For a short time during his adventures in *Master Comics* he fought crime-and-spies without a mask, somehow preserving his secret identity nonetheless, but soon after he got his own short-lived comic he donned a small half-mask as a sop to the comic-reading masses.

Unlike that of some of the other strips, the artwork on the series was generally fairly good — or, if not that, at least somewhat *dramatic*. Most of the stories of Minute Man in *Master* were done by Phil Bard, whose work is at least mildly reminiscent of that done by Simon and Kirby around the same time. There were some eye-arresting villains, too, including some vampires and an unexplained phenomenon called the Skeleton, a ten-foot Nazi monster which somehow managed to be one of the creepiest villains I ever encountered in a comic book.

In connection with Minute Man, a few words might be said about one great difference between National and Fawcett in handling their stables of super-doers. Unlike the D.C. group, Fawcett featured a large number of cross-over stories in which two or three of its heroes would get together for an adventure of especial interest. For example, a Nazi-hypnotized Spy Smasher battled for months with Captain Marvel in the early WHIZ issues; Bulletgirl appeared in a story in *Mary Marvel #8*; Spy Smasher and Captain Midnight teamed up at least once in *America's Greatest Comics*, Fawcett's fat 15 cent answer to DC's *World's Finest Comics*. One of the best of these cross-over stories occurred in *Master Comics #41*.

As the tale opens, the members of the "Crime Crusaders Club" — Captain Marvel Jr., Minute Man, Bulletman & Bulletgirl — all regulars in *Master* — are having a meeting when Junior discovers that the flag-draped one is lost in thought, looking unhappy and perplexed. Upon questioning, it is revealed that Minute Man is in the midst of a bond sale campaign and that "everyone in the country has contributed with the exception of *one* class" ... the criminal class. So Minute Man, seizing upon an accidental suggestion of Captain Marvel Jr., decides upon a treasure hunt of sorts to raise the money he feels hoodlums should pay to the war effort.

Soon afterward, pamphlets are distributed by the other Crusaders saying that Minute Man is selling chances on himself: "Buy a Bond and Get a Shot at Minute Man!" Gathering in an abandoned amusement park, as stipulated, the criminals hand over their guns to Bulletman and Bulletgirl, having been previously promised full immunity from arrest till midnight. To raise additional funds, the Flying Detectives sell back the crooks' guns for $100 apiece, with bullets similarly priced.

The result is a rather interesting chase, with one crook attempting to cheat by using a hand grenade he has smuggled past Bulletman. However, it is caught in mid-air and exploded harmlessly by Junior. Attempting to flee the area in a racer, Minute Man himself crashes into a road-barricade set up beforehand by the wily criminals, and is knocked unconscious. As they line up to shoot the unmoving figure, however, a mysterious cloaked and monocled Nazi with a thick accent shows up and declares that he intends to take Minute Man to Berlin with him. While he points a loaded pistol at the crooks, Minute Man escapes in an airplane, only to be shot down by the hoodlums, who steal their own aircraft from a nearby base and give pursuit.

Parachuting into some construction works, Minute Man figures he can escape before the crooks touch ground, but becomes hung up and helpless. The cloaked Nazi approaches and levels a gun at him — and then turns out to be his old friend Bulletman in disguise.

As the flying crime-buster helps the entangled Minute Man get free, the latter inquires of him as to their exact whereabouts.

"Why, we're on the outskirts of Weston, Pennsylvania," replies Bulletman.

"Swell, I made it!" cries an exalted ultra-patriot as he bolts away. "I'm going to spring my trap!"

"I don't understand" queries a puzzled Bulletman, "It's not midnight yet. Aren't you going to keep your word?" (Comic book characters are very moral.)

"Only an hour left till midnight!" come drifting the cries of the crooks, who are still in hot pursuit. Suddenly, out of nowhere, Minute Man comes rushing at them. Naturally, mere tommy-guns cannot stand against his mighty fists, and the hoods are soon all neatly confined in the jaws of a friendly steam shovel. "Yer a liar!" they cry as one man to a disappointed-looking hero who explains that, to the contrary, he has merely led them eastward into a different time zone. It *is* midnight in Weston, Pennsylvania.

Chalk up $100,000 for the war bond drive, courtesy of Minute Man. And as a small lagniappe of irony, the readers knew that Minute Man's secret identity is Private Jack ... Weston!

Minute Man presents something of a paradoxical figure among these heroes. Evidently popular enough to have deserved for a short time his own comic as well as a featured spot and a number of cover-shots in *Master Comics*, he perished before the end of the war. Outlasting him by some years were a couple of relatively minor war-types from *Wow Comics*, Phantom Eagle and Commando Yank. The latter was a gray-and-blue clad eager-beaver of the Spy Smasher type, except that most of his fighting was done abroad. His secret identity was Chase Yale, war correspondent (and, after the war ended and until his demise, a "roving telecaster").

Quite similar in some ways was a character even closer to the Captain Midnight type, Phantom Eagle. In his regular identity of "young Mickey Malone," the baby-faced soldier whom his sergeant constantly refers to as "too young to fly," he spends most of his time wiping the wings of the airplanes on the English base where he is stationed. However, in his spare time, he has built his own secret fighter plane – a not inconsiderable feat, when you stop and think about it – and has started a career fighting Nazis on his own.

Along the way he picks up a sort of Boy Commandos of the air, a group of youngsters from various Nazi-occupied countries who *all* have their own private warplanes and who, under the command of Mickey, go forth to battle the Nazis under the aegis of the Phoenix Squadron, so named in the confident expectation that their respective homelands will one day rise from the ashes of German occupation. The Phoenix Squadron used to disappear at the end of each story, when their continued presence might prove embarrassing for Mickey. By the way, isn't it funny how none of these enlisted costume-heroes ever got arrested for going AWOL? Steve (Captain America) Rogers and his pal Bucky used to get guardhouse duties galore, but Jack Weston, Mickey Malone … never!

At any rate, in his orange grease-monkey suit with an eagle on the front, Phantom Eagle flew his own raids into Nazi territory, and whenever he flew over, Mickey Malone's Sergeant Flogg was very stern and disapproving. "It ain't good for morale to have one guy bargin' off by himself that way," Flogg grumbled, "but he sure gives those Nazis a headache." Not too articulate, but accurate. After the raid, natch, Flogg usually questioned Malone as to his recent whereabouts and always received the pat answer: "Just catching up on some sleep, Sarge. Anything exciting happen this afternoon?"

After the War the Phantom Eagle more or less abandoned his Mickey Malone identity altogether, and, under the auspices of a private international airline, became a sort of "guardian of the airways," as the subtitle of the strip now read. He also kept up a sporadic hunt for a legendary Golden Chalice on which was engraved the Formula for Peace. He still looked all of fifteen, too; I'm surprised no one ever asked to see his pilot's license. He lasted (as did Commando Yank) into 1947 or so by converting to civilian activities, but there was a noticeable lack of vitality in both these features after the war ended and the editorial stock of war stories (cleverly published as "secret war archives") were used up.

Curiously, one of Fawcett's most interesting "War-Hero" types was not even invented until 1944. In May of that year, in *Captain Marvel Adventures #35*, a young army private named Pep Pepper, during an exhibition boxing match in which the Big Red Cheese is unable to lay a super-powerful hand on his dogface opponent, demonstrates his ability to read minds. He then turns briskly around and slugs Major Stuff, his commanding officer, announcing that his superior officer is actually a Nazi spy. When the real Major shows up, Pepper's wild tale is credited. And so when he announces that he also has "radar vision" (in addition to being able to read minds, which is how he was able to avoid all Captain Marvel's blows) which allows him to see over long distances, Captain Marvel is well ready to believe his statement that a super-missile has just been launched toward them by the Germans so that the Cheese is able to fly and intercept the missile.

Such a talent is naturally invaluable to the Allies, and Pepper is soon discharged from the army and flown by Captain Marvel to a secret meeting-room where he is ushered into a dark room containing the leaders of the Allied nations. Roosevelt, who is present with Stalin, Churchill, and Chiang Kai-shek, explains that the darkness is necessary so that Pepper cannot read their minds and appoints Pepper the vanguard member of an international police force which is to maintain peace after the war ends. Until then he is to work unofficially under the code name of "Radar."

Immediately thereafter the Radar series began in *Master Comics*, more or less replacing the now defunct Minute Man. Ordinarily wearing a green plaid trench coat and an artificial mustache, Pep Pepper had only to take off the lip spinach and reverse his coat to white-side-out and, *presto*, he was Radar, the International Policeman. Now that, by gosh, is a secret identity if I ever saw one, unmatched until the very recent "Mystery of the Jaguar's Missing Mustache."

Captain Marvel appeared in Radar's first story in *Master* to give the new hero a briefing (and to try to see if his own popularity would rub off, or at least assure the new feature a first reading), but Radar soon proved that he needed no help and for the next couple of years he was on his own. When Fawcett started a short lived comic book entitled *Comics Novel* in 1947, the first issue starred Radar in a well-written, feature-length battle with a sinister-looking villain named Anarcho, Dictator of Death. A full fledged Radar comic never emerged, however. The recent *John Force, Magic Agent* comic put out by the American Comics Group was a conscious or unconscious copy of Radar, but it has evidently gone to an early and apparently deserving grave.

Significant among the several magicians which Fawcett carried over the years – and proportionately there were a fair number of them – was Ibis the Invincible, who appeared in *Whiz #1* and all issues thereafter and who, like so many others, had his own comic for a short time in the early 1940s.

For the origin of the this unusual hero, we are taken to about the year 2000 BC, and to Egypt, where the new ruler, known affectionately as the Black Pharaoh, wants as his bride a luscious princess named Taia, who, however, is "under the protection of Osiris, the god of justice." To combat this state of affairs, the Pharaoh summons a master of black magic to conjure up Set, Egyptian god of darkness, who for his part then gives the Pharaoh control over a number of demons which are then used to turn Egypt – "which had formerly been a land of free men," we are informed with more fervency than historical accuracy – into a state of slaves. The good Prince Ibis objects and is imprisoned for his pains, but escapes when he obtains the mystical Ibistick, a sort of magic wand with a silly-looking bird (that's an ibis) represented on it. The demons and the Black Pharaoh are defeated but in the battle the lovely Taia, who is also the beloved of Ibis, is fatally wounded by an arrow, or so it seems at the time.

Grief-stricken, Ibis orders the Ibistick to kill him also, only to find out that the wand can never be used to harm him. As it turns out, this prevents a tragedy of coincidence, for Taia has only been put to sleep for a mere 4000 years by the potion on the arrow. So faithful Ibis uses his super-sparkler to do the same to himself, so that he and the princess awaken at the same time – 1940 – though in different lands due to some meddling archeologists.

After this beginning, which has overtones of *Romeo and Juliet*, the Mummy movies, and Hawkman, Ibis turned out to be a pretty good and durable character. Attired during the early years in a black suit and red turban, he later added a purple cloak (which he still later lost as the strip neared its end). He survived longer than most Fawcett heroes, possibly because of the increased interest in horror comics around 1953. In fact, he survived the Fawcett line altogether, being sold along with a few others to Charlton Publications, who featured Ibis for a time in a comic book called *Danger and Adventure*. Though ogres, witches, *et al* (that *et al* also includes further encounters with various Egyptian deities, Charon and various demons) appeared throughout the career of Ibis, these tales became noticeably more gory and monster-filled in later days.

One Ibis story in particular I remember as having made a deep impression on me at about the age of seven or eight. It concerned a demonic character who was the personification of the fear that mankind has in all ages felt of darkness, and who resembled a skeleton in priestly robes with a cowl over its head. The story began with this Fear killing a frightened caveman in the distant past, and ended in grisly fight between the creatures of man's own imaginings and Ibis the Invincible. When the Egyptian prince managed to utilize the Ibistick to destroy the horror he observe, "Now mankind need never live in fear of darkness again," I recall a complete sympathy and identification that I never felt with *any* character in *any* form of literature. Such stories were the exception, of course, but they did exist.

The other magicians were, by and large, an uninspiring lot when compared to the magnificent Ibis. Warlock the Wizard in *Nickel Comics* was somewhat interesting, though, accompanied by a raven named Hugin which perched on his shoulder. He possessed his own magic wand, called the Golden hand, which resembled a fist-shaped popsicle and which, growing to gigantic size when Warlock spoke the magic word "Abraxas," would carry out the wizard's command by grabbing beautiful girls away from evil ogres and such like. He died with *Nickel*.

Others were a monocled magician named El Carim (spell it backwards) in the bedsheet *Master Comics* and Balbo, the boy magician. There was also Atom Blake, Boy Wizard, but he was primarily a precocious inventor so he doesn't count.

As time went on, the preponderance of costume-heroes in comics of the Fawcett line, as in others, went. There were a number of good characters who didn't fit into this category. Nyoka the Jungle Girl, straight from the Saturday matinee, was one of the most famous ones; Lance O'Casey was a fair-to-middling high-seas adventurer for a long time in *Whiz*; the Companions Three were not bad as general adventurers and Captain Venture was a fairly promising semi-costume hero who somehow aborted after the earliest issues of *Wow*. Fawcett's western heroes make a complete – and large – category themselves, the best and longest-running title being Golden Arrow, the Robin Hood of the West, for many years in *Whiz Comics* and for a while in *Golden Arrow Comics*.

One excellent adventure strip was Doctor Voodoo, a time-travel high-adventure serial beautifully drawn by Raboy in *Whiz* using the no balloons style developed by Hal Foster and Alex Raymond for Prince Valiant and Flash Gordon.

Perhaps it is significant, however, that as ghost stories, teenagers, and war tales filled the pages of Fawcett comics prior to the decision to drop all comics along with the Marvel Family Group, the last adventurer-hero to be introduced by Fawcett was Captain Video, an offspring of television, the medium which many blame for the decline in the comic-book business.

At any rate, in 1953 the last of Captain Billy's Whiz Gang died. They had not been totally without influence, however, nor will they soon be forgotten. There had been movie serials based on Captain Marvel, Spy Smasher, and Captain Midnight; the last named still had a full life on television ahead of him. The Big Red Cheese in particular had enjoyed an immense popularity which had manifested itself in T-shirts and wristwatches (*I* had one and it worked beautifully – I wish I still had it!) and other paraphernalia. And, to quote a letter from *Xero* publisher Dick Lupoff, received in the course of preparing this article:

"Did you know that Fawcett is now publishing Dennis the

Menace? *It ain't much, but at least it's a Fawcett comic and ... someday ... who knows?"*

Who knows, indeed?

UNTITLED, Steve Stiles

EPISTOLARY INTERCOURSE #9

CONDUCTED BY PAT LUPOFF

L. & N. SHAW

Skimming through the latest *Xero*, I chanced upon Fred Pohl's remark re: *A Case of Conscience* that "it went through three editors before *If* had the wit to buy it." In the interest of Truth, I hereby point out that my husband, your friend and fandom's Grand Old Man was editor of *If* and that it was *he*, Larry Shaw, in person, who "had the wit to buy it." Not without, I might add, some objection by his boss James Quinn, who never *did* figure out what the story was about. It was not some faceless crew at *If* at all.
— Noreen

Up till now I thought only H.L. Gold and Lester del Rey had seen *A Case of Conscience* before me (and that Lester had the wit to want it after all ... but I *had* it by then). I wonder who the third editor was.
— Larry

JOHN BAXTER

Interesting cover, as usual, though I think it is a trifle inferior to that on number *8*. Perhaps the choice of color had something to do with it. Bhob's previous effort was visually surprising in two ways: the stripes of green and yellow gave one the horrible illusion of having one's eyes torn out by the roots, and the actual choice of color was also designed to give the maximum possible contrast. The cover on *9* certainly has the brilliant color, but the design is quite mundane when compared with the previous one.

The more letters I read from Fred Pohl, the more irritated I get with the man and his magazine. Both the letters and the magazine seem to rely on a modified version of the big lie technique; i.e., if you say something often enough, loud enough and publicly enough, everybody who hears it will start to believe it is the truth. Lately, in various fanzines, I've heard Fred Pohl claim that editors aren't supposed to teach writers their business, that good science fiction always sells, that *Galaxy* is Better than Ever, that, in general, everybody is wrong except Fred Pohl. The terrible part of the campaign is that there is no way of fighting the man. Like all editors, he controls his readership almost absolutely. He refuses to hold himself responsible to his readers for editorial policy, and so you just have to sit back and bear it, or at the very least exercise your rather futile right of not buying his magazine.

Almost every phrase in Pohl's letter is a distortion of some kind. "Good sf always sells" — what is Pohl's definition of good? If *Galaxy* is any indication, it means anything that resembles what this magazine has been printing for the last three or four years. Does the fact that a story is not written in the *Galaxy* style make it bad? Apparently Pohl thinks so. To claim the all good sf is being published is nonsense. Brian Aldiss wrote a rather avant-garde novel called *A Garden With Figures* and submitted it to three publishers. All turned it down. John Phillifent, a British pro, wrote a novel and sent it to *Analog*. Campbell refused to buy it unless a psi gimmick was written in. Lee Harding, another local writer like myself who sells to the British magazines, wrote a fine short novel that examined the mentality of After the Bomb survivors. Ted Carnell of *New Worlds* turned it down — not because it was poorly written (Lee had made nine consecutive sales immediately before this one) but because the ending was not "upbeat," i.e., happy.

These are just cases from my own personal experience. You only have to look at the field to realize that there must be many others. If all good sf is published, why is James Blish selling historical novels to Faber and Faber, the British publishers? Why is Ted Sturgeon doing movie script novelizations? As for the marvelous stuff that Pohl is allegedly publishing in his magazines, the Bradbury yarn he mentions is a poor rewrite of an old TV script I saw on *Alfred Hitchcock Presents* last year, the Vance novel is a short story blown up with some of the most inept padding I've ever seen in sf, and the Heinlein is either a desperation job or a yarn written as a favor to Pohl.

HARRY WARNER, JR.

Who says that fans can't adapt? Not too long ago I would have broken into a cold sweat at the receipt of a 100-page fanzine, doubting the evidence of my eyes and fearing that I'd never find time to read it. But I've been conditioned quickly by such experiences as Bill Donaho's creations and the 100th FAPA mailing, and I accept this latest issue of *Xero* as one of the more normal manifestations of nature, whizzing right through the pleasant job of reading and commenting on it within a week of receipt.

Good science fiction always sells? I can think of two types of exception to Fred's statement. The first group would consist of the *New Adam*s in science fiction's history, good stories that did not sell in the usual sense, but were put into print after the writer's death because of the affection of friends or the interest that the demise stirred up among readers. The obvious point here is that it's not likely that any writer will produce more than one good science fiction story in this category, and will turn to other types of fiction when he finds he must depend on possible posthumous recognition for the stories. The other group would consist of some novels that I've not read but have heard about. There are supposed to be a couple of Campbell novels in the style of *The Mightiest Machine* that never saw print, because by the time he was in a position to publish his own work, he'd decided that science fiction should publish a different type of story. Dr. David Keller has a whole stack of unpublished fiction, which a correspondent of the old fellow claims are finer than most published work.

RICK SNEARY

You have chopped the tail off one of my favorite lines. In the past when I have been tearfully explaining to some fan editor why his pride and joy has been languishing around my place for months without a word of faint praise, I've told of all the fanzines I do get. Now they go into a box, with the ones I feel are most important (to me) in front. But there are always more in the box than I can answer. The more I answer the more fanzines and titles there are ... And when I whine that as bad as it is, "I still don't get *Cry, Yandro, Kipple* or letalone *Xero*." Now I have *Xero* – and for some time, so I will try to write a few words of thanks. Had you sent me a copy in May, I would be just getting around to writing you about that too, so you see how lucky we both are.

Jim Harmon and Redd Boggs were out to my place about three months ago and we spent a couple of Jolly hours talking about *Captain Roscoe Turner, Little Orphan Annie* (Have you heard Dave Kyle sing her theme song — all the way through?), *Jack Armstrong*, and all the other shows dear to my heart

There was one thing on this Westlake debate that quietly amused me. Now of course I haven't read *Astounding* since the name change (or, rather since the sub ran out 20 months ago), so that might be the reason. But for the life of me I can't think of anything that I remember reading by Westlake. His merely having been a reader of science fiction all those years too, is not a sign in itself that he knows what makes a good stf story. I don't *know* if he does or not, but being exposed to the field is not a sure sign he understands it. There are persons in fandom, who have been around years; publish fanzines; belong to clubs; yet are not really fans. These "not-fans" never really seem to understand the spirit of fandom, or become a relaxed part of it. Yet if you say anything to them they are quite shocked, and run through a list of all they have done. As if editing a fanzine made one a fan. Just so, writing science fiction does not make one a science fiction writer.

RON HAYDOSK

Xero 9 came hurtling in a day or two ago, and many thanks for same. Evidently, after seeing and reading most of the nine issues, what you're publishing is something akin to the *Saturday Review of Literature*, fan style. It'll be a Bad Day at Fan Rock when the last issue comes slipping off the rollers.

The item I found the most interesting was Collins' "Making of a Fantastic Paperback," namely because I've got a vampire stake in the publishing industry myself. His article couldn't help but remind me of the solid year of work, running around name-calling, conferences, digging up sales reports and the like, more work, voluminous correspondence, lawyers and lawyers' lawyers, and (hell) just about everything else I went through before the first issue of *Fantastic Monsters* hit the stands. Anyone who thinks, as Collins subtly puts it, that producing a paperback (or mag, for that matter) is just gosh-wow-loads-of-fun has another think coming.

Seems that Harmon and I started something out this way when we talked a theatre manager into running the *Marvel* serial. Since that particular showing, the serial has been sort of "revived." Three different theatres have picked it up, namely because of the enthusiastic kid response to the initial showing. Ever onward, O Captain of Marvels ...

It's a grand serial as serials go. The Fantasy Film Club has showed it three or four times, to SRO crowds every time. Of course anything above 20 is SRO for the FFC, but another group, The Informal Film Club, recently rented a coffee house for an evening to show the film. They were able to seat something like 112, and they went SRO — and they were charging $1.50 admission, too and it was a no "kid" crowd. —P.L.

RICHARD KYLE

Xero 9 is your best issue yet. It's marvelous from beginning to end. It's been a long, long time since I've enjoyed a magazine as well as this. The great success of *Xero* isn't principally due to its contributors — although they have certainly done well for themselves — but to your own editorial work. I have great admiration for good editors. You're good editors.

My own favorite of the Burroughs novels is *The Mastermind of Mars*. But perhaps that's because it's been so many years since I first read it. I reread it in 1950, just before I was drafted, and then gave away the *Amazing Stories Annual* (which I'd bought in a second-hand store for a dime a few years before) it was in to somebody or other. I must have had rocks in my head. But in 1950, it was still good — so maybe it still is. (I also sold the first issue of *Weird Tales* just before I was drafted. I gave the fellow a cut-rate on it: $7.00. He never did pay me, and I don't know where he is now; but I bet he spends fifteen minutes a day snickering.)

There was an ERB novelette or short novel in the second issue of *Fantastic Adventures* that I liked at the time. I've been told it was lousy. Do you know, Dick? I can't trust my taste at ten too well. Or maybe I was eleven. That'd make a difference. The story was called "The Scientists Revolt," and it wasn't like any of Burroughs' other stories in plot.)

I've scheduled it for the Canaveral book *Beyond the Farthest Star and Other SF Stories by ERB* just to get a copy of that story! Sam Moskowitz maintains that it was not written as an sf story at all, and was completely rewritten by Ray Palmer for the second issue of *Fantastic Adventures*.

> *If this is true Canaveral will be interested to see if the original version can be turned up. Then, if it is, we'll have to decide which version is more suitable for republication at this time. (Not which is artistically superior by somebody's theoretical yardstick.)*
> -R.L.

Since *Stranger in a Strange Land* was published, I've been seeing the phrase everywhere. It's almost a cliché — but one I never noticed before. Kind of gets me.

> *Check. Ever since this discussion sensitized us to the phrase, Dick and I have come across it any number of times. We were watching a 1939 movie of* The Man in the Iron Mask *and it popped up there.*
> -P.L.

It also kind of gets me that me that the book received the Hugo. It didn't deserve it. It won, I think because of its prestige. As did *Warhoon*, which is a good magazine, but which has even more prestige than excellence. Well, I don't vote anymore, so I have no grounds much for kicking, I suppose. But I quit voting because the Hugo is given out about as discriminatingly as the Oscar. If there were more science fiction critics, I guess a kind of Science Fiction Critics Circle Award could be given — but there aren't. Or are there?

Frederik Pohl's letter irritated me and made me feel happy.

The very writers who may have written good unpublished stories are the ones who will never hear Pohl's words — the non-professionals. The professionals, being much closer to the editorial ear, are bound to have a much better chance of selling their good off-beat stories (they're also bound to write more good stories, too, but it doesn't follow that the non-professional will write none). And where the professional will submit and resubmit stories to the market as editors come and go, the non-professional won't, not always.

Personally, I know of at least one good story that was never published. When I lived in Oakland, I met a guy who'd tried writing for the science fiction magazines back in the '30s. He'd thrown away most of the rejects but he kept a couple or three that he liked particularly. One of them was especially good. F. Orlin Tremaine would have loved to buy it then, I'm convinced; it was *Astounding*'s kind of thing. Trouble was, the man never tried *Astounding*, not under Tremaine. He'd submitted it to Clayton's *Astounding* and *Wonder Stories* and *Amazing Stories*, had it rejected and tossed it in a drawer with the others. After trying to sell another story or two he gave it up and went into the insurance business. When I met him as he was a big sf collector, read all the stuff, and was making more money than he ever would have as a writer. I won't guarantee it was a good story, because I'm not a professional editor — and I'm not Frederik Pohl, with his particular tastes — but I think it was. And to say that he would never have been a top writer because he didn't stay with it is faulty. People have to eat. Writing isn't all that compelling.

But I mention this, not only because the story was a good one, but because the writer wasn't a professional. John Campbell had a story, about the same time, that he couldn't sell to *Amazing* or *Wonder Stories* or Clayton's *Astounding*, either. But he was a professional and knew the markets and when Tremaine became editor he submitted "Twilight" to him under the name Don A. Stuart.

There are too many accidents of this kind that can happen for

Pohl to make the statement. There are too many good stories that must just barely make it into print. (I cite Cordwainer Smith's first story, "Scanners Live in Vain," which must surely have been rejected by all the other sf magazines before it ended up in *Fantasy Book*, where it was seen by Pohl and picked up for one of his anthologies. How many writers of other "Scanners" didn't even know *Fantasy Book* existed.)

In 1932 there were four markets for magazine science fiction. There was Clayton's *Astounding*, *Wonder Tales*, *Amazing*, and *Weird Tales*. Today, the sf writer who writes in less than novel length — which means most newcomers — has four markets he can contribute to: *Analog*, *Galaxy-If-Tomorrow*, *Amazing-Fantastic*, and *Fantasy and Science Fiction*. At a rough guess I'd say that no more *words* of magazine science fiction are being published each month than there were in 1932. Those magazines were fat then.

Four markets. I don't think they represent the diversity necessary to guarantee a completely fair hearing for *all* kinds of science fiction.

And, finally, what about the fiction that isn't so very good, but in which there is enormous potential? Heinlein's "Life Line" is no masterwork, but Campbell somehow recognized the talent there. To be sure any sf editor back then who turned down the story wouldn't have been turning down a really good story — he'd only be turning down one of the best science fiction writers we've had. And if Heinlein (and if not Heinlein, some potential Heinlein) had dropped sf in discouragement, any one of these editors could have said, Well, all the *good* science fiction stories that have been written have been printed, or soon will be. Any one of these editors would have been right, too. All he'd written then was "Life Line"...

I'll concede that *most* of the good sf is published. But not *all* of it — and that can make a world of difference.

But Pohl made me happy when he said he didn't expect his magazines to really shape up until the first of the year. So far "Dragon Masters" was wonderful, and now I'm beginning to look forward to Heinlein and Clement. If Pohl comes through with

Galaxy and *If*, maybe I'll change my mind about there not being markets enough to guarantee a fair hearing.

PAUL WILLIAMS

The size of *Xero 9* croggles me slightly.

So Lin Carter can't stand paying 50¢ for a paperback, huh? Perhaps he can remember way back when (like the early fifties) paperbacks only cost a quarter. Perhaps he would like to dig into his collection and pull out a few of those 25¢ books and compare their paper, bindings, and cover artwork with a few of the recent books. Quite a change, huh? And if he's really ambitious, he might try finding out how much paper and printing costs have risen during the last decade. And if he's still disgruntled, he doesn't have to buy the 50¢ books. New York is full of second-hand bookstores.

> *I did pull out some 25¢ paperbacks of the early fifties – and earlier — and their quality stands up quite well against today's products. Fashions have changed in typography, cover design and illustration, but that is not the same as saying that they have improved. Your other two points, however, are well taken.*
> -P.L.

Re: Bob Tucker. The librarian at the Young Adults section of the Boston Public Library is always after me to review sf books, but there's a dividend. I get to keep the books I review. This is sometimes because publishers send complimentary copies to libraries, under the stipulation that the libraries not put the books into circulation, since the publishers fear that this would hurt sales. So the library wants somebody to review these books so that it will know whether or not to buy a copy for circulation. So I review some of the sf books and get the copies I review. The other times my library friend gets her own review copies, since she does reviews for several of the library magazines. When she receives sf books, she gives the galleys, hardbounds or whatever to me, and I write the review. But one way or the other, I get to keep the books, and the moral is: It is indeed better to be a small frog in a big puddle than a big frog in a small puddle, but no matter which way you slice it, we're still frogs. Right, Bob?

JOHN BOARDMAN

I find these Tolkien books rattling good epic fantasy, despite a distaste for some of the underlining assumptions. There is a subtle racism running through them — offhand I can think of at least three uses of the phrase "Then the blood of the Numenoreans became mixed with that of lesser men" or variants thereof. Men are classified by racial divisions into "High," "Middle," and "Low" — and the race called variously Haradrim or Swertlings are clearly Negroes and stigmatized as being little better than Orcs.

Hobbits, Men, and Dwarves are believable because they have characters complex enough to be interesting, and are capable of both good and evil impulses and actions. But Elves and Orcs are too monochromatic to appeal to the reader. Were there never any labor problems at Cirdan's shipyard? Who worked the fields that raised the food that supported Rivendell? Were the Elves always so maddeningly good-natured? Did Orcs never show any affection among themselves?

Together with Tolkien's subtle racism is an equally subtle pre-medieval romanticism of the same sort that permeates T.H. White's *The Once and Future King*. Any craft or machinery dating from beyond the late-medieval period is equated with dirt, noise, unpleasantness, and an Orcish state of mind. We are left with a vision of happy little peasants and craftsmen, sweating out 14-hour days at their fields or forges, and somehow living past 100 despite medieval conditions of health and safety.

BOB BRINEY

I've found out your secret … You're trying to blind fandom! That orange-on-pink backcover of #9 is enough to curdle the eyeballs … Assuming they had not already been a little addled by the phosphorescent red on the front cover, that is.

By now I have read the first of the Tolkien books. I enthuse at you — it's great! I'm going nuts because I can't find a single bookstore in Lafayette or in Chicago that has the other two in the trilogy. I'll have to break down and send for them.

STEVE STILES

I've finally worked up the courage to comment on *Xero 9*; big fanzines always scare me (as well as little babies and black cocker spaniels).

Anyway, thanks for the extra *Xero 9* backcovers, my new stationary which you will notice I'm typing this on. People like it, and I think it's fun to type on, the way I make the typing run down this guy's side, 'n all. I have gained four correspondents this week. Whee!

It goes without saying that all of bhob's artwork was excellent. Although it goes saying, I'm saying it anyway because bhob will be over some night and you can read this to him and make him feel Good All Over. I know what it's like to be a fan artist.

BETTY KUJAWA

Oddly this cover of *Xero 9* didn't faze me or my eyes a bit ... 'twas obviously a credibly realistic reproduction of an earlier Lupoff Party. That's Pat in the middle ... Dick on the left ... doing the twist ... the odd-strange color and distortion is the effect of Lupoff Liquor as I well know from first-hand experience. I'll always try to think of you two looking as you do on the cover of *Xero 9*.

KISS THE BLOOD OFF MY DACOITS

LIN CARTER

CHAPTER I. FOG-PHANTOM OF DOOM

The greenish tendrils of the fog drifted through the knighted streets, as I made my weary way home from a fruitless day of clue-hunting. Fog coiled about the glowing streetlights and brushed clammy fingers against my bobbing cluster of toy balloons, as I clambered, puffing, up a fire escape ladder onto the roof. Must reach my flat unnoticed … and those sinister Oriental Fiends were *everywhere*! Even here, on the rooftops, it was impossible to see your Wembley before your face. Fog-steamers drifted in greenish-yellow whorls, like ghosts, about the hooded silhouettes of water tank and TV aerial. I had made my way thus far by street, but in the fog the White Christian British imagination plays strange tricks, creating shadowy figures from fog and shadow. *Fog phantoms*! Every doorway or alley-mouth seemed crawling with sinister shadowy figures, slanty-eyed, yellow skinned. Filthy disgusting treacherous yellow Chinks! Nips and Chinks! Echhh!

CHAPTER II. THE YELLOW PERIL

Think not, Reader, that I am intolerant of our sneaky Yellow Cousins! Far from it. Why, some of my best friends are Yellow Oriental Fiends. But in the long years that I have struggled (over six continents, seven seas, and virtually innumerable peninsulae), against that fiendish sinister Secret Organization, the *Sci-Fen*, I have come to loath the very sound of such words as "Suzie Wong" or "No Tickee, No Washee" or "Milton Caniff." Echhhh! Slimy devils! Only I know the Yellow Menace hiding at the heart of our White Anglo-Saxon Christian English-Speaking Civilization. Gooks! Nips, Chinks and Gooks! Echhhhhh!

I have been forced to adopt innumerous disguises, to keep free of their nasty dirty Yellow claws! I was, at the moment, cleverly disguised as a one-eyed hump-backed Gypsy Balloon Vendor. Little did they realize my "hump" concealed a duo-directional radio apparatus, my "balloons" were radio aerials, and my "beard" a brilliantly-disguised microphone. I'd track those Yellow Fiends to their secret lair, or my name wasn't Sir Nayland Smith-Dennis! And yet, someday, the very mulitiplicity of my disguises would betray me ... into the slimy grasping claws of that Sinister Oriental Villain, that Criminal Genius, known only to the world as — DOCTOR GHU FANCHU!

CHAPTER IV. THE DEVIL-DOCTOR

GHU FANCHU! Yes, the fiendish Oriental Scientist was at his unholy work again. Armed with his tear-gas impregnated roses, his envenomed cockroaches, his miniature-radio-carrying spiders, his razor-edged-rocket-propelled boomerangs and his Malay dwarfs, he again threatened the peace, welfare, security and White Supremacy of the Western World! GHU FANCHU! I can see him now, his towering figure, his bald brow, the face half-Satan, half-Seraph! In my mind's eye I conjure the memory of those slitted emerald eyes occasionally filmed with deep thought, as he strokes, idly, with a yellow forefinger, the soft fur of his pet platypus ("Ming the Merciless"), whilst his agile but malignant genius busily intrigues new horrors of indescribably filthy Chinese Evil against the peace-loving West! GHU FANCHU! The very name reminds one of slinky Yellow Hordes, or nasty dirty Opium Dens ... and also, it reminds me to get my underclothing back from the (ech!) Chinese laundry across the way, or I shall run out of clean small-linens! GHU FANCHU — blecchh!

CHAPTER V. GHU FANCHU STRIKES!

Ah, what new deviltry was the Mad Yellow Genius up to now? With his hordes to mutated boll weavils, poisoned orchids, sinister *thuggee* and trained scorpions! His nauseating but cunning mind had already worked untold Horrors against the peace of the world! First he kidnapped Warner B. Oland from peaceful Hollywood ... then he saturated the wet concrete before Grauman's Chinese Theatre with live athlete's-foot virus ... finally, the penultimate blow! He attempted to stir the Mysterious (and sickening) East behind his Yellow Banners, by stealing that mighty and legended talisman — *The Mummified Left Ear-Lobe of Mata Hari!*

CHAPTER VI. TREASURES OF THE AGES

Yet, as I reflected, whilst entering my flat through a sliding trap-door in the roof, had I not bested the Mad Doctor's evil-fraught plans before? Had I not restrained him from seizing such Mystic Treasures as the Ring of Cleopatra? The Sword of Genghis Khan? The Toothpick of Holy Buddha? Had I not battled unwearyingly against his sinister plots to use against the West (for what unholy purposes, my White Christian English-Speaking Western soul dare not imagine) the Napkin-Ring of Zoroaster? The Tie-Clip of Confucius? The Pocket-Handkerchief of Mr. Moto? All his Eastern hordes of cannibal-plants, flying fungus spores, radio-controlled cobras and hashish-impregnated Hershey Bars had not availed against True Anglo-Saxon Courage and British Christian Freedom-Loving Integrity!

CHAPTER VII. ROOM OF DOOM

With a sigh of relief, I checked the various locks and seals, and found the flat safe froom the Yellow Monster's slimy touch. I hastily removed my disguise, downed a triple scotch-and-soda, and was leafing through the latest copy of *Yellow Horror Monthly*, when a sensation of urgent pressure on the genito-urinary systems made a quick trip to the Gent's advisable. Propping the seat I was about to Relieve Nature when ... instead of looking down into a porcelain bowl filled with tepid water, I found myself staring at ... GHU FANCHU! Akkk!

CHAPTER VIII. MESSAGE OF HORROR

Yes, GHU FANCHU! As I stared into his slitted emerald eyes (slightly filmed with thought in the upper left-hand corners) I found myself rendered immobile by the Yellow Monster's hypnotic powers! Then it began, the shrill whispering voice that often haunts my dreams: *"Sir Smith Nayland-Dennis! This is Doctor*

XERO 10 - II, Roy Krenkel

ROY KRENKEL was one of the leading illustrators in the now legendary EC Comics school. Talented as both a pen-and-ink artist and painter, he created covers for many paperback books and dust jackets and interior illustrations for hardcovers, all of them now highly collectible.

Ghu Fanchu, speaking! During your absence, my dacoits, thuggee and Malay dwarfs secreted a cunningly devised television receiver in your toilet bowl! I take this means to inform you that my plot to seize the Ear-Lobe of Mata Hari was only a clever ruse! My true intent was to rob England of her greatest treasure, the Royalty Checks of Pearl S. Buck! Yes, I inform you of this, and also that our Sneaky Yellow Agents will strike within one hour! But you will be helpless to frustrate the schemes of the Sci-Fen this time, Sir Dennis Smith-Nayland! As you shall soon discover!" As I stared, rapt with horror, the sneering yellow visage vanished and became a simple toilet bowl again! What did it all mean?

CHAPTER IX. SMITH ON THE NOVEL

Not even waiting to micturate, I sprang into action. I had planned a quiet evening of pasting up my press-notices in a scrapbook, but no sacrifice was too great when I and I alone stood between the slithering tentacles of the Yellow Menace which, even now, curled fiendishly about the White Throat of Western Civilization! Into my next disguise, that of a notch-eared Bulgarian fruit-seller with a limp! Then out — into the night! Put that into your slimy opium pipe and smoke it, Dr. Ghu Fanchu!

CHAPTER X. STROKE OF FATE

A sibilant striation! The telephone! Was it a trick? Perhaps the receiver was impregnated with incurable charley-horse virus? Perhaps it was wired to a clever atomic disintegrator-ray propped in the chandelier! No — I must chance it!

CHAPTER XI. SMITH'S COURAGE IN ACTION

Greatly daring, I *picked up* the telephone!

CHAPTER XII. MYSTERY VOICE

"Are you there?" I said, rasping harshly.

CHAPTER XIII. CONSTERNATION

"Wha-at?" I gasped ...

CHAPTER XIV. THE DOCTOR — STRIKES!

Weakly, I put down the phone. It was useless! The Doctor had outwitted me again. Now I would be helpless — utterly helpless — to prevent his sinister dacoits from stealing the talisman! I had forgotten the date ... tonight was the night that Local Chapter 36 of the John Birch Society met, and *I was host*! I dare not stir from my flat — not with the impending election of Grand High Imperial Arch Wizard, to which high post I aspired! It was awful, to allow the Sinister Yellow Horde to strike at the very heart of Britain, stealing from our very hands the priceless Royalty Checks of Pearl S. Buck, but I was helpless!

CHAPTER XV. HELPLESS!

Yes — helpless!

CHAPTER XVI. "NEXT TIME, GHU FANCHU!"

With a weary sigh, I began straightening the apartment. "You win this round," I grated, harshly, "but — next time, Ghu Fanchu!"

I seemed to hear a hideous gloating laughter, ringing out through the fog-shrouded streets ...

EPISTOLARY INTERCOURSE #10

CONDUCTED BY PAT LUPOFF

JAMES BLISH

I shall miss *Xero*, despite all the comic book stuff.

Larry and Noreen accurately remember the circumstances surrounding the original (novelette half) *A Case of Conscience*. There *were* three editors involved before Larry, but the first was Fletcher Pratt, who commissioned the story for a Twayne Triplet to begin with, and didn't reject it – on the contrary, he was delighted with it, but the Triplets died before he could get it into print. (The other two authors represented in the proposed Triplet were Sam Merwin and Essie Carlson, and part of the deal was that we were all to sell our stories to the magazines before the book came out. Sam sold his story to himself; Essie never sold hers at all.) The yarn was next offered to Horace Gold, whose reaction was: "I like the beginning, and I like the end, and I guess I like the middle, but I run a family magazine — can't we get rid of this religious angle somehow?" I said NO. Les del Rey then offered to buy the story if I would promise him a sequel; he was right about that, and I didn't realize it until years later, and then only under continuous pressure from Fred Pohl. Larry then bought the story, despite the objections of Quinn that Noreen mentions, and ran it virtually as I'd written it (he broke a few of my more Jamesian sentences into several simpler ones, and eliminated one sentence entirely for reasons I still don't understand — the one that mentions Dali, which I restored in the book version). This is only one of several very good reasons why the book is dedicated to him.

Your response to Baxter on why I am writing historicals is also accurate, but Baxter also has a case. My relationship with Faber and Faber began with an sf novel (*They Shall Have Stars*, in England, *Year 2018!* here) which no U.S. publisher would touch until Faber printed it; and exactly the same thing has happened with the historical. For that matter, *Earthman Come Home* was rejected 23 times before Putnam took it; the Okies, despite their apparent popularity

BYE BHOB, Steve Stiles

BOY, bhob, I'll BET YOUR REAL SAD NOW THAT ALL YOUR WORK FOR XERO IS OVER... bhob... bhob?

bhob?

z-z-z-z

with the magazines, have generally baffled book publishers – for whom, my books show, the Okies have made about $135,000 to date and are still going. The moral I draw is that selling sf *at novel lengths* is by no means as automatic as Fred makes it out to be, even if the product is "good" (by the only definitions I know — the public accepts it — that applies to commercial fiction). Nor is there anything automatic in the name that's signed to a manuscript; though my luck has generally been excellent, I have in my files a half-finished novel which is a collaboration with the unforgettable Norman L. Knight, which has been on the market since 1951 and has drawn nothing but sneers. Of course, it may well be as bad as all the editors say it is; but nobody can say it is the product of tyros. One editor thought it good enough to involve another sf writer, one of the best there is, in an unwitting piracy of it — since this was the second time that editor had done such a thing with a reject of mine, I never submitted anything to him again.

I repeat, I've been lucky; sf has made me money and I've been twice honored by conventions, which is more than my due. But if what Baxter is trying to convey is that the field isn't as peachy as Fred claims, then I agree with him, much though I'm indebted to Fred; and I am writing historicals, etc., *both* to broaden my horizons as a writer *and* to lessen my dependence on a set of editors who are, with few exceptions, cranky, absolutist, blinkered. Once a writer has dealt with Charles Monteith and Ann Corlett of Faber & Faber, he *knows* what a *good* editor is like, and the experience is liberating.

RED BOGGS

"Sax" by Bob Briney was an excellent job about a writer who probably doesn't deserve even as much recognition as this. The middle age nostalgia that is sweeping over fandom has given rise to more wordage rhapsodizing about incompetent hacks that one might ever have imagined possible. All the incredible stuff about Burroughs and Lovecraft, two writers who (as James Blish once described it) couldn't write themselves out of a theme on "Why Daddy Buys Life Insurance." Of course Briney keeps firm control over himself and doesn't claim too much for Sax Rohmer. In fact, he praises him so faintly that I am not inspired to Rush Right Out. I am helped, too, by the fact that I have read enough Rohmer to be fairly certain that he is not at all to my taste. Goodbye, Mr. Rohmer. And good riddance.

It is the theory of local non-fan Will Kuhn that "Fu Manchu"

was intended by Sax Rohmer to be a name with obscurely obscene connotations. "Fu" being the first two letters of a familiar four letter word. That "Sax" was also intended to suggest "sex" is also a tenable theory, I suppose. But such speculation doesn't jibe with the fact that Rohmer's pictures of Oriental and Egyptian slums are pretty unconvincing in their depiction of "sin." Rohmer was obviously not a rake; neither was he a Puritan. If he were either, he'd have stronger feelings for "sin." He had no moral leanings either way, I suppose. Too bad. If he'd felt a strong attraction or revulsion for his Oriental hells, the stories would have been more vividly and dramatically colored. As they are, they are obviously feeble fantasies.

Briney did so well on Rohmer as far as he went that I'm sorry he didn't delve into matters of morality in Rohmer — the sexual attitudes, for example, and the racial question. He only touches on that, and it remains for Lin Carter to underline the basic underlying attitudes in Rohmer toward non-white peoples, in "Kiss the Blood off My Dacoits." One of the unfortunate things about becoming enamored of popular writings is that popular writers reflect popular attitudes that later become repugnant. A great writer stands to some extent above popular prejudices; that's one reason we call him great. Popular writers wallow in popular prejudices; that's one reason they're popular. But it doesn't make the task of an enthusiast of Rohmer, Howard, Buchan, George W. Peck, et al, any easier to be forced to accept the writer's outmoded attitudes and try to force them down the throats of people he's trying to interest in his work.

ANTHONY BOUCHER

Just to ease your mind as to why the phrase "stranger in a strange land" keeps turning up so much: It's from Exodus 2:22 (King James version):

And She [Zipporah] bore him [Moses] a son, and he called him Gershom; for he said, I have been a stranger in a strange land.

I never understand why fans ignore the Bible. It has almost as much exegetical appeal as *The Lord of the Rings* or even *Silverlock*.

Very sorry that *Xero* is to be no more. I've greatly enjoyed it, despite the infrequency of my locs. At least you go out blazing with Briney on Rohmer, a most welcome survey and bibliography. Converts to Rohmer might enjoy looking up T.H. Hanshaw's novels and stories of Cleek of the Forty Faces — no fantasy, but similarly superb bad writing and melodrama. (There needs to be a survey of the Great Bad Writers.)

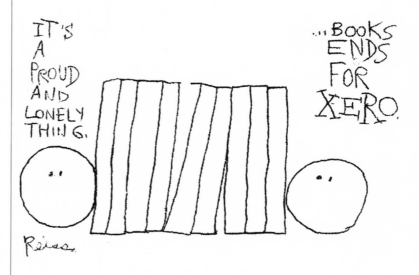

BOOKENDS, Andy Reiss

WALTER BREEN

We come to John Boardman and his nonsense about racism in Tolkien. "Oh, no, John, no, John, no, John, NO!" — In these excerpts from the *Red Book of Westmarch* we are given what is represented not as the view of a modern humanitarian, nor yet that of a racist, but as the views of Hobbit chroniclers of many tens of thousands of years ago; one does not expect them to have viewed their contemporaries as (fortified by cultural anthropology) we look at ours. Haradrim were hated not because they were black-skinned but rather for the more obvious reason that they were barbarically ferocious and moreover in league with Mordor. Numenoreans of the Elder Days seemed to Hobbits to have been a higher race of men than any later ones (save only Aragorn II) because of their accomplishments. These accomplishments were not matched by their descendents nor by *their* descendents who married people of less renown. Elves and orcs seem monochromatic to us because they looked that way to the Hobbit chroniclers, to whom they were more alien than humans or dwarves, and who could hardly have been expected to view them in depth. I can't speak personally for orcs, but the Elves to whom much space is devoted in the Trilogy are quite individualized; Elrond and Legolas, for instance, come out as quite different personalities, as do Arwen and Galadriel.

We are not informed of labor troubles, if any, at Cirdan's shipyard because the Hobbit chroniclers were not witnesses to events of some 6400 years at the Grey Havens. Nor is there any indication of class struggle among members of the Three Kindreds, united as they were by mutual affection and by the need of mutual defense against a common enemy. Nor would Hobbit chroniclers have felt enough disinterested curiosity about folk so foully destructive as orcs to inquire into the personal lives of the latter. In fact, any such digressions as these — whether anent labor problems at Cirdan's shipyards, personal affections of orcs, or farmers who provided food for Rivendell and Lorien communities — would hardly have been in place in the kind of epic Tolkien provides. As for the same reason as the absence of long excurses on the sex lives or the military training methods in use among the Achaians at Troy in *The Iliad*.

I must also disagree with John's claim that post-medieval craft or technology is always equated with "dirt, noise, unpleasantness, or an orcish state of mind." As Doc Weir's study of hithlain in *I Palantir #1* indicated, the elves were farther advanced in biological technology than are we, and their technology was far enough advanced to seem magical to humans and hobbits. Nor could their knowledge of metallurgy have been primitive, either, considering the regions elvensmiths' work with mithril. No, technology that connoted the Dark Land was no more nor less than the kind of chemical technology that polluted atmosphere and water, destroyed growing plants and in general disrupted the local ecology — the kind of thing that has given Linden, New Jersey, a bad name and intolerable odor.

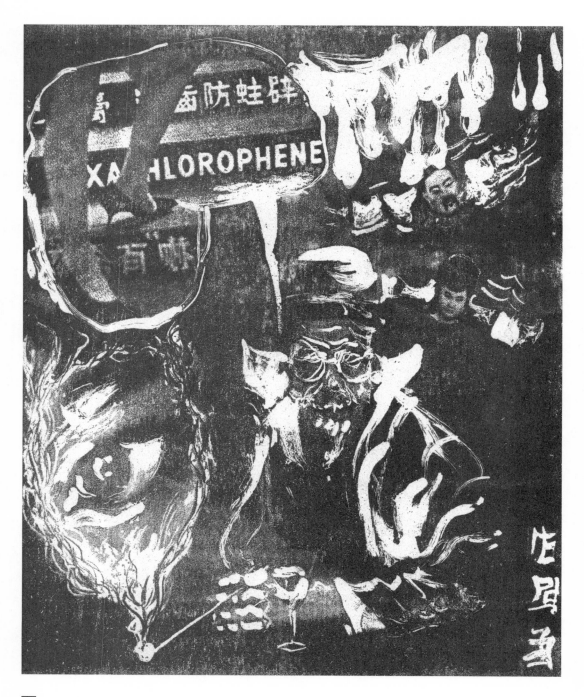

BOB BRINEY

Probably the single greatest thing in the issue is the chapter VII-VIII portion of Lin Carter's parody. I laughed for ten minutes, and when my office mate, a one time Rohmer reader, read it, he too collapsed. The rest of the math department thought we were nuts.

I'll never be able to read that scene in a Rohmer book with a straight face.

DR. ANTONIO DUPLA

Briney is excellent in his complete coverage of Rohmer. As Lin Carter is in his splendid parody of him. And last but not least John Boardman has given me a surprising view to add to my files on Tolkien: racism found and class struggles missed in Middle Earth!

That the books transcended mere fantasy was, I think, agreed upon by many of its fans but to put such down-to-earth problems in it is perhaps a bit too much.

BETTY KUJAWA

I can remember *vividly* hearing one episode of the Fu Manchu series ... hero and pals stuck in the middle of an enormous sheet of fly-paper; the gooey-gummy stuff was sort of animated. It kind of *crawled* up and over them of its own volition. The sound effects were *scrumptious*. Ahhh the sound of that olde gong ... yes. As to the movie with Myrna Loy and all ... must have seen it half a dozen times and would still take time out to watch it again ... the sets, costumes, etc ... real gosh-wow exotic.

Rick Sneary'd better move over and make room for an old woman amid those old men who dug Jack Armstrong and the like ... *me*. S'funny we get a party going here-there or anywhere and if enough of the group is near our age eventually we get around to singing it up ... waving the flag for Hudson High, boys, and asking sweetly, who's that little chatter-box, the one with the curly auburn locks? And booooooming out as Paul Douglas used to do:

YELLOW PERIL, bhob Stewart

"Buck Rogerrrrs in the Twenty-Fifth *Cent*ury ... "

ETHEL LINDSAY

So that's the final *Xero* ... it's all very sad ... and I don't know how you have the heart to do it. I hope you stick to your vow and stay in general pubbing and don't disappear into that awful FAPA. At the thought of no more brilliant *Xero* covers — I cringe.

I never got bit by the Fu Manchu bug even though I read them avidly at the uncritical age. I was probably saved by reading so much *else*. The art section really is good! Lin Carter has quite a sense of humor, doesn't he? I *have* been impressed by his *Spectrum*: and wish I had the time to write and say so. Humor and a good critical faculty — that's a good combination!

Back to the letters section and John Boardman's letter. His remarks on Tolkien made me goggle. Goodness knows *I'm* no rabid Tolkien fan ... but ... but! I've rarely seen a more biased view of a writer's intentions! My goodness ... does John breathe out maledictions like this on *everything* that he suspects does not share his views! Now this is the kind of idiocy to get us so-called "left-wingers" a bad name!

PAUL WILLIAMS

If you've managed to pretty much vent your passionate nostalgics into *Xero*, and are now reasonably cured, this fanzine has done you much good. Perhaps you will now write an illuminating article on "Fanzines as Catharsis" and will throw open a whole new therapy. Fandom could use more people curing themselves by means of spectacular ten-issue fanzines. And — it occurs to me — perhaps the monster fanzines are doing the youth some good after all.

Since when are there only four magazine sf markets, Mr. Kyle? You've eliminated the well-paying men's magazines, you've eliminated the fancy slicks, you've eliminated the literary mags, you've eliminated the Nova pubs in Britain, and most importantly of all, you've eliminated the whole original paperback market, which is thriving. But even the four markets now available that you mention cover the field a lot better, and with more variety, than the titles available in 1933. The only thing missing is a *Weird Tales*-type market.

Well, you'll see me at the Discon, bidding for that set of *Xero*.

Ho there, time-binder! We did enjoy seeing you; that Saturday night progressive party was a ball; and Freddy Norwood surely appreciated your passing on the Gospel according to Leman Monday night. Sorry you missed the bound set — Frank Prieto got it for $28.
-P.L.

FAREWELL (AFTER THE STYLE OF BILL ROTSLER), Steve Stiles

LARRY IVIE was the illustrator for the bold and somewhat sinister cover of Xero 5, which is featured as the cover of this edition. Ivie worked in the comics field as both a writer and an artist. He was well-known for a series of cover paintings that appeared on so-called "monster magazines," and still works in that area.